OSIRIS

Tim Ward Tales
Book 1

JAMES T ABBOTT

Ribblesdale, Lancashire, February 17th, 1634

Lucy yelled her thanks as her two children filed quietly out of the house. Mistress Small, the woman who looked after them when Lucy had calls to make, sent back a muted 'I'll have 'em back when church bells ring two' and then silence descended on the tiny, two roomed hovel that Lucy was pleased to call her home. The Lord of the Manor, Sir Robert de Ridesdale, would probably call it a midden, but it was Lucy's home and she loved it. She kept it as clean as it was possible to maintain cleanliness in an old wooden shack whose thatch was a constant challenge and whose walls were regularly eaten through by mice. But she kept the walls almost entirely wind and waterproof and was thankful the roof now suffered from only a single leak. From outside, came the clatter of horses' hooves on the cobbles of the main street, intermingled with the loud greetings and mock-insults of shopkeepers and tradesmen at the start of another cold February day.

The tiny wood-fire she'd lit earlier to take the edge off the early morning for the children was now just a heap of warm ashes. She threw some dry soil over them and turned to scraping and tidying away the breakfast platters. Goodness knew the children did not get much but they were not starving, they had a roof over their heads, and Lucy was earning a modest but steady income from her herbs and remedies. She gazed around again as she straightened from her chore. There was another crack in the wattle-and-daub wall near the main - the only – door. It was a recent development which let in frigid gusts and dribbles of ice cold rain, probably caused by old Alfred when he bashed the door with the wood he'd brought for her last week. She could not complain at his clumsiness. The gift of some free wood was a blessing. She would try to fix it herself before calling in Sam, the carpenter. Every ha'penny counted. She smiled to herself at the thought. Every farthing counted!

She let her eyes range around the place. It was a good home and a good life now she had come to terms with the loss of her husband, Jacob. He'd been a thatcher and slater – a top tradesman – but one day, up at the Hall, he'd slipped on wet roof slates and fallen three storeys to his death. Up to that terrible day, they had been reasonably well-off, living in a modest but warm cottage on Sir Robert's estate. After Jacob's accident Lucy had to move into town and find much less expensive property. Her life now was dominated by trying to keep body and soul together for herself and the children.

In spite of its hand-to-mouth nature, she enjoyed helping her neighbours and townsfolk with their health problems. She'd been a healer all her life. Her mother had taught her the art. Indeed it was her mother's old box, now containing her own herbs and potions, that she now picked up in preparation for leaving. She grabbed her shawl and a threadbare cloak and turned for the door, just as there was a firm knock. To her astonishment the figure that loomed in her doorway was that of the vicar. He was already moving to enter the house and Lucy barely had time to step out of the way. He'd never visited before. She'd never heard of him visiting any of her neighbours in this poor area of the town. The closest Lucy had ever come to him was at the Sunday service when, from her lowly position at the back of the Nave, he was merely a distant figure behind the lectern.

He was a tall man. As he stooped beneath the low beams supporting the straw roof, he glanced around with an expression that took no pains to disguise his disdain. Lucy took the opportunity to take a closer look at him. He was not a displeasing man to look at. His features were even and he had a strong jaw. His complexion was clear but dark – almost olive. He wore his jet black hair long over his high white collar. His eyes were a dark colour that Lucy could not identify - brown or very dark grey, she was not sure. A neat black moustache reminded her more of a nobleman than a country vicar. When he turned his face towards her, his eyes bored into hers.

'You are Widow Lucy Brimham?' She nodded and such was his presence that she had to consciously stop herself from bowing. 'I have seen you on many occasions as you were about your errands around the town. May I set myself down?' Lucy waved at the only stool. The rough bench in front of the fire was too uncomfortable for a clergyman. As he sat, Lucy became even more aware of his eyes. They scanned her up and down - especially down – coming to rest on the belt at her waist. With an inward sigh she also noted he now blocked the only route towards the door.

'How may I help you, Vicar?' Even to her own ears her voice sounded a little shrill and urgent.

'Please be calm, Mistress.' He smiled. It was a reassuring gesture and Lucy felt ashamed for her suspicions. 'I have come to assure myself that you are well and secure here since your husband went to his doubtless well-deserved rest.' Lucy briefly wondered why then he had not come earlier.

'Thank you, sir, yes I am.'

He grunted. 'That's as may be but a pretty young widow living alone is never completely secure, as you must be well aware. Your husband was a good man and he was your protector. You no longer have a protector.' Lucy took a deep breath remembering how strong and active Jacob had been, and how good a husband.

'I have good neighbours, sir, and several of their husbands would come to my aid if I needed them. They are good people.'

He stood and moved closer to her. 'I am pleased to hear it, Lucy.' He took her hand. His smile was now not so reassuring and his eyes were on her lips. 'God has blessed you with two fine children, but I have to warn you that the lack of a man in your life, at this young age, is a sign from God that you are in error. He is displeased with you.'

'I do not need a man in my life, vicar. Jacob's memory is still too fresh.'

She tried gently to remove her hand but he gripped even more tightly. 'Look into my eyes Lucy and let me see your soul. You need to be cleansed of sin. God has sent me to be his instrument to lead your erring soul back to grace and righteousness.'

Taking her face in both hands, his dark eyes still devouring her features, he bent closer and kissed her roughly on the mouth. Lucy was well able to recognise when a man was beyond his own control. The vicar was urgently pressing himself against her, trying to kiss her neck. His aroused state was only too evident. Lucy knew there were only two things she could do, and for the first, she was most definitely not going to become the Reverend's mistress. He was now desperately pulling her towards him as she resisted with all her strength. So, it had to be the second. She considered for a moment and then suddenly stopped resisting. Instead of pulling away from his embraces, she jerked his hands from her shoulders and pushed him as hard as she could in the chest. He had been pulling her strongly towards him, and, without his grip and her resistance, he could not help himself from staggering backwards. Lucy's push, and a foot behind one of his, sealed his fate.

His stumble turned into a crashing fall and, even though he put out his arms to save himself, it was a bad tumble. Lucy watched dispassionately as long arms and legs flailed but failed to save him. There was a nasty crack as his shoulder hit the stool. His body continued its journey to the floor where his head hit the hard-packed earth with a thump. He yelped, gripping his shoulder with one hand and rubbing his head with the other.

'You have broken my shoulder, you harlot,' he whined.

Lucy shook her head. 'I think not. It looks to be dislocated. Do you wish me to re-set it?' The Reverend took one look at the smile on her face and shook his head. Slowly, he crawled to his feet, in very obvious pain.

'You will not touch me, Widow Brimham.' He sucked in a breath as he tried to move his dislocated arm. The sweat was pouring from his brow. 'Be warned, I will not forget this. You will pay dearly for your insolence.' He stumbled out through the door grasping his arm tighter.

Over the following week, she tried to put the incident out of her mind. Apart from a distant view of him with a sling at Sunday service, she did not encounter him, and he did not come near the house again. She carried on with her life but, a week later, she became aware from an old friend that there were rumours circulating in the town - rumours she was a witch. Lucy was astounded but another friend told her the source - the church verger. His master, the vicar, was getting some revenge. Her friends were staunch and true but even they admitted they had been made to wonder at the detail in the stories. The verger was retailing some lewd and lurid tales. They involved nocturnal trysts with demons, naked prancing in the woods with other witches, the casting of malicious spells, the seduction of 'good' local men, and using occult means to drive magical wedges between them and their God-given and long-suffering wives. The men of the town began looking at her in very different ways. None of them good.

For a while she was confident the people knew her well enough to ignore such rumours. Then she found herself having to fend off men who accosted her in the dusk and whenever she was out after dark. They wanted to see whether the rumours were true, caring not a jot for their immortal souls. She was forced to stop work early and return home in daylight. Then she was arrested.

The children were playing on the floor with some crude wooden dolls when the door burst open and the town constable with two helpers strode into the room. She was allowed to send her children to Mistress Small but then she was taken to the town lockup and left for two days, seeing no-one and not knowing with what she was charged. On the third morning she was given a rough escort to an upstairs room at the lockup where two women, unknown to her, stripped her and then examined every square inch of her body. The excruciating embarrassment was made worse by their occasional cackles and giggles and the lingering touches they left on her private parts. While she was still naked, two men came into the room announcing that it was 'time'. She'd known both of them since they had been children but that seemed to make no difference now she was a predatory witch. They watched with obvious pleasure while Lucy dressed herself, offering lascivious comments and making suggestions as to how they could rid her of her witchy-ways. They escorted her to the town court where she was pushed and groped all the way to the front through the throngs of local men. The women were at the back jeering their condemnation. Calls of 'Hang the witch' echoed in the room. The Justice of the Peace and two Parish officials sat at the raised bench. One of them, of course, was the good Reverend.

Witness after witness was brought forward. 'I saw her last week gathering poisonous mushrooms in the woods, your honour', 'She charged me a whole penny for a poultice for my boil and it didn't work,' 'My child was sick but died after she'd suggested a potion,' 'My stomach cramps were cured by her but my cat died the day after she'd cured them'. Lucy vaguely knew most of the witnesses and their testimonies were usually true or partly so, but no-one listened when she tried to explain. At one point she was told by the Justice to keep her mouth shut or be gagged. Those were just the introductory witnesses, though.

The two women from the searching were brought forward, smirking as they told the court in salacious detail how they had found marks near the top of her inner left thigh. The Justice frowned at them.

'Why were you searching her in this way?'

'The Reverend asked us to do it.'

'I am aware, your honour that the Devil marks his own among witches with secret signs. Once so marked a witch is the Devil's forever.'

'How do you know this Reverend?'

'My authority is nothing less than the great work 'Malleus Malificarum' - a seminal scholarly work by the devout Dominican monk Kramer, two and more centuries ago. It has become a central reference in the Church's battle against evil. In his treatise he lists the ways in which the Devil claims silly women in nocturnal … er … escapades.'

The Justice was obviously a practical man, thought Lucy. 'What sort of escapades?'

The Reverend looked a little sheepish but Lucy could tell he was putting it on for effect . 'I would rather not explain in this room,' he said. And then, more quietly, 'Perhaps I could enlighten your honour in private?'

'Never mind that now. Is there any more evidence against this woman?'

Again, the Reverend spoke up. 'Yes. There are two more matters. A witness who saw the accused conducting a seance in the woods and the matter of her husband's death.' He waved forward another young woman who Lucy did not know. She was obviously a servant of some sort but her eyes were shifty and did not meet anyone else's except those of the good Reverend 'Tell the court what you saw on the first Sunday in November.'

The girl looked at the Justice's chain and insignia of office and spoke in a sing-song voice as though coached. 'I was coming back to my master's house from my father's home on that Sunday evening when I saw the accused dancing naked in the woods. She was chanting something but I was frightened so I ran.'

'How did you know it was the accused? Do you know her?' the Justice was studying the girl with narrowed eyes.

She blushed. 'I have seen this woman in town many times and people have named her to me. It was her in the woods.'

It was an outright lie but Lucy was not permitted to question witnesses.

The Reverend waved the girl away and spoke directly to Lucy.

'Your husband of five years was a good man and had a reputation as an honest and capable tradesman. I believe you wished him dead.'

'I dare say there are a good few women who would mirror her sentiments.' The Justice's comment drew laughter from the room but the Reverend vicar kept his face straight.

'Of course, your honour, but few genuinely wish such a heinous thing and even fewer have the witchery skills to make their wish come true. This woman,' he pointed dramatically to Lucy, 'has both the skill and the intent to kill.'

'And how did she make this happen, pray?'

'We have heard from witnesses who saw her in the woods, one of whom has testified that she witnessed the accused conducting a dance and chanting spells last November shortly before the husband died. I do not wish to understand how her depraved spells work but work they did and her husband, a skilled and experienced slater, somehow slipped on a roof he had worked on many times. His colleagues testified at the Coroner's Inquest that they had never before seen him slip and that no-one else had ever fallen from the roof. I believe she cast a curse upon him in order to be rid of him so she could consort with other men.'

He called as a witness the church verger – an odious drunkard who had tried to court Lucy prior to her marriage. The man testified that he had heard Jacob complain about his wife's strange knowledge of plants and herbs, her constant nagging, and her regularly-stated wish that she had never married him. Lucy listened to these untruths with mounting anger. She attempted to make several interventions but was always silenced by the Justice.

There was an interlude while the bench considered the verdict among themselves. At one point she heard the Justice say, 'I am inclined to a heavy fine and a sentence of thirty days in the lock-up.' The Reverend coughed politely. 'Your charity and merciful nature do you proud, sir, but I reluctantly have to plead for the death sentence in this case. There are too many weak women in the parish who would take a merciful decision as a licence to emulate Widow Brimham. It would be remiss of us not to set a firm example. I believe our God-given duty to be clear.'

The Justice pondered a moment. It was difficult to oppose a plea backed by the Church. His bleak countenance warned Lucy of her fate and her legs almost gave way under his gaze.

'Mistress Brimham you have been convicted of malicious witchcraft and the murder of your husband by malicious magic. You will be taken from here this afternoon to the usual place of execution. There you will be hanged by the neck until life has expired. God have mercy on your soul.'

The next two hours were a blur of experiences that Lucy felt were happening to someone else. She had retreated deep within herself to a place where nothing mattered. Men shoved and groped. Women spat on her. Even children were encouraged to strike at her legs with sticks. Many times she had to struggle to her feet after falling.

Eventually she was standing precariously on the top rung of a ladder that had been placed against the hanging tree. Her hands were bound behind her back. A man had been deputed to climb the tree. He perched on a higher branch from which position he forced the stiff, hemp noose over her head and tightened it. The Justice was standing with a crowd of senior citizens looking up at her. Townsfolk crowded behind. All were silent.

'Do you have anything to say before you are sent to answer to your maker?' the Justice asked.

Lucy did not look at him. All her attention was directed towards the smirking face of the Reverend vicar. Lucy gathered all her strength and spoke loudly and clearly so all would hear - 'I curse you, Vicar, false man of God. I curse you and all your line for all eternity. I will ...' -

'Enough ...' shouted the Justice. 'That is not going to gain you the good grace of God.' He nodded and the man who had been stationed at the bottom of the ladder yanked it away.

Lucy kept her eyes on the vicar as she choked and struggled against the tight hemp biting into her neck. The chokes grew more and more violent as the air failed to get to her lungs. Her legs thrashed beneath her. Soon she could not see. The pain was agonising but it did not last long before consciousness dimmed and the life left her limp body. The last thing Lucy saw was the shocked look on the vicar's pale face. He had never witnessed a hanging, but more to the point, the curse had struck home.

2

RAF Sneddon Downs, 2026

I'm told by people I would normally trust that it's traditional to begin stories like this with a phrase like 'It all began on that fateful June day in London ...' or 'I remember it so vividly ... that morning when the policeman knocked on the front door.' But I have to say, my beginnings weren't like that. To be truthful, I couldn't find clear-cut beginnings even if you were to write me a large seven figure cheque for them.

Over a great many years, little things happened. And then more little things happened. I took decisions and made apparently unimportant choices until, one highly traumatic day, I realised that they'd all been connected. All those tiny things and unimportant decisions had brought me to disaster. In the most innocent process you could imagine I had - not to put too fine a point on it - found myself up the proverbial creek with a paddle nowhere to be seen.

It's no use now, but from my current position I can see that some of the decisions were pretty pivotal. In fact, a good few of them turned out to be Everest-sized pivots. But, at the time, they either seemed of minuscule importance or completely logical in the then scheme of things. I'm sure you'll have found the same thing in your own life - things that seemed innocent when the decision was made but turned into monsters that caused untold trouble. If it were possible, we'd all go back and un-decide them.

But that's it, isn't it? It's entirely possible a major event will change the course of your life. A stranger calling at the door can change things forever. The new person in your life can sometimes send you down a completely different path. However, these mega-changes don't happen quite as much as the fiction writers would want you to believe.

No, it's the scores of things you do yourself, almost without a second thought, that imperceptibly influence the path you tread. For most of us it's those micro-changes that shape our lives. You start out on your own familiar garden path but, after dreaming half a life away, you eventually wake up and discover yourself in the middle of a six-lane highway with a fifty-ton truck bearing down on you.

That's what happened to me. I wasn't an innocent bystander, far from it, but I had no idea the multitude of things I'd done and the choices I'd made would result in the car-crash that became my life.

3

A winter night's dream

My final shift at RAF Sneddon Downs was on February 6th, 2026. After working my way up the slippery promotion ladder, I'd been the Flight Lieutenant in charge of Team Bravo of the Cyber Warfare Squadron at Sneddon for the past two years. I'd come to the end of my seven year contract and - for reasons which I will come to – I had decided not to renew it.

The day had been uneventful and ordinary – a total anti-climax. It was so ordinary that I even had to give my regular 'disappointed' speech to Flying Officer Wainwright. Brian was okay but he was in the wrong job. I'd told my boss, Squadron Leader Sean Tallis, and we'd come to an agreement that Brian would be better off in an admin role. Sean was going to think about it and make any potential changes after I left and definitely after he'd found a new team leader.

Four o'clock came around far sooner than I'd wanted. The clock showed two minutes past four and it suddenly hit me hard that I was now surplus to requirements. The whole of my team were there, of course, four going off-duty with me and four coming on for the late shift. One guy was not there. He was still in bed, waiting his turn. He had the unenviable job of covering the night watch. I was surrounded by them, all making their farewells in different ways and with different levels of enthusiasm and sincerity. Well, not everyone loves me in spite of my own propaganda! There was one person I particularly wanted to speak to and I spotted her and manoeuvred her away from the others. Pilot Officer Linda Grover was not what you'd call prepossessing. She was overweight, short, stubbornly stuck to a hairstyle from three decades ago, and had the sort of skin that girls (and boys) have nightmares about. I guess a lot of it was down to the two or three doughnuts she was wont to put away in the mess at lunchtime and while working at her desk.

'Don't take any nonsense from the rest of the team, Linda.' She gave me a look which asked: What else am I supposed to do? I put on my most serious face. 'Seriously, do not take any crap from anyone – senior officers as well.'

'What do you mean, sir?'

I sighed and glanced around to make sure we were not being overheard. 'Linda, you're worth three or even four of the others on this team. You obviously don't know it, even though I have told you so during your last three appraisals, but you are vital to its success. You have everything it takes to excel in this job and I've told the boss in no uncertain terms.'

It was tentative at first - as though she suspected that I may be pulling her leg - but eventually a small smile became a wide beam of joy and understanding.

'Thank you, sir … Tim … I'll … that is, we'll miss you a lot.' She was so flustered she almost fell backwards over a desk.

I steadied her arm and nodded encouragingly at her. She wandered off to her station without a backward look but I could almost feel her grin from where I was standing. She was embarrassed and distracted but I could only hope that she'd take my advice. She was one of the best programmers and cyber-sleuths in the team - arguably *the* best apart from me. If she could just acquire some confidence from somewhere she'd be really good and might even be a team leader and senior officer in the making. I realised I was staring at her and tore my gaze away to find Sean standing right next to me.

'You need to go now, Tim. I've got to get the evening shift briefed.'

'Look after Grover, Sean. She's special - she can spot a coding error better and quicker than anyone else - and you'll need her ability to track a hack. Wallace is inconsistent and Khan can be distracted by false trails.' He nodded patiently. I'd told him all this three times already.

I shook his hand and, after waving to my crew, sorry, those who used to be my crew, I turned for the door. There was a wrench in my gut that I had not expected. It was a real stomach-churning rip and, for a second, I felt that I'd become disengaged from the world. There was a sense of unreality and the room turned to black and white. I breathed deeply and forced myself to leave and to focus on my new life.

Outside, the freezing air cleared my head and my breathing became easier. I was not used to having 'turns' like an old man. I paused for a moment at the side of the standard-issue concrete roadway to gaze around. I'd left the Cyber-Warfare Building hundreds of times but this was my last. I could not even turn around and re-enter. My security code had been disabled before I left and the system would not only not let me back in, it would trigger the alarms. Which would be just a little embarrassing.

I walked down towards the officers' mess just as an ear-numbing thunder of afterburners signalled the departure of a pair of strike fighters. I could imagine the word-stream on my old monitor announcing a ready-alert scramble and the need for vigilance on all electronic channels. The pair were off the ground and standing on their tails within seconds. They disappeared to the north-east. I wondered if my pal Archie was one of the pilots. He had given me several vivid accounts of the G-forces he had to deal with in those beasts. That's why he had to be so fit. Anyone not at peak fitness would probably die under the strain or through blacking out for a long enough period to crash. It was almost certainly another Russian test of the RAF's readiness - the stop-watches would be running and the pilots would be hoping this was just another test.

It was my last evening on the base. My last in the RAF. I chose to wander slowly back to my quarters - surprisingly torn between seven years of mostly good memories and the prospects I'd lined up for myself. RAF Sneddon Downs was an old World War One Royal Flying Corps base that had flown Handley Page biplane bombers from a grass field in the early years. In the second contretemps Sneddon had hosted squadrons of Lancaster bombers and Hurricane fighters. Everything from the overall layout to the old brick-built officers' mess and the non-commissioned officers' quarters, as well as the concrete squash courts and guardhouse screamed of standard RAF practice from 1943 and, as I meandered down the paths and roadways, I began to appreciate how much it all meant to me. It wasn't just familiar to me as an RAF officer, it was a direct link to my father who'd served on bases just like this. It temporarily shocked me to realise that I had failed to check whether he'd been posted to Sneddon during his career. I can be a thoughtless idiot at times.

But, in the winter darkness, with the wind swirling the mist under the dim yellow glow of the nearest sodium streetlight the scene became increasingly unreal, as though I was drifting through time. Looking back, the correct term would be ethereal. For that brief period I felt like I was floating in another world. There was no sense of dread or threat. In fact it felt warm and somehow comforting.

I knew I was feeling very emotional about everything but, as I stood outside the officers' mess gazing at the clouds of freezing mist drifting past, I sensed the ghosts of long dead airmen and women bustling around me. Except that this time, they slowly resolved into recognisable but insubstantial figures lit not by the yellow sodium lamp but by the dim warm light from the battery torches carried by everyone. A remote part of my mind remembered that the blackout rules would not allow any other form of light outside after dark. My whole attention, though, was on the figures of young people in uniform walking quickly or standing briefly in small groups. They shouted to each other about drinks later that evening, about the upcoming rugby match, about driving into the town of Sneddon for a meal. One couple had their heads together, no doubt planning a secret rendezvous. They all seemed companionable and close. The vision widened so that I saw pairs of old Lancasters lumbering into the air, each laden with tons of fuel and high explosive, piloted and guarded by those same young people. I saw the wounded air gunners and pilots being ambulanced away after their aircraft had limped back to a crash landing. The clamour of their bells echoed through the mist into the distance, each old-fashioned ambulance bearing its load of life-changing agony. Then, right in front of me, there appeared the lifelike face of a young airwoman. Her breath whispered down the wind like tiny fleeing ghosts. She was staring directly at me from a pretty face surrounded by curls of light brown hair. I felt myself flinch with the realisation that she could see me.

'Who are you?' she asked. 'Are you the replacement for Dicky Spencer?'

Suddenly I was very afraid. I shook my head and the apparition faded in the dismal chill of a winter's night. The dream had evaporated but I was cold and, yes, not a little scared. I could still hear the sound of those vintage ambulances and I had a very vivid memory of the face of that young WAAF. I recall the apprehension and grief in her face – she'd liked that chap Spencer. I was being far too emotional and the result, it seemed, was a waking dream right there in front of the officers' mess. I took another deep breath and the cold air brought me back to earth. I dearly wanted to shrug it off and wipe the episode from my mind. But that didn't happen. I remember it to this day but at least I now know why I saw that pretty young WAAF. At the time, however, I pretended to forget and strode off into the freezing February drizzle towards the relative warmth of my quarters.

4

Breaking up is hard to do

When it's your last evening, you see everything through fresh eyes. It was disturbing to see my quarters as though it was my first visit - the discoloured paint in the corridor, the scuffed skirting boards, the paint peeling away from the cheap doors, I even noticed the squeak of hinges on most of the doors. And it wasn't just the sense of sight that suddenly woke up. The single officers' quarters smelled of old socks, stale sweat, and a weird combination of burnt bacon and cheese. The combination is not to be recommended. I guess it was the volume of pizzas brought back from the mess, and the rooms with their individual baskets of dirty laundry waiting, too long, to be dragged down to the base launderette. The recent switch to LED lighting - as efficient and modern as it was - had not helped the place. With the old mixture of incandescent and flickering fluorescent lamps it had been as dim as a cheap doss-house. The stairwells had been pitch-black, the corridors just a series of barely illuminated patches separated by long dark sections. Now, however, bright new LED lamps cast a cruel, pure white glare on everything and revealed every single scratch, scuff, and imperfection. Even the small balls of fluff and dust stood out clearly on the ancient hessian that had once been a real carpet. Each cast its own tiny shadow. It was not pretty. In my own room I kept the lighting dim. A few visitors assumed I was trying to make it look romantic, but it was really because the walls and furniture were so old and pathetic that it was physically depressing to look at them in bright light. I'd bought myself a decent mattress and a few small pieces of furniture and equipment - including a good microwave. They helped to make it bearable as a place to live, but nothing except total darkness could hide the years of neglect and underspending.

Depressing, but not my problem any more. I gave myself a spruce up and answered the soft knock at the door. It was Emma - my significant other - a Flight Lieutenant from the Ops Team. Her room was just down the corridor from me. I'd first encountered Emma Dawson-Keen when Ops had experienced what they thought was a viral attack a few years ago. They'd acted entirely correctly in the circumstances - running around screaming with their hands waving in the air while they sent a diminutive airman to try to get help from the Cyber team. Someone had had the sense to hit the air gap switch which isolated the system from the outside world but that just meant that every machine now flashed dire warnings of the end of civilisation as we know it and the whole of the Ops section were almost eating their own arms until I got there. On that particular morning, Emma was the senior person. It was she who had hit the emergency switch and it was she who managed to explain what had happened to me in a reasonably coherent fashion.

As I explained later, it was not an external piece of malware or a denial of service attack but just what we experts call 'the system getting itself into a fankle'. Those events are almost impossible to diagnose but occasionally a bunch of code will be skipped during a procedure for some weird reason, and then the system thinks it's a microwave oven, forgets its own name, and descends into temporary insanity.

The reason it skipped the code in the first place is never revealed by any searches no matter how careful. In some mysterious way the system seems to do its best to distract any analyst from looking into it in any depth. The only way out is the equivalent of a solid slap around the face. Cut it off from the outside world - mainly for the safety of the latter - shut down all systems and then begin again with the simple stuff until either the cause becomes apparent – unlikely - or it just regains its sanity for no apparent reason. After an hour I had found the problem, replaced the corrupt section of code, and - within two hours - they were up and running again with a system that knew not only who it was but also had a fairly firm grip on the day and date. When I had time to notice, I found myself sitting beside a very beautiful brunette with startlingly green eyes and a smile that made even rational humans forget who and where they were. She bought me a 'thank you' drink in the bar that evening and we've been what they call an item ever since.

Emma was one of those hugely ambitious girls who'd set her sights on getting to senior rank in record time. For that reason we'd agreed to not get 'involved'. Well, you know what it's like, we never really agreed anything specific, it was more a sort of series of half-finished sentences that left both parties confused and determined never to bring the subject up again.

Our arrangement, therefore, was everything romantic - it was loving, caring, sensual, highly sexual, and exclusive. If you ask me how that differs from a fully committed relationship, I'd have a job answering. We liked each other - quite a lot I think - we enjoyed each other's company and we were great in bed. We'd go to the cinema together, have meals out, spend a few days in London on leave, and we acted as the plus-one for various events in each other's lives. On two occasions we'd spent a couple of weeks together on a beach in the Greek islands. Sheer bliss. But we did not allow ourselves to get any closer than that. I know you are laughing yourself silly but it seemed sensible and believable at the time. No introductions to other people as boyfriend/girlfriend, no over-the-top endearments, comedy birthday cards only, no contact with her parents, and we told anyone who would listen that we 'were just good friends'. The irony is that she was just that and more. Emma did not have a clue about what I got up to in my secret life, but, if anyone could lay claim to that dubious honour … she understood me.

We exchanged a long kiss and I then nodded towards the suitcases on the bed. I got a grin and a punch on the shoulder before she made a start on the small piles of t-shirts and shirts I'd folded up ready for her. To be fair, there wasn't much to pack. She rolled and stuffed her piles in a few minutes and I added some jeans and chinos and my only two decent civilian jackets and that was it. I'd already placed my few framed photos under layers of clothes. I threw in my rowing and running gear together with the shoes I'd wrapped in a couple of plastic bags last night. I reviewed my stuff. It seemed pitifully little for seven years of my life - just a couple of medium suitcases, a duffel-bag, my personal laptop, a three-year old cell phone, and an e-book reader. Even my washing and shaving gear was minimal - two small hotel bottles of shampoo and shower gel, some shaving oil in a tiny bottle, and a five-year old electric shaver that badly needed a new foil and cutters. Somewhere I had a beard trimmer but I only used it on leave and, for the life of me, I couldn't remember who I'd loaned it to.

I walked over to the battered chest of drawers and pretended to check that it was empty. There was no need of course. In reality, I was painfully aware of all the false signals in the room - the loving couple doing some packing, both of them lying to the other about the future. I'd assured Emma that I would call her once I was settled so that she could join me for a spot of her leave. She'd told me she'd fit into that vision and would be sure to spend time with me. Neither of us, I thought, was being genuine. I convinced myself that each of us believed they were telling the other what they wanted to hear and that it was 'better that way'. Have I told you that I can be a bit of a wally at times?

I gave the room a scan. Yes, just my laptop, cell phone, e-book reader, and my toothbrush and razor remained. Those would go into the duffel-bag in the morning. That sorted the downside of the evening, now it was time for fun. I lifted the two cases off the bed and replaced them with Emma. It was an inspired move.

The next couple of hours surprised me - but then again what was *not* surprising me at the moment? Our love-making was usually fun, active, innovative, and exciting. There was rarely a moment when our faces were not lit up with smiles. But this was unlike anything I'd ever known with Emma. The only words I can think of are … intense … needy … incredibly caring and … gentle. We were like a different couple. I lay there afterwards with her silently nestled into my shoulder, her arm wrapped around me, and it hit me like a steamroller. I was such an idiot. I should have known. This evening had been exactly like it would be our very last together … and now, staring up into the darkness with her fragrant hair tickling my face, it sank into my soul that it was. Someone had thrown a bucket of ice-cold water over me.

We lay there not speaking for a long time until Emma stirred and kissed my cheek.

'Take care of yourself Tim, and please keep in touch. I mean it.'

I nodded in the dark and squeezed her hand. She got out of bed. Well, actually she did what she normally did and virtually fell out of the narrow single bed. I heard her scramble from the floor and watched the silhouette of her body as she slipped into her knickers and bra and shrugged on her robe. She grabbed her other clothes and then stood waiting while I stepped up to her and pulled her to me.

'Stay a bit longer?' I felt her move into the embrace but then the sensible Flight Lieutenant from Operations climbed back into the driving seat and her body stiffened.

'Best not, Tim. I have the early shift and you've got a long day tomorrow, too.' She gave me a long, soft kiss. 'I'll see you around, eh?'

I did not trust myself to do more than nod. Her tears on my cheek felt cold as the door clicked quietly behind her. I stood there for a very long time staring at the faint outline where the corridor lights leaked through. I wiped her tears onto my finger and tasted them on my tongue. They would have to last me a very long time.

I'd been shaking my head a lot that day and I did it again as I straightened the bed. In my imagination … in my plans … today had been a boisterous and fun-filled day from start to finish. But nothing had been like that. My colleagues had been sad to see me go but had covered it up with a few weak jokes. There had been a little banter but the whole day had been a shadow of my anticipation. It had all been strangely low key and somehow dissatisfying. The intense time I had just had with Emme was a painful memory. No, I mean it – on top of the disappointment of the day, this evening had been heart-wrenchingly, agonisingly painful

As my head touched the pillow, I remember thinking that it just went to show that you can never predict things. I did not know just how right I was. Yes, I know, I've already told you that I can be a complete moron – get used to it.

5

Nightmare at Sneddon

I awoke after an indeterminate time, to see the door to my room opening. In a distant and very vague way, this puzzled me. I was sure I'd flicked the lock after Emma left. As it swung wide open, it let in a gust of frigid air that instantly enveloped the entire room and pierced me to the core even through the bedcovers. The influx of chilly air was accompanied by a weird, dark cloud. It began at the door and slowly crept into every corner bringing with it a terrifying sense of dread and despair. It was like watching those time-lapse films of cloud formations - the puffs of cloud growing and combining and reforming until they create a gigantic thunder cloud. The black cloud expanded in an apparently random pattern and, from my frozen bed, I became aware of something nameless and utterly terrifying creeping across the floor towards me.

I was shaking - whether with cold or fear I am not sure - but at the same time I was paralysed. I couldn't move my hands, my arms, my legs … all of them felt completely numb. My head seemed to be locked onto the dim shape of the open door and my whole being trembled in anticipation of the things that were now coming towards me.

A series of forms materialised from the dark cloud. One

second there was an amorphous black, swirling cloud of ink. The next it had become a figure which walked towards me, becoming more definite and recognisable as it approached my bed. More apparitions glided out of the cloud and turned to move directly towards me, joining those already standing there. It was pitch dark in the room and yet I could see the features of each form very clearly. They were frighteningly familiar as they glided to a halt in a semi-circle around my bed. There were my dead mother and father, there was Emma, Sean, Miller, Grover, and the rest of the team. My father stood towards the back. He was in full Air Marshall's uniform, his gaze accusing and grave. At the back of the group were a couple of pilots from the squadron with whom I was friendly. The Wing Commander stood to one end and his beautiful PA, Helen, was glaring at me from his side.

None of them was smiling. I could feel the disapproval and disappointment radiating from every single face. I kept returning to the puzzle of why it was so dark and yet I could see their faces so clearly. The weight bearing down on me was a physical manifestation of their expressions. Every one of them looked sad, betrayed, and thoroughly disappointed. And even as I watched they began to glide closer. Each figure held out its arms as though to strangle me. They glided silently closer and closer. I wanted to fend them off, to call for help, to move away from their embrace but I could not move a finger. I was going to die, smothered and absorbed by the darkness. Illogically it was my father who reached me first, my mother was alongside him and Emma and Sean were also beginning to get their hands around my throat. The darkness had now reached down my throat, making breathing almost impossible. It seemed to be clouding my vision as well. I could feel strong hands around my throat, squeezing and squeezing. I don't know how long not being able to move, see, or breathe lasted but I was going mad trying to speak, trying to say sorry for whatever had annoyed them so much, trying to suck in air, trying to make them stop their attack and remove that fear-filled darkness. I was voicelessly shouting at them before the blackness began to break up. It did not fade away, it pixellated - breaking into smaller and smaller bits, each slowly falling to the floor like motes of black dust. The most heart-wrenching thing of all was watching my mother break up and fall into a black wisp of dust.

I woke with a start as the final pieces of the dearest people in my life disappeared. My breath came in ragged gasps, as though I'd been running for hours. The room was silent and no-one was banging at the door so I assumed that I had not actually screamed during the nightmare. But I was drenched in sweat and the bed was a disaster area.

It took me more than a few minutes to regain some composure. I was trembling – well and truly spooked. Once my breathing had slowed and I could think fairly clearly again, I got up – slowly - and made myself a cup of hot chocolate. My hands were still shaking a bit when I sat myself heavily on the moth-eaten excuse for a desk chair. I wrapped my bathrobe around me and used the hand towel to dry my face and hair. After all that had just passed, my brain focused on the fact that I hadn't packed the bathrobe. It was almost new, a present from Emma last Christmas. So, I'd need another carrier bag in the morning! The mind does crazy things in tense times.

Confused I might have been, but not so much that I ignored the implications of that nightmare for my future. It seemed like a warning of disaster to come, and I did not need disaster. I had a very strict rule - nothing was ever spoken or written down about my private life anywhere on or near the base, whether physically or digitally. It was a good rule. That way nothing could ever be found to incriminate me. I had encrypted digital files stored deep in the dark web and on a couple of servers in countries that could never be accused of being compliant with international IT regulations. But not a single thing in writing or digitally in my room or on the base.

But the nightmare had shaken me and I urgently needed reassurance about the new life I had created – the reason I was not renewing my commission. I took a very small piece of paper and wrote out the names and locations of my various bank accounts. Beside each one I wrote the rough amount of money that should be residing in each and fired up my laptop. I used a complex ten-leg, triple-VPN route to hide my identity and location as I checked each and every account and ticked them off on the list. When I had finished I totalled it all up - £119.7 million - more than I'd thought. I ran the calculation again and the figure was right.

I'd been hacking and stealing that cash for the past five years and not a single other person in the entire world knew that I'd got it. No-one. The police still did not know who had robbed banks and large companies across the world. Some I'd robbed while on postings to places like Singapore, Sydney, Cyprus, and even Washington DC. I'd covered my cyber-tracks perfectly. At the time I thought I'd been super-careful and very lucky.

Tomorrow, after signing out with the Wing Commander, I'd be heading for London and eventually to a final identity as Hans Breitner. In a few months he would arrive at Grantley Adams Airport, Barbados as a long-term emigrant from Brazil. In spite of the risk, I checked the accounts again and double checked the safe deposit boxes in London, Newcastle and Edinburgh where I'd stashed fake passports and a pile of spending money. To my profound relief, everything was in perfect order.

I grabbed a cereal bowl from the cupboard, tore the piece of paper into tiny bits, and burned them thoroughly before washing the oily black mess down the sink. I totally erased the history and other caches from the laptop, and triple-checked the systems and hidden files. Even I would not be able to recover any of the activity from this evening.

When I sat down again I stared at the scratched and worn surface of the tiny desk. I was checking that I'd not left any indentations from my scribbles on the piece of paper but I was still in a state of shock. The few patches of remaining varnish reflected the light from my little LED desk lamp. It looked as depressing as I felt and, unbidden, the thought pushed itself to the front of my mind that I had another choice if I wanted it. After mid-morning tomorrow, sorry, today, my life would irrevocably take a new path. I would not need to work, there would be all the travel I wanted, and all the money I could ever use – sheer luxury. But I also had a choice, right here and right now, to dump all that; to tell the Wing Commander I wanted to re-enlist for another five years. He'd bite my hand off and in that extended enlistment I'd probably make Squadron Leader or even get my own cyber-warfare group as a Wing Commander. I'd be able to stay with my friends and in a job I enjoyed. The thought initially felt like stepping into a warm shower after a long January morning in a single scull. But that was the problem I suppose. It was too easy to stick to the familiar, too tempting to stay with Mummy and Daddy in their nice comfortable home.

I tapped the pen lightly on the desk as I pondered the choice. Stay and be comfortable but always strapped for cash … or leave and be even more comfortable and rich. Plough the same old furrow until retirement and a pension or take advantage of five years of what I thought had been very clever thieving and strike out for new and exciting shores. It was a genuine, gold-plated no-brainer. Who in their right mind would turn down a lifetime of trying to spend the pile of cash I'd got locked away? Even at modest rates of investment interest I'd have upwards of £3.5m to spend every year. It was not going to make me a member of the super-rich but I'd be able to do everything I wanted and stay below the radar of suspicious police officers. And the clincher was that, should I really want it, I could always re-enlist a few years down the line. Just because I was rich did not mean the RAF would reject me.

It was 3.30 am when I finally breathed a sigh of relief. The nightmare had been the result of the massive life-change that was facing me in the morning, but that is all it was. I'd managed to clear my mind of the doubts. I'd checked my pots of money and my go-bags in those safe deposit boxes. I grinned to myself as I got back into bed. I was lucky enough to be young, reasonably good looking, intelligent, and rich. I had a doctoral degree in Quantum Information Theory. I'd worked hard to acquire the wealth, and now a whole new life awaited me. Missing out on shifts in the Cyber Warfare Centre, spending hours trying to track down a foreign hacker, struggling to get certain members of staff to do their jobs properly, watching the money to make sure it lasted until the end of the month ... suddenly all of it seemed a very small price to pay for a life of well-planned wealth and leisure.

6

Brave New World

The alarm on my watch woke me at 6:45 am. I snoozed it three times and still felt foul when I forced myself into the world of the living. I shuffled to the cramped bathroom and turned on the shower. Today was THE day - the one I'd been working towards for the past five years. The flat was cold, but the shower soon warmed me up. By the time I'd had a shave, I felt half-way human. I dressed carefully in my full uniform and brushed my cap. I wanted to look my best for the final few hours. I lined up the civilian clothes that I'd be changing into later, threw some last bits and pieces into the duffle bag, set the suitcases and bag by the door ready for collection, and checked myself one last time in the bathroom mirror. I looked the business. Three very minor medals on my chest, my Flight Lieutenant's cuff stripes and shoulder flashes, and my shoes polished to a deep shine. I spent a few minutes getting my cap angle right. I wanted a stylish rake but not too much. The WingCo would be very displeased by anything that seemed arrogant in a young officer. When I'd got it tilted just enough, I sucked in a deep breath and reached for the door handle. This was worse than going to the dentist.

The sky was overcast but it was a sullen threat rather than

the harbinger of an imminent downpour. My stomach was churning as I walked the familiar route to the CO's office. Partly nervousness and partly a lack of breakfast. I'd have time before the taxi to pop into the mess after seeing the WingCo. The officers and the airmen and women I passed generally smiled and waved. I knew almost all of them. In the distance I saw Emma turning to look as she disappeared into one of the hangars. I threw her a salute and blew her a kiss. In spite of my nerves I was walking into familiar territory, with familiar people. In the outer office would be Helen - the fabulously attractive PA to the CO. She was the one that got away. She would wave me through with a frown and I'd enter Mike's office, salute him, and stand to attention while he ran through the routine. He would hand over my discharge papers, I'd sign a few forms to give them permission to deduct mess bills and other spending from my final pay, and then I'd shake hands, and throw him one more salute. I'd then return to my room, change out of my uniform into civvies, grab a quick bite in the mess, and meet the taxi booked for 11:00 at the main gate. Nothing too onerous - just a series of easy fences to be negotiated.

And I was there. I winked at a lovely girl from the mess who had probably just been bringing coffee to the CO and skipped up the steps and through the inner lobby. The door in front of me was marked 'Commanding Officer - Wing Commander Mike Miller, DFC, MBE'. I swung it open and, with my very best and broadest smile, asked 'What ho, young Helen. How're you managing without me today?'.

And that was the first shock of the longest day of my life. She wasn't there. In her place sat a large, thirty-something chap in a dark suit reading a newspaper. He didn't smile or acknowledge me in any way, but his eyes flicked to the Wing-Co's office and I took the hint.

I was daunted neither by the lack of the ravishing Helen, nor by the smartly-dressed robot sitting in her chair. I breezed through the inner door and into Mike's office. Before I could register much of what I was seeing I came to attention and began to intone my rehearsed line: 'Sir. Flight Lieutenant Ward reporting for discharge.' I got about two words out before it struck me that Miller was not in his chair. He was standing behind and to the side of a portly character who was now filling the WingCo's desk chair. Mike did not meet my eye. His face was like thunder. Something was badly wrong but, in my innocence, I had no idea just how badly wrong it was.

My attention turned to the chap sitting at the Wing Commander's desk as though he owned it. He was expensively dressed in a top-quality suit, blindingly white shirt, and red silk necktie. Almost completely bald, what little hair fringed his head was well cut. At that moment he removed his reading glasses and looked up at me.

'Ah, there you are at last'. His voice was deep and cultured. He turned his head to Mike Miller and continued, 'Thank you Wing Commander. We don't need to keep you from your duties any longer. You may go now. We will finish up here and be out of your hair within an hour.'

I was baffled. I glanced at Mike Miller. He hesitated for a second and then walked quickly past me to the door. Not once did he meet my eye. He opened his door and turned back to look at the chap who had taken occupation of his desk. The man looked up from the file he was reading. 'Don't be concerned Wing Commander, I will abide by our agreement. Out as quickly as possible and no uniform. The documentation is signed. I will leave copies. Thank you again for the use of your office.' Mike nodded once and left, closing the door quietly behind him.

Mike's office was old-fashioned. Masses of wood and lots of shelves. It smelled very strongly of polish and musty books, with a mild overlay of aftershave. I stayed very still and watched. The bloke exuded civil servant from every pore. If he was senior enough he could certainly waltz into a Wing Commander's office and take over. But what did he want with me? He was a mind reader, too.

'Flight Lieutenant Timothy Ward, my name is John Reid. You are under arrest.' My jaw must have dropped open but I was thinking quickly behind the dumbfounded exterior.

'You must have the wrong person, sir, I am here to be discharged after a seven-year enlistment.'

He pursed his lips as though he'd expected something similar and was disappointed. 'You are certainly being discharged Mr. Ward but not to be set free into civilian life.'

'What am I charged with, sir? I haven't done anything.'

His head dropped and I was dazzled by the bright reflection of the ceiling lights off his pate. He did not invite me to sit down. 'Mr Ward. We have evidence that you have been using your cyber skills to enrich yourself to a considerable extent. We have photos and documentation that, in any court of law, will see you receive a period of incarceration not less than ten and not more than twenty years. The actual term will depend on how a military tribunal regards your besmirching the uniform and betraying your duty to uphold His Majesty's laws.' He gave me a lengthy gaze. 'I would place good money against them being minded to let you off easy.'

'Why should I believe these preposterous charges? And please give me my correct title in civilian life. I am Dr Ward.'

He tossed a fat folder towards me. 'Take a close look Mr Ward. I think you will recognise very quickly that you are in no position to make empty denials behind fancy titles.'

The contents of that folder were astounding. It was true. They'd got a lot of evidence. They had photos of me in a few places outside and inside some of the banks I'd used to hide the proceeds, they had documents which listed the amounts of money and the dates on which I'd hacked millions of dollars, and they had everything indexed and summarised so that even military police officers would be able to compile a highly damning charge sheet. My mind simply couldn't cope with it all. He had evidence on a total of about £40m in hacks. How had they done this? I'd been ultra careful. Sensibly for once, I opted for silence.

Reid stood up and retrieved the folder from my suddenly weak hands. 'I see you are convinced. The evidence is solid - a total of over £40m and a list of five separate overseas accounts containing that sum.' He opened the office door and shouted for his man to bring them in. Bring what in? Things were moving too fast but I had time to register that he did not know everything. They'd missed a number of bank accounts and a goodly sum of money. Just then, Reid threw a bundle onto the visitor chair and told me to get changed.

'What, here?'

He did not dignify that with an answer. He took up a position in the open doorway looking out into the PA's office. I had no choice. I stripped off my uniform down to my t-shirt, pants, and socks, folded everything up and placed it neatly on a corner of Mike's desk. Only then did I actually look at the bundle that Reid had tossed me. It was a set of plain brown overalls that had seen too many washing machines. I sighed deeply but put them on. They were too large but it was not difficult to guess that complaints would be met with total indifference.

Reid looked back with satisfaction and his man stepped into the room to complete the final act. He pushed me roughly around to face the back wall and handcuffed my hands behind my back.

'Come along then,' ordered Reid. He immediately set out and we followed - a stunned and bewildered me next, and the silent goon at my back. I was absolutely stunned but I'd learned a long time ago to remain calm. There was always a way of escaping and my guess was that I'd get an opportunity sometime on the car journey they were taking me on. There was money left and the folder had not contained details of passports or go-bags. Things were not great but, where there was hope, there was a way. I tried to focus on potential escape plans.

Which was impossible during the walk of shame that followed. I made the mistake of looking around as I got outside and was unfortunate enough to catch the eyes of a number of my erstwhile friends and colleagues. Disappointment was the main look but there were also a few - mainly blokes - who looked quietly satisfied. Ward had got his just desserts. Miller and Helen walked quickly away. I saw young Linda Grover wipe her eyes before doing the same. After that I kept my eyes to the ground, and hoped desperately that Emma was not seeing this. I couldn't wait to be put into the back of their car.

And that was yet another of my many mistakes that day. They didn't have a car. They'd brought a hulking great military police prison van. Roughly the size of a ten- or fifteen-ton delivery truck it gleamed in the weak sunlight that was now emerging from a clearing winter sky. Regulation grey, plain sides except for barred windows, its only adornment was a thick, bright yellow strip down the side containing the words: 'His Majesty's Military Prison Service'. The goon opened an almost invisible door on the side of the truck and shoved me into a tiny cell. He threaded my handcuffs through a chain, kicked one of my feet deeper into the cell and slammed the door. I remember at least half of me being relieved that I did not have to face my friends any longer. The cell was an upright coffin which had the benefit of a tiny, barred window high up. This was a high-tech prison van. Each cell had its own external door but prisoners were shackled to a chain which was welded to the door on one side and disappeared through a hole in the back wall. The chain was ratcheted tight and the door could not be opened without it being released by a lever somewhere inside the truck, beyond the cell. Even if I could somehow pick the lock on the handcuffs, which I probably could, I could not unlatch the chain to open the cell door to the outside. To say that I was clinging to the hope of escape would be just plain wrong. There was nothing to cling to. From what I could see, the prison van was escape proof unless the Mafia staged an armed attack and remembered to bring an oxyacetylene torch.

Surely, Reid had to stop somewhere before we reached a military prison? Perhaps a comfort break? All I'd need to do would be to disable the guard chap and then steal a car. Off the motorways the police would have a job catching me and all I had to do was grab a go-bag, buy a change of clothes, and get to the private airfield at Drifforth. Alec Masters was an old friend - a pilot who had left the RAF to launch a charter service. As long as the news had not preceded me I could cadge a flight in one of his aircraft to get me to the continent and ultimately to Switzerland. In Alec's Gulfstream - elderly as it was - it would take me just a few hours and, once there, I'd be able to use two more go-bags and several million dollars to get me to Brazil.

My excitement rose as, about an hour into the drive, my arms and legs stiffening painfully from the confinement, I felt the truck leave the motorway and begin a slow crawl which I hoped was leading us into a service station parking lot. In truth, I hoped to hell it was a service area. If it was, this was my chance - they'd have to let me go to the loo. I reviewed my elementary hand-to-hand combat training. I'd not be able to get the nerve in his neck. I was never able to do it even in training when the instructor carefully pointed out the pressure point and guided my hand to the right spot. It would have to be a heavy object to the base of the skull. A small fire extinguisher, perhaps a soap dispenser, maybe I could grab some heavy crockery from the diner? I'd only get one chance and it would have to be taken with gusto. And then I'd have to leg it into the car park, hijack some poor sod's car as they were getting ready to drive off - and hope they had enough fuel to get me the fifty or so miles to the first go-bag. A change of clothes, a new hired car, and then to the airfield. Narrow chances are better than none at all, and my hopes were high.

The truck rocked to a stop with a hiss of air brakes and everything went quiet. I braced myself for the external door being opened. There was the whirr and clunk of the chain being released. I turned towards the external door, expecting to hear footsteps before the door was unlocked from the outside. Instead, the loose end of the chain was fed through the hole behind me and another click resulted in a second door being opened into the interior of the vehicle. Was there nothing that worked the way I needed? The goon was standing in the entrance to the cell beckoning me into a larger space. I was stiff from sitting on the narrow prisoner's seat but that was soon forgotten when I struggled to my feet and saw the inside of the truck. There were no rows of cells, just what looked like two behind me plus my own. The rest of the interior was done up like a luxury camper van complete with two toilets at the rear. Mr Goon nodded to one of the loos and let me in after removing the handcuffs. And no, no windows in there either.

When I emerged, I found Reid sitting in a very comfortable armchair working on a laptop. He indicated the seat across from him and his man pushed me down and attached one wrist to a loose shackle in the chair arm. The chairs were heavily padded, the tables and fittings were wood veneer. The smell of new leather was heavy in the air and there was a blank but expensive large screen TV against one wall. That was probably the moment when I mentally gave up. Their security arrangements were superb. I could not escape from this truck. I'd not be let out until I reached the prison. But I reminded myself that all prisons have their weaknesses. I was just a bit puzzled with the luxury prison truck. The Military Police would never be able to afford such an expensive piece of kit.

Reid closed the laptop. 'While Mr Black goes to get us some refreshments I have a proposition for you. The choice you make is entirely up to you.' I inclined my head to indicate that I was listening. 'We are currently about thirty miles from a major military prison. My paperwork and the proof of your crimes is completely in order and I can take you there and drop you off into the gentle custody of people who tend not to relish the idea of serving officers enriching themselves while wearing the King's uniform.'

The word 'proposition' was music to my ears. 'There's an alternative?'

He nodded. 'There's always an alternative. In this case you could avoid all that by working for me for a year, possibly less. I have use for a bright young man like yourself. You'd be closely guarded - I have great respect for your ingenuity - but you'd live in decent accommodation, with good food and the chance to exercise regularly.'

I frowned. 'Sounds like another prison.'

'Yes. It does and to an extent it is. But the living arrangements would make your recent RAF quarters look like a slum and I can assure you of two other things. Firstly, you'd be very interested in the work, and secondly it would be the closest thing to freedom you could expect as things stand. Within the confines of the job and the base, you'd be free to do whatever you like.'

A year? That sounded much too good to be true. 'So, what's the catch? What's the job? And why me?'

'None, I can't tell you yet, and because you have the right skills.'

'Would I get paid?'

He cracked a small smile. 'No. Not a penny. But I would allow you to keep the cash you've stolen, after you leave my employ.'

'How long? You mentioned a year.'

'Given that you'd be looking at ten to fifteen years in a

military prison, I think twelve months - less if I have my way - would be a bargain.' He paused as his man deposited some pastries and two coffees on the table between us. 'So, what is your decision? HM Forces Prison Wood Grange or working for me?'

I think you'll agree that I did not have much bargaining power. I wolfed a pastry and sipped the delicious coffee while I pretended to consider his offer. There was really no choice of course. He had me bang to rights on some very serious charges, he had all the proof he needed, and there was no way I wanted to spend the next half of my life eating prison food and trying to avoid the soap falling to the floor in the showers.

I nodded once. He nodded once. He indicated that his man could drive on and that was the last thing I remember of that journey.

7

Hogtied

I woke up in bed in a darkened room with a pounding headache and the immediate realisation that the bastards had drugged me. If I felt like a fool before this, I was climbing rapidly towards my gold-star idiot badge.

It must have been in the coffee. I remembered nothing from Reid starting to get up from his chair in the prison van. I lay there befuddled. My mouth felt like the inside of an incontinent rabbit's cage. In deference to my head, I lay completely still, trying to sort out my thoughts. Feelings came first because they took less effort. I was annoyed they'd been confident enough to drug my coffee *before* I'd taken the decision to join up. I was ashamed that my plans to escape had been so easily thwarted. I was puzzled that my crimes had been recorded. And I sensed, beneath all of that, a desperation born of being thoroughly trapped. Having got all that listed, I dragged myself to a sitting position and considered my surroundings.

The bed was a double - the sheets were soft, cotton, and well laundered. The pillows medium firm - just the way I liked them. I was dressed in the shorts and t-shirt that I usually wore for bed and I was covered by a sheet and a duvet on top - again just the way I liked it. This was more than spooky. Was there nothing they didn't know about me? There was a dim glow in the room - street lights? What I could see of it was fairly large and there was more light coming into it than I was used to at the base. It also smelled clean, unlike my musty RAF quarters. Chests of drawers, fitted wardrobe, a blanket box and an easy chair - it all looked and smelled fairly new and of good quality. With a little effort I sat on the edge of the bed and waited for my head to stop spinning before standing up very slowly. I needed a glass of water and something for the throbbing pain behind my eyes. There were two smart, wooden doors. One led into a small sitting room. The other into an en-suite bathroom and shower. The bathroom alone was almost as big as my old RAF quarters. The fittings were of the latest fashion and very clean. The cabinet contained everything from my brand of toothpaste to pain-killers. I took two with some water and then gulped down three full glasses of tap water. The clock on the bedroom wall said 4:27 am. I took a quick look around the sitting room and peeked out of the windows through curtains that had been neatly drawn. The window in the sitting room looked out from the second or third floor onto a narrow, concrete street. There were buildings of three and four storeys further up a shallow hill. The view from the bedroom was of a side alley between two brick buildings. Unremarkable in both cases and eerily like the sorts of buildings I was used to on military bases.

I made my way carefully back to bed and pondered. Was I on another military base? If so, how had they managed to get the budgets to offer such comfortable quarters? I did not ponder for long. My head barely touched the pillow before I was being roused at 9:35 am by loud knocking on a door and constant ringing of the doorbell. I felt much better, the headache had gone although I suspected the doorbell would bring it back pretty soon. The external door was at one end of the living room, shielded by a smart wooden screen. Standing on the doorstep in a wide, brightly painted corridor was none other than my old friend, Mr Goon. He wasted no time.

'Get dressed. Mr Reid wants to see you immediately.'

'I haven't had breakfast yet and I'm not feeling terribly good after your little potion yesterday.'

He treated me to a 'not my problem' shrug and pushed past me.

'Come on. Move it.'

I sighed. 'Look. I need food and tea. I can't function without them.'

'My orders are to drag you by the hair if necessary but, if it makes you feel better, there may be a bite to eat in Mr Reid's office.' I needed no more encouragement - stick and carrot had worked very effectively.

After a short walk, with me feeling extremely underdressed in jeans, t-shirt, and a sweater, he presented me in a super-plush office on the second floor of a building about seventy or eighty yards up the street. There were people everywhere, all of them wearing jump-suits in a variety of colours. It looked like something straight out of a James Bond film - colourful henchmen and women striding purposefully up the street carrying folders or clipboards or just staring fixedly ahead and not meeting anyone's eyes.

When I say the office was plush I'm not exaggerating for effect. The carpet was about six inches deep, the sofas and chairs looked like they could swallow you whole, and there was a smell of polish and a light but expensive perfume. There was also a strong aroma of food which reignited my intense hunger. I'd thought about it walking down the road. I'd eaten one small Danish pastry since dinner with Emma the day before yesterday. It was long past Ward's feeding time.

Reid was in a massive desk chair reading a thick document. The chair was more like a throne than the sort of desk chair most of us are used to. It spoke volumes about his ego. He handed the document to his man.

'I've initialled the right places. Get Carla to organise the actions right now.' Mr Goon disappeared almost instantly and Reid seemed to notice me for the first time.

'Sit down, Ward. There's breakfast on the sideboard there. Help yourself to as much as you want. There's a selection of juices, and the usual tea and coffee.' I was stacking a plate with a huge fried breakfast even as he finished speaking. I chose to sit on the far side of what was probably his meeting table so that I could see him while I stuffed myself. He read some more from his pile of papers while I put away the monster meal, only lifting his head when he heard me sigh contentedly and clink the knife and fork onto the large, expensive, and now empty china plate. I'd also managed two full glasses of his wonderful orange juice.

'Right. Come and sit in front of the desk and I'll brief you on your role here.' I did as I was told, being sure to take a cup of tea with me. His eyes followed me all the way. There was a very slight delay and then he dropped the bombshell of my life.

'Yesterday you agreed to work for me and signed a contractual document. It requires you to work for my company – Reid Research - for a period of up to five years with compensation only in the form of bed and board.' I must have frowned. 'You will not remember the signatures but - trust me - you signed and initialled every part required.'

'So, why am I here? Why do you want me for five years? You said yesterday that it was a matter of months, a year at most.'

'That's true but contracts always err on the cautious side. I need someone with intelligence and the proven ability to plan well, think on their feet, and possibly to steal things.'

For some reason that gave me renewed hope. If he wanted stuff half-inched he'd have to let me get out and about and that meant I'd get chances to escape. I still had my three UK go-bags. If I could get to even one of them I was free and clear - albeit with less cash than I'd originally counted on. Still, freedom would mean more opportunities, so my optimism rose accordingly.

'I'm your man. What do you want me to thieve? I know the jewellery stores, the richest citizens, and the biggest banks in a score of world cities. Take your pick.'

He gave me a very strange look and then said. 'Mr Ward, you will not be required to leave this compound. The base you will see in the next couple of days is all you will ever be needed to see. You will simply be asked to act as part of a time-travelling team.'

I'd been eating a chocolate croissant while sipping my tea and it almost choked me. 'I'm sorry, that sleeping draught last night must have affected my hearing. What did you say?'

'I said that your role here is to act as part of a time-travelling team. I have other teams working from the south but,' he coughed significantly, 'given your penchant for subterfuge, I thought that you should be kept closer to home. Yours will be the only team operating from here and that affords me the chance to keep you under extremely tight security.'

I was still floundering. 'You're not making sense. Have you been sampling your own knock-out drugs?'

When his eyes met mine it was patently clear that was not the case. He was deadly serious. 'Your tasks will be similar to all the other teams in operation - to acquire for the company information and insights on events and people from the past.'

'You're serious aren't you!' He just stared back at me as I tried desperately to absorb his words. It was a minute before I felt strong enough to continue. The man was clearly mad but if anything brought me closer to escaping, I was all in. There were a million questions hanging in the air, but I went with something comfortingly physical. 'So, where's my team?'

He must have pressed a hidden button because, instantly, the leather panelled door opened and he asked for someone to be shown in. The person who entered the office was probably the largest man I had seen in a very long time. In his early-thirties, about six feet three, fair haired, and almost as wide as he was tall. Reid watched him stride to the desk and stand to attention. He was wearing a black jump suit.

'Sir, you asked for me, sir.'

'Mr Ward, this is ex-Sergeant Major Richie Deutzinger. He has been with us for a couple of years now. Joined us after leaving the Royal Marines after ten years' service. Mr Deutzinger this is the other member of your team, Mr Timothy Ward, ex-RAF.'

Deutzinger did not take his eyes off Reid. 'Sir. I read Mr Ward's file outside. Your secretary has the folder.'

Reid nodded. 'Thank you.' He turned to me. 'When he is not nursemaiding you, Ward, Mr Deutzinger is a valued member of our security section. He will be in charge of your team. You will have two days to get acclimatised to the base and to become reasonably familiar with Mr Deutzinger. Following that, I will supervise your first mission briefing and you will get to work.' He scanned our faces. 'You do not need to like each other but I insist on you working effectively together. I must also emphasise to Mr Ward that people here at Barrow Briggs are discouraged from speaking to members of other groups.'

I felt that I needed to impose myself just the teeniest bit. 'What groups, Reid?'

He stopped dead for a moment but clearly decided to ignore the insult for the time being. I'd probably have to pay for it at some point.

'All staff are allocated to colour groups which correspond to their overall purpose. You may have noticed the uniforms on the way here. At the bottom are the Yellow Group whose roles are generally extremely simple and junior. Green coveralls denote administrative people. Blue is for staff working directly to me. And Black is worn by those who supervise and conduct operations. Brown overalls are the uniform of the support staff - cleaners, maintenance staff, caterers, and so on. As you can see Mr Deutzinger wears a black jumpsuit. That is because security is considered part of the overall operational function.'

I waited but he remained silent. I desperately wanted to laugh. Was he serious? 'Okay, and me? What colour do I have to parade around in?'

'That would be yellow, Mr Ward. You will find sets of jumpsuits in your wardrobe into which you should change as soon as you return to your quarters. Any questions?' I glanced at Deutzinger but he stared stolidly ahead and kept his lip buttoned like a good non-comm.

'I will probably have a hundred questions,' I ventured, 'but I'm still reeling from your sci-fi revelations.' I wasn't joking - I could not begin to think of any other question than 'Time travel? What?' So I let it go and followed the giant out of the room. As soon as we were outside in the roadway he turned around and gave me a wide grin.

'Can I call you Tim, sir? I've read your file and I have to say your exploits would be legendary if I was allowed to speak of them around the base.' I smiled back - probably in relief - he was the first person who'd been friendly to me since Emma - but not in the same way of course.

'Of course. It's Richie, is that right?' He nodded rapidly while stepping up the intensity of the grin to solar levels.

'I've got to get back to the security section to finish today's shift but then we'll be able to schedule some meeting times. We have to run through the things you won't yet know.' He went to pat me on the shoulder but pulled back at the last second and sped off. I wandered back to what appeared to be my 'quarters'.

When I emerged for a run about half an hour later wearing my running shorts and top I was almost instantly accosted by two black-uniformed guards carrying automatic weapons. They informed me that I should really consider returning to my rooms and dressing correctly. I was bold enough to ask what would happen if I refused. One of them sniggered.

'Oh, please, please do. I've been looking forward for months to someone not appearing in the correct jumpsuit. We're allowed to lock you in the base jail for any length of time we feel appropriate and, believe me, bread and water is sheer luxury in there. He grinned at his companion. 'Getting out without at least one limb broken is very rare.'

'That seems fair enough gentlemen. I shall return and change without delay.' I could hear them chuckling as they watched me walk all the way back. I changed quickly and emerged again for my run looking like a giant banana. There were very few yellow jumpsuits on the street and my own outfit was so brand new that people had to shield their eyes from the glare.

I ran myself ragged that day, consumed by a deep anger. I ran as far as I could through the grounds and depressed myself to suicidal levels with what I saw. When I ran east I soon encountered the two main gates. They were separated by about fifty yards and covered with enough cameras and lights to shame the security at Buckingham Palace. They also possessed sets of upright poles along the roadway which looked vaguely electronic but I'd never seen anything like them before. To each side and stretching away into the distance on either side were three separate security fences, each about ten feet high and with double layers of razor wire on the sides and top. Each fence was separated by about thirty feet from the others. The East Germans would have loved this stuff. I ran west until I got beyond the main buildings and into a semi-forested area which extended for about a quarter of a mile. At the end of the roadway - now an unpaved track - were the same three lines of fencing but with no back gate. My exploration of the rest of the site's roadways and paths confirmed that the fencing, cameras, and lights encircled the whole base. The cost must have been enormous but I could now see why Reid wanted me here. There was no way out except through the front gates, and if what he'd said about me not being required to leave the base was true - and he did not strike me as the frivolous type - I was well and truly buggered.

The main restaurant was fairly easy to find. I just followed my nose. After a light lunch - which was free – I checked out the base cinema - small but comfortable - the gym - large and very well equipped - and the medical centre - tucked away but apparently modern. I noticed signs to the spa and the bowling alley and I'd already seen the tennis courts, football field, and squash courts. Apart from the main restaurant there were also three small cafés and what looked like two speciality restaurants. The base lacked for nothing it seemed. I estimated total population at between two and three hundred people.

I spent a good part of the evening lounging in a small café which had been placed conveniently between my residential block and the gates. The reading matter - on every interest from stamp collecting to astronomy was up to date and plentiful. The TV in the café played old soap opera videos and a few music videos. The drinks were very good and the pastries and sandwiches top quality. I may have been trapped but this beat RAF Sneddon Downs into a cocked hat in all other respects.

I had an early dinner and spent an hour checking my stuff. Someone had brought all my clothes and washing stuff. My towels had been changed since this morning and my bed made. My robe - the one that Emma had bought me in my fast-fading other life - was hanging on the back of the bathroom door. The only things missing were my laptop and my cellphone. I'd spent a lot of money on those machines. The laptop was specified to the hilt with all the latest tech and, unlike almost everything else on the market, had batteries that could be easily replaced. It was cutting edge. The phone was good too. You never realise how important those things are to your life until they are taken away.

Looking on the bright side, they'd left me my e-book reader but they had disabled the wifi connections. If I had been the crying type I'd have sobbed into my pillow that first night. The worst of it was that not a single thing got any better.

8

A tall, dark stranger and a small one too

As I emerged from the restaurant after breakfast the next day I ran into Richie as he was coming in. He barred my way and you'll understand that there was no way I'd be trying to push past. I stood quietly while he grinned at me.

'Glad I caught you, Tim. We're to be briefed tomorrow at 1100 hours. I've booked a meeting room for us to get to know each other - Room 14 in Building Black, at 1500 hours today.' I smiled back. There was almost nothing else you could do when faced with Richie's joviality.

'Okay Richie. I'll see you there.' He was actually twitching with excitement.

'I can't tell you how much I'm looking forward to getting some real operational time, sir, it's just so … exciting.' I smiled some more and he carefully manoeuvred his massive frame around me.

I was still thoroughly depressed about my situation. Smiling did not come easy. I'd lain awake for a couple of hours the previous night unsuccessfully trying to think of escape possibilities. That morning I had gone for a walk to the west fence and used the time to study the security arrangements up close. The fences and gates I've already described.

You'd need a main battle tank to get through them without the correct passes. I stealthily surveilled the rest of the base during that lazy stroll while regularly holding my face up to the pathetic imitation of sunlight coming through the massing rain clouds. There were gimbal-mounted cameras on every street corner, often two, and I noted several infra-red sensors above doors leading into certain buildings. Notably, the ones labelled Blue and Black. Reid had not only segregated the people into colours there were also separate buildings for each of them. Two Black buildings, one Blue one, several Greens, and a lot of smaller Brown places. The gates and fences were covered with laser and IR sensors as well. Could I forge passes or hack the system to get out? I'd need a different coloured jumpsuit but, I guessed, that would be the easy bit. Without a decent computer and connection to the internal network I wouldn't be able to arrange a digital pass. There were almost certainly biometric checks at the gates and possibly inside the high security buildings. It was all too much for a Yellow with no tech equipment.

In the past I'd learned that a problem rarely solved itself at the first pass. One needs to ponder and generally harry the thing to death. So, I put it to one side, stored the information I'd gained and went to have a nice scone and tea before joining my team leader in the Black Building.

Richie had an excellent memory and was very efficient, but he was also very mechanical. He went through the rules for the team as laid down by Reid. Rules numbered one to twenty could be easily summarised. He was to be the boss at all times and in all circumstances. Richie was all apologies - he was not used to bossing officers around - but he stressed that Reid would have his guts strung out on one of the security fences if he did not do so. He then spoke for a while about the time travelling bits and this is where I perked up a lot.

'I've never done it but I hear it's easy. Just a step into a new time and place, then you does the business and then you comes home.' I questioned him for almost an hour about 'the business' but he was only able to say that the London teams and this new one up here were given people and places to research and that the reports had to be 'really detailed'.

I watched him closely. I could see him being very effective in most situations. He was a trained soldier and now a trusted security officer. As long as I could make him think that all the good ideas were his he'd be a reasonable team leader. He was nobody's fool, though.

'You blew it, sir, didn't you. They got wind of what you were doing and stitched you up good and proper.'

I gave him a rueful look. 'That would seem to be the sum of it, Richie, yes. But I am totally flummoxed as to how they did it. I was very careful.'

'Mr Reid is a clever sod, sir. He's got a reputation for being a hard horse too. My guess is he used one of the London teams to suss you out.' He honoured me with one of his most serious looks. 'Still, I've got to go now.' He grinned again. 'Dinner with a lady from Planning.' I grinned back.

'Go, then, Richie and have a great time.'

'I'll meet you in Reid's outer office at 1045 hours tomorrow.' And he was gone.

I sat for a while and considered my situation. The more I did so, the angrier I became. I was angry at myself mostly, for being so stupid. Richie was right - I'd thought I was being clever, but – somehow - I'd blown it. I was even angrier that I couldn't do anything about it except keep thinking about ways to escape.

There was so much adrenaline in my system that I had to go for a run. I went back to my rooms and changed into a Yellow outfit that I was now keeping just for this purpose. I set off in the drizzle and darkness, immediately aware that the temperature had plummeted during the day and was now hovering around freezing. I turned my face into a sloppy mix of sleet and snow. I ran down to the gate, garnering a little jolt of pleasure as the guards got jumpy as I ran determinedly towards them. About ten yards short I wheeled 180 degrees and set off up the hill the way I'd come. As if anyone would attempt to run two heavily fortified security gates dressed like an over-ripe banana!

I jogged all the way past the residential buildings and the various working ones and then out into the pitch dark towards the west end where the fence blocked the path. For a minute or so I was a little concerned that I might run into the fence in the darkness - that would be bloody and very painful - but the security lights flashed into existence thirty yards before I reached the inner fence. Conscious of the cameras watching me, I did the same again. Ran up to about five yards short and then wheeled about, the visual and IR cameras moving on their mounts to follow my antics.

I ran steadily back down the rough path and the lights went out behind me. I switched on my head torch to counter my loss of night vision and plodded on through the sleet, soaked to the skin and thoroughly depressed. In the distance, the base lights were visible as I rounded a shallow bend in the track and suddenly there were two people in front of me, standing beside a cleaning trolley. One was holding a broom. I hadn't passed cleaners on the way up the hill but I supposed they'd come out of a building behind me. But what were they doing up here halfway into the woods in this atrocious weather? I stopped, panting a little, just in front of them.

'Hi.' I said. Always the one for the incisive introduction. 'I'm Tim Ward, who are you?'

The smaller of the two spoke first. In the dim glow from my head torch I saw that it was a little old woman dressed in a brown overall. 'Hello,' she said brightly. 'I'm Mrs Biddle and this is Henry. We're cleaners.'

I looked them up and down again. Henry was the tall one presumably. A black guy, he was as tall as Richie but slender. It was he who was holding a broom as though it was a poisonous snake. I nodded at them. 'Not the night to be out here in this muck, can I walk back with you?'

When Henry spoke it was an instant surprise. His diction was perfect and his accent almost cut-glass English. 'Thank you, but we are walking up to an old lodge so we will not detain you.'

Mrs Biddle smiled - the sleet dripping from her lined face. 'It's good to meet you Dr Ward. We'll meet again I think.' She waved Henry forward and they began to push the old trolley up the hill into the darkness. I was grateful it hadn't been a long meeting - the cold was knifing into my arms and legs in spite of me jogging on the spot to keep my muscles warm. I ran down the hill towards the bright lights of the base. It wasn't until I'd reached my own doorway that I realised that Mrs Biddle had called me Dr Ward. I was in the shower when it struck me that the cleaners around here would have lists of residents and that my name - Tim Ward - must have triggered her memory of my Doctoral title. Still, it was good that the official records offered that tiny crumb of status even if Reid did not.

After I'd showered, I slumped onto the sofa with a bottle of beer, my mind filled with the calamities of the past forty-eight hours. It had all looked so promising. Since then, my entire world had been turned on its head.

I could feel the drastic situation slowly eroding any confidence that remained in me. A black mist was engulfing me. I closed my eyes and saw only endless captivity. I had no assurance that John Reid would abide by the contract – the one I had not seen but I could not survive a future of captivity. When I opened my eyes it was to see my room as a comfortable prison cell – as devoid of light and hope as the deepest stone dungeon. I took another sip of beer. I could always drink myself to death.

Somehow, that single thought broke my depression and I smiled. Becoming a drunken sot was not in my repertoire.

Things might look bleak, Ward, but you've never let that stop you. Life has been easy for years and you've gotten maudlin in your old age. Pull yourself together. I roused myself from the sofa and went to sit up straight in one of the dining chairs. It made no difference to the depressing list of problems I was facing but it sure as heck made a difference to my determination to get past them.

It had been a traumatic period but the main thing was that I was not in a military prison. I was still thinking, and my go-bags and the majority of the money were still out there waiting for me. I guessed from the name of this base that I was in Northumberland, probably near the Scottish border. The go-bags in Newcastle and Edinburgh were only fifty to seventy miles away. On these roads, about two to three hours by car. Once I got a go-bag I'd have the cash, cards, and documents to get out of the country immediately. I looked at the clock. It lifted my spirits to think I could be in Lisbon by tomorrow afternoon.

I was Tim Ward and there were few problems I could not solve. My top priority was to escape.

9

How's your karma?

I had time for breakfast with Richie before the briefing with Reid. Richie was a hoot. He knew everyone, seemed to be very well liked, and had a limitless store of amusing stories. I didn't need to say anything - he just talked the whole time. To my surprise, no-one commented on my Yellow jumpsuit. Back at Sneddon Downs I'd have been a laughing stock for a month but here at 'the Briggs' as it was known by the residents, curiosity was discouraged. I was grudgingly impressed by how effective Reid's rules were.

When I got back to my room I pondered what to do to fill the spare hour and a half before the briefing. I got hooked when I cast a glance out of the window. Just up the road was the Blue Building and about fifty yards further up was the main Black Building. I watched people entering and leaving them and was fascinated by the contrast. People wearing all sorts of colours went in and out of the Black Building but - and I watched for some time - no other colours but blue jumpsuits accessed the Blue Building. I walked past the doors on my way to the briefing and, still, no colour other than blue was coming out or going in. A quick look into the lobby revealed a very high level of security.

Even in that second or so I noted people swiping cards and could see retina-scanners and possibly fingerprint scanners in the background.

I also rewound the meeting with those two weird cleaners. The tall one, Henry, seemed a very strange choice for a cleaner. He was clearly intelligent and was certainly not used to handling a broom. And the old lady had piercing blue eyes and a most penetrating stare. And why were they pushing that trolley up the hill towards the forest? As far as I knew there were no buildings up there. I smiled inwardly at my own silliness and pushed the matter out of my mind. It was not my problem, but apart from Richie, they were the only people who'd been friendly to me.

The 11:00 am briefing turned out to be with Reid and his Security Chief John Marshall. Richie was instantly on his best behaviour and went very quiet. Marshall was a wiry individual of medium height – about five feet nine - whose hooked nose and pronounced brow ridges made him look like a predatory eagle. Mutual dislike was instant between us. Also in attendance was a white-coated male doctor and a female nurse whose biceps would make two of the doctor's. First impressions are not to be relied upon but she seemed bluff and good natured while the doctor - whose name was Dent - turned out to be a miserable article.

'Right,' announced Reid as soon as we entered, 'let's get the medical bits over with.' He motioned for Richie to sit in the chair in front of his desk. The two medics descended on him and began doing things with his scalp. Richie said 'Ouch' a couple of times but within a few minutes the doctor stepped away and told him to vacate the chair. It was my turn.

'What are they doing?' I asked Reid before sitting.

'Four very simple implants under the scalp - front, back, and both sides. They are electronic and necessary for the time travel process.'

I sat and, apart from it stinging like mad, it was straightforward. The doctor and nurse left the room immediately they'd finished with me. My head felt tender.

Marshall was next on the stage. He approached Richie and me and handed over two leather wrist straps. His voice was like broken glass. 'Put these on your left wrists where you normally wear your watches. If you examine them, the watches underneath are covered with the leather strap. To a casual observer in the past they will look like innocuous wrist bands but, if you peel the leather back in a certain way, you reveal the control screen for the time travel system.'

I peeled mine back. The screen was a larger version of a modern smart watch. He handed over two sheets of paper to each of us. 'These are the instructions. Learn them by heart tonight without fail.'

Reid motioned him to seat himself and took up the running. 'The system is very simple and you will not need to concern yourselves with any technicalities. Your control panels will be wirelessly programmed the night before a jump. The settings will be treble-checked during the two hours before you go. All you need to do - and this is Ward's job because only he has the button - is to press the red button. No matter where Deutzinger is, you will both be transported to the correct time and place. When the mission is complete the same routine applies and you will be transported back here.'

I frowned at him. 'That's it? No spinning flywheels or flashing lights?'

He ignored me. 'The system is working but is not yet fully stable.' He must have heard my 'Knew there'd be a catch.'

'We have already operated about twenty missions and it all works well. Occasionally the system will yank the team out of the time period and back here without warning. It's unfortunate and a little nauseous but not dangerous.'

It was Richie who asked the obvious question. 'Is there anything we can do to prevent that happening, sir?'

Reid shook his head. 'The engineers don't know why yet

but it happens so infrequently that we don't worry about it. They call them Rapid Involuntary Returns – or just IRs - but I understand the teams in London use the term 'whip-backs'.'

'So, what are we supposed to do - assuming that whip-backs don't get us first?' I winked at Richie.

'You get briefed on a specific mission - time, place, issues, etc. Three days is usually sufficient to acquire all the information and recordings we need.' He paused for effect. 'And then you come back, laze away the week that we insist upon as a break between missions, and then go out again.'

I held up my hand. It was intended as a sarcastic gesture but Reid took it seriously. 'No need for that Mr Ward. If it answers your question you have four missions to complete.'

'Is that all?' I was genuinely amazed.

'Yes. We have around one hundred missions to fulfil and your quota is four. We want quality not quantity.'

'Why are we doing this, sir, if I might ask?' Richie didn't hold his hand up but he could not be more subservient if he had got down on his knees.

'Good question Mr Deutzinger. We are under contract, for a lot of money, to several top universities. In effect we are selling the data to them although it is analysed first by the Blue section.'

'Why are there no other teams here at the base?' Reid stared at me for a while. His eyes were cold and I'm sure he'd have shot me on the spot as an over-inquisitive nuisance if he'd had a gun handy. He glanced at Marshall.

'I think I already explained this. You are a slippery customer, Mr Ward. Having gone to such trouble to acquire your services I am not inclined to risk you … how can I put it … deciding that the grass is greener …' I smiled but he did not. 'Your team is an exception. The others work from London. Yours will remain here under my direct supervision.'

'Could you indulge my curiosity as a tech-head and

explain who invented this time travel gadget, please?' I was genuinely interested – which explains the politeness.

He sighed. 'It was the result of a couple of government programmes during the 1990s. The government shelved them as partial failures - too many problems and dangers - but I managed to get a licence to continue development and to work for the universities.'

'Dangers?'

'Dangers to the time continuum. The government of the day decided that they were too great to risk. We have established this new system so that those risks are minimised.'

I took him up on that final word. 'There is always the danger that someone will do something to change history.' He shot Marshall a look that was unreadable. 'We send disciplined teams with tightly specified objectives. Are there any other questions? Your mission briefing will be tomorrow at 0800 and you will be off on your first mission by about 1030 or 1100 hours. You are free to go, Mr Ward. Mr Deutzinger please remain here. Mr Marshall would like to brief you further.'

I smiled to myself as I strolled down towards the gates. Marshall was telling Richie how to handle me if I got feisty. No problem. I had no intention of getting feisty on the first mission. I had to know what was going on first. I settled myself in the nice café half-way to the gates. It was warm and had comfortable furniture. Crucially, the triple glazing meant that the windows did not steam up. Sounds inconsequential but it was important to me that I had a clear view from here at all times. I'd been to the café for three relatively short visits over the past two days but, much as this particular café attracted my professional attention, I'd made sure that I also lazed about in the other two cafés and spent good time in the restaurant. I pretended to read a magazine while I noted the comings and goings at the gates and the routine at the café itself. In the absence of a modern tank those gates were the only way out of this place. Slowly, an escape plan began to take shape in my mind, gradually becoming something that might work. I ran through it a dozen times in the quiet hours before bed. I was going to get out of this place. Within a day I would fly to Switzerland and then Lisbon and from there it was a simple hop to South America on the 11:30 pm TAP flight to Rio de Janeiro. There were one or two wrinkles to iron out but I was darned well going to get out of this luxurious prison.

On my afternoon run I met those cleaners again, as they emerged from the lane beside the spa. They seemed to be arguing about something. Henry was saying something about speeding things up and urgency but I could not hear what the lady was saying. They appeared to be surprised to see me.

'Hello, Dr Ward. How nice to see you again. On another run I see.' The old lady was pretty much like any other - they tend to look the same, don't they? Except for her eyes. They were like those bright shiny blue buttons that served for eyes on an old-fashioned Teddy Bear. It crossed my mind that they could probably be patented and sold abroad as the latest death ray weapon. The black chap, Henry, glowered.

'Good morning, Mrs Biddle … Henry. How's work today?' Their brown jump suits were neat and clean, so I guessed they'd not really done much work yet.

'We are just starting,' said Henry, clearly noting my glance at their jumpsuits. 'But Mrs Biddle thinks we should wait for a while. What do you think Dr Ward?' It was a weird thing to say and what made it even stranger was the way he said it. More a challenge than a question. I frowned a bit. They actually expected an answer. I decided to go for deep and mystical.

'Waiting is good if it clarifies things and makes the final work more effective.' Wow, I'm good sometimes! Henry looked surprised but Mrs Biddle nodded.

'Are you a Buddhist Dr Ward?'

I tried not to show my shock at the turn of the conversation. 'No. But I have to confess that I find their philosophy quite compelling - the focus on peace and karma and the objective of ultimate goodness.'

'And how do you feel your own karma stands, Dr Ward?' Henry had stepped a bit closer. His stare was almost as daunting as Mrs Biddle's. What on earth was this? I'd come out for a run, not a debate on life, the universe, and everything.

'Not too good, I'm afraid, Henry. Tattered with some pretty significant moth-holes I'd say.' He nodded sagely as though I'd confirmed his own conclusion.

'You seem anxious Dr Ward,' interjected Mrs Biddle. 'We must get on now but we must speak again soon. Please be very careful. The work you are doing can be dangerous.'

I was about to ask what she meant but they turned immediately and walked quickly away. I resumed my run up the hill - slowly at first because I'd gotten quite cold but mainly because I was very distracted. It had been the weirdest conversation I'd had in a very long time. I was grateful they spoke to me but they were strange to say the least. Highly intelligent and totally incongruous for cleaners. The conversation had been cryptic - even arcane. The word 'karma' kept reverberating through my mind as I picked up the pace.

But it was her warning that came back to haunt me later.

10

What did I say about decisions?

I confess I was quite nervous the next morning – it's not every day you prepare for a time travelling mission. The initial process went pretty smoothly. Richie and I changed into suits that would probably not stand out too much even today. Short jackets with tight, narrow-legged trousers were still in vogue but the highly polished black brogues were not. And I hated the starched shirt and its starchier collar. It was slow strangulation and I complained accordingly. The wardrobe lady was kind enough to suggest a softer shirt and a cravat. It would make me look a little Bohemian but comfort won. I laughed out loud when they brought in two tiny suitcases in which they'd packed a spare shirt, socks, garters (don't ask), period underwear, a spare cravat and a simple toothbrush with a tin of toothpaste that looked like ground up dirt. If we needed anything else, they said, we should buy it.

Our mission was David Lloyd George in 1913 London. I asked why 1913 and not during World War One when he was at his peak, but no-one could throw any light on the choice of date. We were to watch and follow him for three days and record everything on tiny recorders in our pockets linked wirelessly to minuscule mics and cameras in a small 'old school' badge on our lapels. The equipment recorded everything, visuals, comments, times, people, events, etc. Three staff briefed us and tested the wrist controllers. Both Richie's and mine had ways of controlling the surveillance equipment, keeping track of mission time and communicating via text with each other but only mine had the red button A mystery for me but, again, no-one could say why this was so.

We were given plenty of money. I found out later from Reid that it was all forged but was so accurate it would probably never be discovered. I probably missed half of what I was told because I was so nervous and - yes - excited. They told us to close our eyes for the transfer but, when the time came, it was so smooth that I didn't know when to open them again. It was only Richie tapping me frantically on the arm that did the trick.

The noise and smells hit me like sledgehammers. Richie and I were standing underneath some trees on the edge of St James' Park looking out over a narrow road towards Horse Guards' Parade. Horse-drawn hansom cabs and cumbersome motor vehicles rumbled across our vision but it was the smells that really hit me. There was a lot of petrol and exhaust in the summer air together with strong elements of horse dung. Underneath all was a hint of vegetation and cut grass. Richie might be the nominal team leader but he was out of his depth here. He gazed in stupefied wonder at the scene in front of us and I had to pull his sleeve to get him to move.

About an hour later we'd found ourselves good rooms at the Albert Hotel in Derby Gate. The street in 1913 was not as plush as I remembered it from my occasional visits to the Ministry of Defence in my own time, but it was respectable and within yards of Whitehall and Westminster – smart but not luxurious. The worst thing – worse even than the chamber pot - was getting used to going down the corridor to wash and bathe. You met lots of interesting people but personal hygiene was not among their strengths. In view of the smell and the condition of the cast iron bath, I washed but did not bathe for the three days we were there.

We took lunch at the hotel – terribly formal and incredibly slow service – and then got to work. In 1913, David Lloyd George was still a backbencher - a firebrand Welsh MP. He did not become Prime Minister until 1916, so we tracked him down at the House of Commons. Given our backgrounds in twenty-first century security, we found it stunningly easy for two smartly-dressed men to enter the building and find a particular Member of Parliament. Once we knew where he was, we split up. I took the first shift through to five pm and Richie took over from then until Lloyd George retired for the night in his modest residence.

And that was how it went for the next three days. One of us stayed close to the dark-haired Welshman every second he was not in bed or on the toilet. He was a busy little bee. We recorded who he met, when, and where. We recorded as much of what he said as we could - generally it was just his Commons questions and a few snippets if we got close enough to him while he was speaking to constituents or visitors in the Parliamentary lobbies. His accent was deep Welsh and his talk was almost entirely about what the English should do for the principality. In fact he was saying what an old friend of mine at Sneddon Downs used to say - sorry, will say – about how badly done-by the Welsh were/are. We noted where he travelled around the precincts and across Whitehall and Westminster. Richie was particularly made up when Lloyd George took a boat down to Blackfriars - even though Richie said the river stank. Three very tiring but fairly straightforward days. I'd done the same sort of thing when planning some of the robberies I'd pulled off. The recorders must have had multiple memory cards because there was not a single sign of them running our of space when we called it a wrap at about 7 pm on the third day. It had been a smooth and successful mission.

We'd arranged to meet back at the hotel. Richie arrived

with a broad grin. Did he ever stop grinning? 'That's it then, Tim. All done and we're ready to go, but I want to do something before we jump back. Won't take long.' He was like a kid at Disneyworld. I think he'd have jumped up and down in excitement except that he knew he'd have caused a small earthquake. Turned out he wanted to have a 'real' pint of bitter in a 'real' pub. I pointed out that he'd had one in the Brewer's Arms in Regent Street yesterday, but that, evidently, was too 'posh' to be the legitimate article. I further pointed out that such jaunts were against Reid's policy. He returned serve by reminding me that we'd been good boys up to now and that we deserved a pint. It was only a drink, for goodness sake, what harm could it do? I expressed my reservations, he played the team leader card, and we were on our way. We walked for what seemed like hours but was probably only half an hour until - in a back street in Bloomsbury - he found the place he wanted. The rotting wooden sign outside announced in faded letters that this was the 'Duck and Drake' and it looked every inch as insalubrious as its sign.

It was a chilly evening, so the small fire in the bar was welcome. The single room seemed to be all the pub offered. I was dismayed to see that the place was pretty rough and the clientele looked even worse. From what I could make out through the smog of tobacco and coal smoke they were a mixture of draymen and builders' labourers, with a good smattering of costermongers - those tough, hard-drinking, hard-fighting, street merchants. Dickens had reported that even the costermonger women used to fight with their fists.

All noise ceased when we entered. A man I took to be the landlord - a big man in a very dirty apron - came straight up to us, blocking the way.

'And you two can piss straight off, if you know what's good for you.'

I was all ready to turn tail but Richie was bigger than the landlord and his bluff good humour seemed to make a difference to the atmosphere - well, a tiny difference. He was obviously used to lying through his teeth because he went straight at it.

'A bloke down the street told us this was the best beer in Bloomsbury and we wanted to try it. I'll pay you double the normal price.' The landlord gave us both another good looking up and down.

He sneered. 'He's talking through his arse.' He spat a large gob of half chewed tobacco at a spittoon but missed. 'It's the best in London.' One of the smaller labourers at a nearby table sniggered and received a smack round the back of his head for his trouble. 'Sit your posh backsides at that table over there and I'll bring you two pints for a florin.' It was an outrageous price and several customers almost fell of their chairs laughing. Richie just nodded and guided me to the table. The stools and table were filthy. The table top would have been covered in dust and bits of food except that spilled beer had created a surface of dried mud upon which at least twenty flies were feasting. I swallowed and said to Richie that we should not outstay the meagre welcome we'd received. He grinned and examined the room.

'This is what I'd expected. It's wonderful - like something out of a Sherlock Holmes film. What do you call it when something like this is … you know … right?'

'Authentic?'

'That's it. Great isn't it.'

The landlord returned with two large overflowing mugs. They contained a dark brown liquid. I tried not to let my disquiet show on my face but Richie handed over the two shilling coin and was already slurping away. In between slurps he gazed around him like an American tourist at Windsor Castle.

'Richie,' I said, 'don't stare. The natives are getting restless.' He frowned at me.

'No probs, Tim. I've handled worse than this lot before dinner.'

'Don't forget that they may seem primitive to you but they are used to pub brawls and street fighting.'

He gave the room another scan and I noticed two or three of the costermongers glaring and nudging each other. 'Anyway, they fight with their fists only. They aren't used to real martial arts. I've handled far worse in fights in Hong Kong and Limasol. How do you like the beer?'

I'd taken an experimental sip and was surprised at how good it was. It looked like sludge from a sewage works but it was all hops and alcohol. I was astounded to see that I'd almost finished it.

'It's good. Let's finish up and go.'

'Nah,' his grin was even wider now. 'I want another. We've got the cash to pay whatever old misery-guts asks.' Something dark was stirring in my stomach and it wasn't the beer. The locals were watching us more regularly now. I had a bad feeling and told him so. He simply brushed it aside and played the team leader card again. For a second I considered just initiating the return without warning him but we were in the middle of a bar and, anyway, could one more pint really hurt? It was good stuff. I sighed my agreement and he scraped his chair back and wound his way through the crowded room to the table on which two beer barrels stood. I watched as the landlord came over, bargained, got given two silver coins, and handed over the two refilled mugs. Richie grasped them both in one beefy paw and started off back to our table.

I looked away for a second so did not see exactly what happened but suddenly there was a loud shout.

'Oi, you posh bleeder, you've got beer all over my best smock. You'll pay for that.'

I must be very naïve. It was only then that I realised that Richie was actually spoiling for a fight. Without more ado he very deliberately poured the rest of two whole pints of the land-lord's best all over the speaker and his three friends . It also splashed onto several other customers who were quietly playing dominoes. The result was instantaneous. I counted seven men whose chairs crashed backwards as they stood. They lunged for Richie as one. My valiant team leader stood almost a foot taller than most of his opponents and his first blows were telling. Two went down and stayed down. The problem was that they crashed across other tables spilling more beer and multiplying Richie's troubles. He was doing okay as far as I could see but he'd forgotten that martial arts tend to require lots of room and - in this crowded space - he could not use most of the moves. Nevertheless, two more opponents went down. One, who Richie had straight-armed in the throat looked to be terminally down. I was no use at all. I stood up but a couple of groups at nearby tables growled at me to sit tight if I valued my life. Unlike Richie I did not have the hand-to-hand fighting skills to argue. I sat.

It seemed to go on for a while but it could only have been seconds before I lost sight of Richie in a crowd of assailants. What worried me was that I could not see his head and shoulders any more. Suddenly the room went quiet and the crowd around Richie backed away. He was still on his feet, but the hand that clutched his stomach was bloody. I shouted to him to come to me and told my neighbours we'd be leaving. Richie staggered towards me. He was too heavy for me to support but I did my best as we pushed through the door into the street.

'How bad?' I asked as he fell against the wall outside.

'Bad, I think.' I took my jacket and shirt off and ripped the shirt down the seams.

'Use this to apply pressure. Where are the wounds?'

He was slumping down to the floor. 'Belly and chest ... bastards had knives ... too many of them.'

I pressed a wad of shirt against his chest and put his hand over it. But the hand fell away and I went to pick up the piece of shirt from the floor. When I tried again Richie was staring at me with eyes that would not see anything ever again.

I pressed the return button and we were back at Barrow Briggs in disturbingly familiar surroundings. I still knelt on the floor holding a wad of very bloody shirt partially covered in 1913 dirt, while Richie's blood covered body slowly folded back ... because the wall he'd been leaning against was no longer there.

11

It wasn't my fault!

The doctor gave me a sedative and I slept for four or five hours before waking and spending a long time in my sitting room remembering Richie's last hour. I felt guilty for not vetoing the pub idea, I felt guilty about not going to help him in the fight, and I felt even more guilty about not using the return button while he was still unwounded. He would have been annoyed but at least he'd still be alive. At the time it had seemed like a very reasonable request. What could go wrong with having a pint? I discounted the second guilt-trip. If I'd attempted to intervene, the men at the nearby tables would have seen to me in no uncertain fashion. But I certainly could have used the return button earlier. I thought for a long time about that. But I just did not think about using it in the immediacy of the pub and the fight. It did not cross my mind while I was trying to think of physical ways to help him. Stupid, eh? Blameworthy? Definitely, and it had cost Richie his life. Marshall's words as he gazed at Richie's body kept coming back to me. 'If you did this, Ward. I'll kill you with my bare hands.'

The doc came to my rooms early the next morning and prescribed a couple more sedatives to alleviate the shock. So, when I walked into Reid's office I was almost sane. Marshall was there.

Reid went straight for the throat. 'Did you kill Deutzinger and fix the recorders? Did you manoeuvre him into a fight?' He slapped his desk. 'Is this your doing Ward? Because if it is …'

'Of course not,' I shouted. 'What do you think I did - knife him to death and then bring the body back for you to see what I'd done?'

'You both switched your recorders off - why was that?'

I sighed. 'Richie wanted to have a traditional pint in a traditional working man's pub. He was determined to see a real 'Sherlock Holmes' pub as he called it. He deliberately spilled beer over some locals and they called him out. He did okay but it spiralled out of control and in the end he was fighting seven or eight of them.'

Marshall stepped forward as though to hit me. 'He was one of my best, Ward, and you did nothing to save him.'

I nodded. 'True, but in my defence I had two tables of builders' labourers telling me to sit still or I'd get the same treatment.'

'Even so, you could have at least tried.'

At that point Reid intervened. 'We would have lost both of them.'

Marshall was not giving up. 'But he was one of my best men - someone has to pay. I've known Richie Deutzinger since he was a corporal.'

I looked him in the eye. 'Then you should have known what he was like. I liked Richie. He was a lovely bloke. But if that's what you call your best, I'd have a think about your choice of men if I were you. He wanted the fight. He spoiled for it, He spilled a little beer over them, but when they complained, he didn't try to buy them off - even though he had pots of cash. Instead he poured the rest of two pints over the whole group.' They'd both gone very still. 'He was a nice chap and I'll really miss his grin and his gung-ho attitude, but he was ninety percent to blame for that fight. He was so cock-sure that he'd beat any bunch of primitive, Edwardian Londoners. Unfortunately, he forgot they were practised street fighters.' I paused as my mind was taken over by the images of him staggering towards me, his chest covered in blood. 'He was so friggin sure they'd fight with fists. Your briefing failed to cover the fact that knives were the order of the day back then.'

Marshall had gone pale but whether with shock or anger I never knew.

'I'll be sending a London team back to check your story. I want them to interview the landlord.' With that simple state-ment Reid waved me away and I was released.

Two days later I was summoned again. There was no sign of Marshall this time but I'd seen him around and he was defi-nitely not forgiving me. Reid indicated the usual chair.

'The London team confirms your version of the events and I consider the matter closed. Deutzinger did well it seems – two of his opponents were killed and another two badly injured. That, evidently, is why the rest of them resorted to knives. The police searched for the pair of you and would have charged you with murder if they had located you.' I waited and he shuffled papers to the side of his desk as if to prove that the case against me was settled. 'I have been giving thought to Deutzinger's successor.' I waited some more while he did the thing with the button under his desk. The door opened a few seconds later and my jaw must have made a clang as it hit the floor. Into the room walked one of the most beautiful women I'd ever had the pleasure of seeing. About five six, fair hair in a bun, a body that would grace any swim-suit catalogue, and a face that would certainly launch a thou-sand ships. She moved like a cat and by the time she reached a point about four feet from the desk I was in love.

'Thank you for coming Major.' Major? 'Please take a seat.' He turned to me. 'This is Major Sarah McKenzie. She is Mr

Marshall's deputy here at Barrow Briggs. She has been with the company for three years now.' I noticed her nodding as Reid spoke. 'Major McKenzie joined us straight from ten years in the Royal Marines, five of which were in the Special Boat Service.'

I sucked in a breath. The SBS was the sister organisation to the SAS - basically a bunch of highly skilled, elite troops who would slit your throat given the slightest excuse - and sometimes without it. Reid introduced me as Mr Ward, the man you will have been reading about. I smiled my very best smile at the Major and extended my hand.

She ignored the hand and gave me a look that turned my blood cold. You know when people look at you as if you are a great mass of very smelly dog poo on their favourite sneakers? Well this was far worse. Possibly because she'd been ordered to undertake this child-minding job and resented it.

'Major McKenzie volunteered for this assignment and I was pleased to accept her offer.' Reid's voice seemed mildly surprised by this turn of events but I guessed he'd take it any day of the week. He'd now have an extremely competent killer to watch me, and, of course, she'd also remain on her normal security duties as far as possible. Win-win.

So, somehow, Tim had gotten off on the wrong foot with this stunning, green-eyed Major. Had Marshall turned her against me? Had she been a friend of Richie's? Both? I thought about it. I was certain I had never met her before but there was something vaguely familiar about her. Whatever, from minute one I was persona non grata.

To show she'd not fazed me, I grasped the nettle. 'Have I met you before Major?'

She didn't look at me as she shook her head and got up to go. 'I will let you know when our first briefing will be held. Do not miss it.'

I got up myself and glanced at Reid. He gave me a quick look but it seemed he had not noticed the arctic conditions that had descended on his team. But if he had, happiness would probably be coursing all through that little fat body of his.

The next stop was my favourite café. I needed time to think about what had just happened. This outfit was a madhouse - a luxurious prison for a couple of hundred people, time travel missions for unspecified academics at what would be eye-watering cost, led by a man whose 'Goldfinger' approach would win him an Oscar, staffed by people who obediently wore specified colours to mark their corporate tribe, and with the strangest cleaners I'd ever encountered. And that little list did not include the latest lunatic - a psychopathic Major who'd taken an instant dislike to me.

Reid had told me that no-one would be leaving the base for any reason at all until all the missions were complete. Everyone, including me, had signed contracts in which they agreed to this stipulation. The only ticket out of the base before his deadline was death. I'd not thought about it before, but wasn't that a bit strange? Possibly, but, if time travel was top-secret, such restrictions could be justified. And what about London? Did the people down there work under the same rules? Knowing Reid, I expected so. Another puzzle was the cost. None of this was being done on the cheap. The base, the people, the training, the time travel missions, all would cost a fair amount. And Reid would not be shy of making some profit. So, where were universities getting the sort of money that would be needed to satisfy Reid's weakness for pots of loot? Very little of it made sense.

I finished my pot of extremely good tea and gazed up the roadway. And that was another crucial element of the enigma. Why was the Blue Building so special?

On a whim I left the café and wandered up to that mysterious place - the one where no-one who was not wearing a blue jumpsuit could get in. I stuffed my hands in my pockets and, whistling quietly to myself, innocently ambled up the steps and into the blue-fringed double doors. They swished open for me and I found myself in the wide lobby that I'd seen part of from the road. I also found myself surrounded by blue-clad security people with their guns out and aimed.

'Stay exactly where you are. Put your hands behind your head.'

I looked up in feigned surprise. ''Oh, my goodness, I thought this was the Black Building.' They physically turned me around and pushed me violently out the door. I had my work cut out not to fall down the steps but, true to my story, for I knew they'd be watching. I put my hands back in my pockets and strolled to the Black Building. I went in and asked for Major McKenzie, knowing full well she'd not be there because I'd seen her marching down to the gates while I'd been finishing my tea. I eked out the search for her as much as I could. By the time they'd tracked her down to the gates and told me where to find her, I'd spent fifteen minutes in the Black Building. I was sure that, even if someone in blue was still watching, they'd be convinced that I'd made an innocent mistake.

The ruse had worked, though. I now had a much better idea of the security inside the Blue Building and it did not make me feel optimistic about any chance of getting inside. The security was incredible. I'd seen the usual optical, finger-print and facial scanners but there were also voice checks and something that looked very like what the Ministry security people called a 'gait walk'. A Lidar system scanned people as they walked down a short corridor which had another security gate at the end manned by armed guards. If, by some miracle, you passed the voice, fingerprint, iris, and facial scans, you still had to be cleared as having precisely the correct gait for the person you were supposed to be. I'd been through security where you needed three greens to get in … but five?

Later I went for my usual run. It wasn't just for fitness – I needed to burn off the frustration-fuelled adrenaline that built up during these unusual days. I estimated - mainly by the time it took - that I could get about five miles by circling the base a couple of times, doing some convoluted detours through different roads, and then doing two runs from the gates to the west fence. Not taxing, but at least it was exercise. I tried to do it every other day and to do some workouts in the gym every day. The activity was good for me but it was also a great way to do some thinking and spying. I used it to locate cameras and sensors and estimate their range and span, and to watch the repair crews who worked on those sensors. A couple of times I saw maintenance people filling in rabbit holes underneath the fences. On that particular day I made sure that I passed the gates three times. I was intrigued by the posts that formed an alleyway which ended just before each gate. The posts were metal - probably aluminium - about eight feet high and twice the thickness of a standard lamppost. There were no lights or antennae so I put them down as infra-red scanners. They were probably there to scan cars and vans as they entered and left the base picking up the heat signatures of anyone being smuggled in or out.

I was still pondering those posts when I almost crashed into Mrs Biddle and Henry. They came out of nowhere but I had been deep in thought about escape plans. I just managed to avoid Mrs Biddle - but crashed into Henry.

'What the ...' Henry staggered backwards and rocked the cleaning cart they were standing beside. He righted himself and treated me to his standard glare.

'Sorry, Henry, I didn't see you,' I panted.

'You don't need to do all this silly running to keep fit, you know.' His arm was grasped quite firmly by Mrs Biddle.

'Now, Henry, we don't go into that do we.' She smiled gently up at her grumpy colleague. 'Dr Ward is just doing what he enjoys.' Henry took a deep breath and subsided a fraction while Mrs B swivelled to face me.

'Hello Dr Ward. How are you today?'

I don't know why but I suppose it was because they were now the only people on the base who spoke to me. I blurted out what had happened to Richie, my being suspected of killing him, the intense dislike exuded by Major McKenzie, and my general anger at being kept in this place. I even expounded on my visit to the Blue building and my hostile reception. They stood and listened patiently.

'I can see how that would upset you,' Mrs B offered. 'But you can't get out of here until your tasks are complete.' Henry gave her a nudge which almost knocked her over.

'That's right,' he agreed. 'None of us can.'

I was cautious. 'Yes, that's true.' I was not going to reveal my escape plans to a couple of cleaners. Instead, I changed the subject to the Blue Building and wondered aloud why it was so strongly protected. I got the very strong impression that Henry was about to say something but Mrs B spoke quickly.

'We wouldn't know, Dr Ward. We are not allowed to clean in there.' She gave me a sly smile. 'I would think you'd know more about it than we would because you speak to Mr Reid often.'

'Mmm,' murmured Henry, 'but not using the right methods.'

My head must have snapped towards him. He looked startled. 'What do you mean by that Henry?' He pursed his lips and looked at his colleague, who again stepped in.

'Henry is a scholar of human nature, Dr Ward. He is often critical of others when they do not appear to meet his expectations.' She flashed Henry a 'you dare say any more' look.

'Even so, it was a strange thing to say. What other methods?'

Mrs Biddle grasped her end of the trolley and used her head to tell Henry that he should do the same at his end. 'That is for you to find out, Dr Ward.'

12

Here's to sun, sand, and money

That night I took a quick dinner at the base restaurant and retired to my rooms. McKenzie, I'd taken to calling her 'Mac' (in my mind but not to her face) - came into the room about halfway through my meal. She saw me, ignored me, and took her meal to another table to join what looked like some other security people. I was missing Richie badly.

Back in my sitting room I felt positively lonely. Apart from a couple of mad cleaners I had no-one to speak to about anything of any weight. Everyone was friendly enough and the waiting staff were jolly and ready to exchange a little banter but there was no-one to *talk* to. And, on second thoughts, none of the people I had to work with - Reid, Marshall, and McKenzie – even liked me. I opened another bottle of beer and meandered across the room. I toyed briefly with the idea of watching a DVD film. There was no cable TV and no streaming allowed on the base but it boasted a really good stock of DVDs of which I had about a dozen lined up on my bookshelf. I could find no enthusiasm, though. Richie's death had put me off action thrillers and I was in no mood for a comedy. I found myself at the window, staring at the entrance to the Blue Building. Looking at the building as a whole I was shocked to notice that the roof was lined with razor wire. I was good, but there was no way I was going to blag or climb my way into that building.

Then I reminded myself that I didn't need to get into the Blue Building. I was going to escape and that's what my thoughts and energy should be directed towards. Whatever was in the Blue Building was Reid's problem.

Did you know, there are ways your mind can actually think for itself? You can try to convince yourself of all sorts of things but the mind sometimes disagrees. You should listen to those messages. In my case I told myself very sternly that the Blue Building and what went on inside it was of no importance to me. That particular night, I probably thought it twenty times while wandering with beer between the window and the couch. Yet I always ended up near the window and I always felt the tingling of my senses which accompanies an apparently unsolvable problem. It would be nice to know.

I gave in to my inner self. If there was a way to get into that darned building it was only going to be by using the computer networks. I needed a good laptop but getting one was about as likely as me winning the 'Most Popular Man at Barrow Briggs' competition.

Reid gave me the full week and a bit more to get over Richie's death. McKenzie wanted to see me a couple of times. She booked a meeting room in Black and harangued me about protocols and processes and correct procedure, the need to follow her orders at all times, and about a dozen other things. I didn't mind too much and remained silent and attentive at all times. What she was saying flew right over my head but she was great to look at and I enjoyed the opportunity to have her to myself – so to speak. I was careful to keep my face neutral and impassive, but it was a tonic just to watch her. The more I saw of her, the more I saw her as a cat in both the way she moved and in the way she could stare at something without blinking for ages. By the end of the second meeting, I understood why she was a good SBS soldier and I determined never to get on her bad side. Sorry, to be accurate I hoped not to get any *further* on her bad side. Her attitude towards me was like that of a university professor who thinks you're a waste of space and should not have gained entry to the institution in the first place. She was brusque, she never engaged in banter or side talk, never hung around for a chat afterwards, and never suggested a drink or a dinner to get to know each other. I was entranced by those deep green eyes but there was never any warmth in them when they looked at me.

For the rest of the time, I did as I usually did. I went to the gym by myself, did my runs alone, ate alone in the restaurant, and had tea or coffee in the cafés around the base – you've guessed it – also alone. I met Mrs B and Henry three times during the week. One of those I've already described. The others were just superficial hellos and fleeting chats about the weather or about me. They seemed very interested in how I was feeling and getting on. Mrs B approached it in a motherly, concerned sort of way. Was I sleeping well? Did I have bad dreams after my somewhat unusual capture? Henry tended to be the disapproving father - as though I was disappointing him in some way. Their arguments were a familiar feature. The two seemed to have more disagreements than common ground. If I hadn't been in such a frustrating situation it would have been hilarious.

I was careful to spend longer periods of time reading in the other cafés on the base but I managed an hour – give or take - in the one by the gate on a reasonably regular schedule. I even waved to McKenzie and a couple of her security guards when they came in for a take-away. I got the impression that being waved at by a Yellow was not something they enjoyed. The key thing in my life was how I was going to escape and, as I have said, a plan had been almost hatched.

On that particular day I occupied a table well away from the windows. The gates were of no interest now that I had sussed them out. I'd noticed however that a delivery truck brought ice cream, Danish, waffles, and cakes to the base three times a week - Saturday. Tuesday, and Thursday. The main freezer-room for foodstuffs was behind this café. The supplies were then raided by the other cafés as they needed them.

The delivery truck was a standard refrigerated ten-tonner. After it had cleared the gates it drove up to the café and turned around in the roadway to back into the loading alley between the café and an admin building. The men's toilets had a window that overlooked the alley and through it I noted the driver's routine. Open the rear shutters, get the barrow from underneath the truck, open the internal insulated doors to the fridge and freezer compartments, wheel the supplies into the refrigerated store behind the café, shut the internal doors, put the barrow back, leave the rear shutter open and go for a free coffee, Danish and a chat in the café. Nothing was locked and he only closed the shutter once he'd emerged from the café and was ready to leave.

My problem was the yellow jumpsuit. I could not get any other colour and could see no way of stealing one. In any case no one was allowed off the base without very special permission from Reid. I'd seen only one chap in black go out in a car and he was accompanied by two very burly Goons from security. They'd returned in less than two hours. Hiding in a car or an ordinary van to escape would not work because the infrared detectors would spot me in the trunk or wherever else I was hiding. There were commercial ways of fooling an IR detector but I did not have access to the suits. The only way seemed to be to cool my body to a level that would barely register on the detectors. I couldn't actually freeze myself so I'd have to get very cold and then hide myself behind stacks of ice cream boxes. I'd overheard the driver telling the waitresses that his next regular stop was about twenty minutes away. That meant that I would have to persevere through about ninety minutes of being trapped in a fridge. I was young and fit. Once I was released at the next stop I would look for a car to steal, orientate myself, and then head for my go-bag and my friend's airfield.

The final part of the plan was how to get into the truck. I had taken to carrying a bag to the café - my small duffle bag from RAF days. Anyone could see that it contained my running sweater and shoes, e-book reader and charger. For the escape it would have to hold a bit more – but I will come to that. When the truck arrived it took the driver about half an hour to transfer the ice cream and cakes boxes. I then had about the same amount of time to get into the back. The café had a back corridor which led to the toilets. They were either side of the corridor which ended with a push-bar door opening to the loading alley. The staff used it to collect supplies from the refrigerated storeroom.

Recently, on one of my runs I had 'accidentally' run up the alleyway. I threw my arms theatrically in the air to signal the error but there were no cameras in the alley.

My mind kept returning to the refrigerated compartment. I had given the van a good deal of thought. Some of the stuff that was onloaded was very obviously frozen – it steamed as it was removed by the driver. But stuff like the pastries was just chilled. So there were two internal compartments – a fridge and a freezer. To beat the IR scanners I'd need to be in the freezer part – and that's very cold – minus eighteen Celsius. Life threatening if endured for a long period but bearable when wearing the right clothes. My problem – as I constantly reminded myself – was that I was going to be trying to deliberately cool myself down first and then spend a minimum of an hour and a half in those conditions. The more I thought about it the more images I had of me freezing to death. Hypothermia is dangerous. Once the body starts to shut down you are almost powerless to do anything about it. Even if I did not die, there was every chance that I'd end up unconscious in hospital and then be returned to the base.

It took me a while to come up with a solution. It was watching the waitresses serve tea that did it. They had little pre-formed tea cosies that fitted over the tea-pots to keep the contents warm. When I did a simple test it was possible to touch the tea-cosy whereas you'd burn yourself trying to do the same to the pot itself. Keeping warmth in, if done efficiently, would also mask me from the IR detectors. The next issue was how I could get enough insulation into the van – I could hardly wander into the café with a trunk full of winter clothes. I wondered whether the driver had warm gear in his cab and watched him again. Yes, he had a jacket and gloves, but I could not see how to steal them without him noticing – they were hung from a hook on the other side of his cab and occupied a highly visible chunk of his normal world. He'd notice their absence straight away. The solution came when I watched him unloading one day. The compartment must have been full because thick insulation blankets began to be thrown out. His final act before closing the fridge and going for his coffee was to fold them up and pile them in a corner. It was a risk, but if I could build myself a thick tent with them, my heat would be sealed in the tent, there would be no IR signature, and I would not freeze to death.

So, the plan was that I would drink my tea and read while I waited for the driver to finish transferring the boxes. As soon as he came into the café for his free drink and cake I would take my bag and, as though visiting the loo, slip out of the back door and into the back of the truck, shutting the door behind me. The driver would then simply do his usual thing - pull the shutters down, get into the cab, and we'd be off. I wasn't quite as confident as that sounds. I knew a hundred things could go wrong. But I had been trapped for too long and it was worth any risk to get out. The thought of sun, sand, and money was a constant and powerful motivation.

13

Ward strikes again

Two days later - a Thursday - was when I made my move. I knew that I would be expected to go on a mission with Mac within the next few days. I wanted to be long gone before that could happen. The previous evening had been filled with trying to anticipate every possible contingency. I'd kept strictly to my routine - everything that I would normally do. I even paid McKenzie an unscheduled early visit to ask her for another meeting on Friday. I told her I thought maybe another mission would not be far away and I wanted to have enough time to prepare. Her face was a treat. She frowned and squinted her eyes, she hesitated and used what was probably her only tell. She had a habit of rubbing her bottom lip with her right thumb when she was a little confused or undecided. I kept my face serious and professional and, eventually, she accepted that my request was genuine. As I left a slightly confused Major to return to my flat, I whistled a happy tune.

I did my usual session at the gym and then ambled down to the café and settled myself at my usual table at the back next to the entrance to the corridor. As well as the usual facilities, there were staff changing rooms at the end of the corridor, so it was in fairly constant use. I would be lying if I said that I was totally calm. My pulse was certainly raised as I sat pretending to read my e-reader and it leapt to another level when the delivery truck arrived and began to reverse into the alleyway. I forced myself to calm down, ordering another pot of tea for show. There was no way I could hear what was going on in the alley and I could not visit the loos to see.

I wasn't being paranoid in believing that Reid had me watched all the time. I was not inconspicuous in my banana-suit. Even the laziest security guard could spot me on a monitor. There were cameras everywhere and somewhere - probably deep within the Black building - would be a central security room fitted with all the surveillance monitors and sensors you could wish for. Ever since my 'arrest' and the trip in the prison van it was evident that Reid was not a chap to be underestimated.

The entrance door opened and the driver - thank goodness it was the usual one - walked to the stools at the counter. He took the one he usually did and pulled a menu towards him. On a whim I walked up to the counter and politely asked for some more milk. I glanced at the driver and smiled.

'If you've got time you should try some of that apple pie with the single cream - it's absolutely delicious.' With that tiny, complimentary bit of upselling, I winked at the waitress and went back to my table. I sat down and then got up again pulling the duffle bag across my front as I casually turned into the corridor. It was as easy as I had hoped. No-one glanced up, and the corridor was empty. I slipped out of the back door and held it against its usual habit of slamming. The truck was humming to itself as I climbed up into the back, opened the door to the freezer compartment and squeezed through. It was bone chillingly cold after the warmth of the café. I allowed the door to shut solidly behind me and took out my little torch. The only way out, now, was when the driver opened it or by using the emergency switch which would beep an alarm in the cab. Unless I was feeling suicidal, it would not be used.

My greatest fear was that there would be no insulation blankets. At first it looked as if this was the case. My plan then was simple. Emergency exit and back to the café hoping the driver would think the alarm was a glitch. I was looking for a pile of four or five. What I eventually spotted was a whole corner of the freezer stacked with a couple of dozen. Wood and trees. I got to work building a tent towards the front, in between two stacks of boxes which were also covered with blankets. There were similar stacks down both sides with a gap towards the rear where, I suppose, the café's boxes had been.

I placed three layers of blankets on the floor to sit on, wrapped four around my shoulders in a double layer and then put another three over my head. It was a fiddle to get the shoulder ones to stay in place but when the head ones were on top, they helped to weight the others down. The secret was not to move too much. I switched off my torch, opened my e-reader and made myself comfortable. It was cold but it is amazing how cosy I became under all that insulation.

I was beginning to get stiff already and I regretted suggesting that extra snack for the driver. You've no idea how fidgeting is built deeply into human DNA and how much effort it takes to stop yourself from doing it. Then I heard the shutters rumbling closed and thanked my lucky stars. Either he was a fast eater or he'd resisted the apple pie. I heard the cab door open and close and less than a minute later we were on our way. To stop my heart beating and try to stay still I concentrated on what I would do when we reached his next delivery stop. I would probably be cold by then, but stiffness and cramp were more likely. I could stand once we were on the open road but, even then, I was not at all sure I'd be able to move easily. Once we were through the gates and the truck's movement showed that it was on the main road I would put on the two extra sweaters in my duffle bag to augment the little home I'd built. If necessary I could march up and down the eight foot space with blankets over my shoulder to keep warm. I imagined the poor driver's surprise as he opened the door. I'd say 'thanks for the lift' as I let myself down and revealed the carving knife that I'd stolen from the restaurant last week. Swapping clothes with him would take roughly ten minutes and I would also, very reluctantly, have to rob him of his cash. I'd had a brilliant idea. Why steal a car when I had a nice truck and a driver? We would just drive the truck to the go-bag and I'd steal a car to get to the airfield. The company would be informed of the missed delivery and they'd be puzzled but would have no reason to worry if I got the driver to tell them he'd forgotten something for the Barrow Briggs drop and was going back. That might buy me an hour – possible two. We would take the back roads because there are fewer police patrols on those. If my luck held I'd be in Lisbon by this time tomorrow.

I'd been so engrossed in my thoughts that I hadn't noticed the short drive down to the first set of gates. The truck wheezed to a halt and braked so fiercely that I almost toppled over. I waited for the driver to be given his usual all-clear. There were muffled voices. I supposed the guards were checking the delivery notes. Meanwhile I stayed as still as I could in my tent. My feet felt cold but I wasn't going to get frost bite. I wiggled my toes and fingers and tried to concentrate on the book. Some hope. Come on, come on.

Then the engine noise increased and the truck began to move again. I breathed a sigh of relief. One down, one to go. In my head I could see the vehicle heading down towards the second gate as I had watched it several times. We had to negotiate the narrow corridor of IR detectors mounted on the steel crash barriers. This was the big test. Would the insulation shield the heat from my body and would the barriers of ice cream boxes around me be enough to fool the infra-red detection system. I would surely be virtually invisible.

The truck stopped at the gate and, once more, I heard the guards talking to the driver. I shivered some more and waited for him to be given the go-ahead. Then my heart fell as I heard the sound of the driver's door opening. There was no need for the driver to leave the cab. He'd never had to do that before as far as I knew. Apart from the rumble of the engine and the refrigeration system there was silence.

I began using my watch to count the seconds. It took four agonising minutes but then the vehicle rocked slightly and the driver's door closed. I cannot remember ever being so relieved as I listened to the air brakes being released and felt the truck begin to move. We were outside the gates and on our way!

The truck had travelled only a few yards when it rocked violently. The wretched driver must have misjudged the chicane below the gates and got his right rear wheels onto the kerb. I did not have time to register what was happening because the inside of the fridge suddenly became the centre of an earthquake. One of the towers of boxes beside me fell on top of my tent accompanied by the crashes of piles of boxes falling. The noise seemed to go on for minutes but eventually all was quiet. Nevertheless, I recognised defeat when I saw it.

It took a minute as guards came running down to the truck and the driver joined them. I heard one tell the man that he would have to move the vehicle down the road so that he did not block the gate. It was a split second of hope. I might be able to deal with the driver when he came to re-stack his truck. Hope was crushed by the driver refusing until he'd seen the damage. The door opened and I think two men climbed up. The driver uttered an extremely crude expletive and a guard said, 'What's that?'

'That' turned out to my shoe, which was now sticking out from beneath a pile of boxes of frozen croissants. I heard the men shifting boxes to get at the shoe. The guard called to his mate. When I was eventually revealed as a stowaway there were three faces staring at me. The driver looked shocked and amazed. The guards were pale. I guess they had already imagined what Marshall would do when he heard that, but for a total freak of bad driving, I would have been free and clear.

Two of the guards dragged me to the door and threw me to another two who were standing outside. They grasped my arms and dragged me painfully back to the guardhouse where I was zip-tied and dumped in the corner.

I sat there for a long time while radio conversations took place. At least it was warm. Everyone was getting their oar in. Marshall was up at the Black building and he exploded as expected, threatening the guards with punishments that would never be permitted even in Henry VIII's time. Soon the guards took their walkie-talkies outside where I couldn't hear the ear-bashing they were receiving.

I was wondering what Reid would do when I looked up and saw McKenzie staring down at me. She scanned me up and down in her usual disdainful way.

'You are a complete fool, Ward. And now you will pay the price.' She nodded to her men and left. The 'pay the price' bit was ominous. As the three security guards stepped forward I saw the 'price' in their faces. Two of them dragged me up and held me while the other gave me a good beating. He was wearing gloves to protect his hands so he had no qualms about hitting me in the face as well as treating my torso as a punch bag. I actually heard one of my ribs crack and they had to pause for a moment while I wretched up the meagre contents of my stomach.

Then they swapped places and another one had his fun, after which I fell to the floor spitting blood and fearing for at least four cracked or broken ribs. Finally the third one used his boots to kick the shit out of me while I lay on the floor. They were efficient and professional, beating me up methodically and painfully. I was going to have two closed eyes, a broken nose, and several ribs in poor condition. I just hoped there was no serious internal injury. I was just a mass of pain.

I lay there playing dead so that they didn't start again. I tested my teeth with my tongue – none were missing but my mouth was full of blood. I had probably bitten my tongue and cheeks several times. I could not breathe through my nose – which was also spewing a stream of snot and blood. My face was numb. Yet even through the pain and nausea I noted academically that they'd been professionally retrained about it. They'd broken no vital bones – just some ribs and my nose - and they'd carefully avoided doing serious damage to my kidneys and liver. But the third guy hadn't finished with me. I felt his boot connect with my upper back. He gave my stomach another wallop and I wretched again. At what point I passed out I couldn't say but I distinctly remember welcoming the darkness.

14

Lesson learned

I woke under sedation in the sick bay. A pleasant-sounding female voice told me not to worry that I couldn't see anything. The swelling around my eyes would reduce in a couple of days. They gave me painkillers but there were times when those wore off and the pain became unbearable. And alongside the discomfort, temporary blindness, pain, and the humiliation of having a nurse check my stools and urine to see when the blood stopped flowing, I had to endure rounds of furious accusations and blame from the usual suspects.

McKenzie came in and verbally attacked me again for being a fool and - more than anything else - for delaying her first time travelling mission. Reid stood beside the bed and fumed. He told me he'd seriously considered letting me die under that beating but that he'd been persuaded out of it – by whom was never made clear but, looking back, I have a good idea. He had had to bribe the driver of the delivery truck with a considerable amount of money.

I couldn't speak properly but I slurred a few words about it being his lucky day. Reid agreed. The driver had been told that he'd witnessed a dangerous prisoner being stopped from escaping into the community to cause untold harm and that the whole episode was subject to the Official Secrets Act. Reid's main beef was that I had delayed the project. He'd have to set back the timetable. I was not then past the dribbling stage - my lips were still hugely swollen. He gave me a disgusted look and left. Marshall was a real laugh. He accused me of hurting one of his men, going on at length about how the bloke in question had failed to wear decent gloves. He now had dislocated fingers and might have broken a small bone in his wrist. People who watch action movies think that fist fights are simple affairs. But the human hand is extremely delicate and the human head is heavy and pretty robust - apart from the jaw that is. Unless you are very lucky, very skilled, or have exceptionally robust bone structure it is almost inevitable that you will break something if you hit someone with your unprotected fist. Marshall expounded on that theme for a long time and only gave up in frustration when it became obvious that I couldn't speak properly. He'd have hit me himself, there and then, but the nurses kept coming back and I think he'd been told by Reid not to do any such thing.

After a few days, they released me from sick bay, to what they called 'room arrest'. I was to rest and recover but not to leave the flat under any circumstances except fire. Just shows how incredibly stupid I am because it did not cross my mind for a second why Reid should be so solicitous of my welfare. If I thought I was lonely before the escape attempt that was nothing to what I went through under room arrest. My only visitors for at least two weeks were a male nurse who looked like an all-in-wrestler and the chap who brought my food. Neither was allowed to speak to me. The nurse simply examined me and checked my ribs - none too gently – replaced dressings and replenished my painkillers and ointment. He came every day at 10 am. The youngster who brought my food - about which I was given no choice - was so frightened that he never brought a single tray without spilling the juice or the tea. Sometimes even the gravy was soaking into the tray cover when I lifted the stainless-steel lid. Only McKenzie, who appeared at random every third day or so, was allowed to speak to me and I very quickly got fed up with her constant moaning. The general theme was 'disappointment' but she occasionally threw in a new strand along the lines of …

'I had hoped for a few more brain cells, Ward. Surely you must have seen that, while you were unlucky to be caught outside the gates, we'd have been onto you like greased lightning? A couple of fast cars would have caught the truck before it got to its next stop. Even if you had got that far, Mr Reid has a helicopter. We would have caught you within a few hours at most. '

You can see, I hope, that I was not getting the usual comfort and care that an invalid should be able to expect. McKenzie may have looked like an angel but that was just a shallow front. I got so fed up that I missed talking to Mrs B and Henry and I badly missed getting out to the restaurant and flirting with the café waitresses. I was getting to the end of my tether when the Major graced me with another visit.

'You're getting better now, Ward, and Mr Reid will soon allow you out - under supervision - to start to get your fitness back.'

I grinned lopsidedly at her. 'That's good news, Mac. Will you come for a run with me?' She shook her head and narrowed her eyes.

'Don't call me Mac. And no. You are to be supervised by one of my men in the gym - no runs for you for a long time I think.'

I was angry. 'But why not? I'm not going to be leaping the fences or storming the gates and I'm certainly not attempting the smuggling trick again.'

'Not a chance. Mr Reid is teaching you a lesson and I think it's almost been learned. But you are to be kept on a very short leash for a while yet.' She smiled in a nasty way.

'You are lucky to be alive. If Mr Marshall had had his way you'd be cold in your grave by now.'

She left and I looked at my lunch as it lay congealing on a plate. The anger built up in me like a flood. It was not just about Mac and Reid - nor was it about Marshall. A hefty chunk of it was anger directed at me. I was the one who had concocted that little plan and I was the one who had missed the vital message in what lay all around me on the base. Reid had spared no expense to seal it up tight. He was not going to skimp on cars, or a helicopter for that matter. I'd assumed that once I was out of the gate nothing would catch me. Anger, loneliness, frustration … they had been building up in me for weeks. I felt like a dam under mounting water pressure. Unless I was able to release it somehow, something was going to explode.

They say that all things come to an end and I have always thought it an asinine statement. But, as usual, I was wrong. Even my recovery came to an end. I could soon hobble around the flat a bit, my ribs could move with my breathing without too much agony, and even the doctors could find no reason to prolong it. Reid was forced to allow me out of the apartment to get some proper exercise. I was restricted to the gym and two runs per week but Reid made sure I understood that any further attempt to escape would attract the ultimate penalty.

After about twelve days of incarceration, the front door was officially unlocked and my keys given back to me. The ceremony was touching. Marshall and McKenzie came to the door, unlocked it, threw the keys on the floor inside the door, and told me to watch myself … or else.

I found out the hard way that being able to get from my bedroom to the sitting room and back a few times was not the same as walking the roads of the base. I needed a stick and I perambulated, not without pain, like a seventy-year old. The mere thought of anyone bumping into me made me stand well back from doors and hobble on the quietest side of the road. On the first day I managed a very slow walk to the café. The occasion was thoroughly embarrassing. Everyone knew what I'd tried, everyone knew what had then befallen me, and everyone tried their best not to look as though they knew. I steeled myself to endure the sea of insincerity. I smiled a lot and even managed to wink at a couple of the waitresses. All empty show but it made us all feel a bit better. If everyone was playing the game, we could all get on with our lives.

Over the next week I worked up my fitness by walking a bit further every day. Within four days I could walk to the west fence and back and by the end of the week I managed a very short run up to the Black building, back to those hateful gates, and then back up to the café. It must have been a few days later that I made my first run to the west fence. My bruises had gone but the ribs were still quite sore. The doctor had no sympathy. They'll mend and you need to get them working again was his very supportive comment. It was on that run to the west fence that I ran into Mrs Biddle and Henry for the first time since the failed escape. They emerged from the side alley of the Black Building, waved at me, and stepped back into the alley where I stumbled after them a second or so later. I was about as unfit as I could ever remember being. My breath came in deep gasps as I bent over to clutch my knees. They murmured appropriate sympathy and greetings and regarded me silently while I recovered a semblance of dignity.

'How are you Dr Ward?' Mrs Biddle looked genuinely concerned. Henry just glared as usual. Whether that was a special glare or just the normal one ramped up a couple of notches I could not tell. No, that's wrong. I didn't care.

'Thanks, Mrs B, I'm getting back on track slowly. How are you two?'

'We are well, thank you, but we have been very concerned for you. That was an immense risk and - if you don't mind me saying so - it was not really necessary.'

I shook my head. 'You don't know how much I want to get out of here. It seemed like a risk worth taking.'

Henry shifted his weight. I could tell he was angry but did not understand why. After all, it was me who'd taken the beating. 'You're being very slow, Dr Ward. There are more ways of skinning a cat.' I sucked in a breath to steady my own anger.

'Look, Henry. With all due respect you really have no idea what my situation is and what I have given up to endure this … wretched … base. I'm perfectly aware of how cats should be skinned but occasionally I select the wrong method.' I shot him an exasperated glare. 'Anyway, how would *you* suggest I get out of here?'

I noticed Mrs B place her hand on Henry's arm. She was telling him not to lose his temper, I think.

'I suggest you think, Dr Ward, that's all. Think about what has happened to you and not just the events concerning Mr Reid.'

'And you assume that I have not been doing just that?' He inclined his head the way an adult does to a child to wait for the penny to drop. 'Don't look at me like that. You really don't know why I did it.'

Henry was nothing if not a straight-talker. 'I know far more than you think. You were a complete idiot to try it.'

I flashed a look at Mrs B and turned on my heel. I didn't want to say something I'd regret.

As if that was not enough, Mac came to see me in my rooms that afternoon. She had not forgiven me. The conversation was sharp and short, consisting of her berating me once again for delaying 'her' time travel experience and being a fool to think I could evade their carefully designed security systems and the raft of backups they'd created. For my part I fired back a few barbs about whether she'd enjoyed watching me being beaten up, about her being too impatient for the mission, and why she was working for a couple of nasty pricks like Marshall and Reid. She stormed out in the fashion that I was getting used to and I tried to calm down by considering which of the stack of DVDs I'd watch that evening with my 'doctor's orders' dinner - which was incredibly healthy and even more incredibly boring. I'd read most of the books in the flat except for two – one on South Atlantic Molluscs and the other on the intricacies of Victorian needlework – both kindly brought to me by a smirking Mac. The DVDs failed to ignite any genuine interest either. For a fraction of a second I considered watching the Blue Building some more. But I'd got a very good idea of everything that could be seen from the outside - including the heavily protected roof. I'd counted people in and out and found a rough correspondence every day and I'd noted the fact on numerous days that the Blue people did not often talk to or otherwise interact with the Black crew or, indeed, any of the other colours of the rainbow.

The only thing left was another walk and, to avoid running into the cleaners again, I walked slowly down to the café and stood outside looking down at the scene of my recent humiliation. I seemed to be making a habit of being humiliated lately. Soon there'd be no-one in the country who was not sniggering behind their hands at the tales of Tim Ward's stupidity.

My mind's eye focused of its own accord on a vision of the ice-cream truck. I remembered that feeling of being trapped, the more powerful feeling of having screwed up, the increasing frustration at not being able to get out of the base, and the fear during the beating that Reid had told them to finish me off. Now even Henry was having a go at me. For no apparent reason, my head suddenly became full of images of the Blue building lobby. I saw it as I'd seen it the day I'd 'accidentally' wandered in. The image was sharp and clear. All the security systems stood out. But then I was moving past the lobby. No-one stopped me or put me through the checks. I even went through the Lidar scanners and past the second set of guards without setting off any alarms. I was just floating through everything. The images changed at that point. I found myself with a sign ahead of me saying 'Second Floor', and saw two open plan offices, their entrances leading off from the lift well. I moved into the first, which was large and airy with several pairs of desks down the middle. Papers and plans were pinned to the main wall. They all had a standard pre-printed header - 'Orwell' - and I was able to read excerpts from extremely detailed project plans. There were dates and 'targets' and team allocations. Each completed mission had a sheet underneath containing a summary of the mission. I even recognised my own mission with Richie and there were several rows of blanks where I presumed the summaries of yet-to-be-completed missions would be pinned.

There seemed to be blanks for all teams, but not many. Further down the rows of missions and summaries was a point at which the project lines for all the teams came together in an arrow-like point. It was labelled with a red tab marked 'Orwell' and another single arrow to the words 'Mr Reid'. After that there was a series of blank red cards with 'action teams' numbered and labelled. The cards were labelled with the names of each of the individual targets - but the rest was blank.

I was about to explore further but a car horn shocked out of the daydream. I'd been standing in the middle of the road. I shook my head and waved an apology to the driver who I belatedly recognised as one of the guards who'd beaten me up. I walked across to stand in the café doorway where I felt safer. It had been a disturbing experience. I'd had daydreams before but never one as vivid or detailed. Was it the beating? Had they damaged my brain? I gave the matter some thought but discounted it because they had given me all the scans the medics could think of. Nevertheless, it could be some sort of delayed concussion. Or I could be exhausted after everything that had happened, followed by my relatively hurried efforts to get fit again.

That evening in the flat I reviewed it all again and came to the very sensible conclusion that I had had too much thinking time. I'd been injured, isolated, bored, verbally attacked, and I was still quite tired. A daydream was the least of my problems. Tomorrow was the initial briefing for the second mission. I was barely fit enough but only someone like Hercules would have had the nerve to tell Mac that it was going to be delayed again.

15

The lodge in the trees, or is it?

Another day, another briefing. All pretty boring but it contained one tiny bright spot. For the very first time, McKenzie did not immediately object to my calling her 'Mac'. I took that as progress even though she remained thoroughly hostile and brusque. My ribs still hurt after a night in bed, my back was still bruised, and my face still bore the scars. So, only about 80% normal fitness. Mac, on the other hand, seemed to be firing on all cylinders plus a few that I didn't know she had.

The target of the mission was William Pitt the Elder. I didn't know much about him but the people in black gave us all the intel. It seems he was the chap whose competence and ingenuity saved the country during what was called the Seven Years' War. We have him to thank for beating the French on a number of fronts in the US, Canada, India, the Caribbean, as well as at sea. Happily married to Lady Hester Grenville, he had a son - also called William - who went on to emulate his father's proficiency by becoming Britain's youngest Prime Minister and successfully negotiating a way through the Revolutionary and Napoleonic Wars at the turn of the nineteenth century. In laying the basis for what became the British Empire, Pitt the Elder was such a skilled orator that he was known as the 'voice of England'. Our target date was in late 1754, just after he'd married Lady Hester and before he became Prime Minister for the first time - there was a second time too. Strange choice of date but the black crew told us the 'clients' had specified the date.

The next morning we skipped back to 1754 and found lodgings in a reasonable Inn off what is now Regent Street. Still a bit delicate, I felt almost physically assaulted by the noise and smell – different to the 1900s and highly offensive. The accents were so thick at first that we could barely understand one word in four. We claimed we were Americans to explain our lack of comprehension and most people then spoke to us slowly. Mac was her usual cold, efficient self but I could tell she was excited to be standing in the straw encrusted sludge of a London street in November 1754. Her only gripe was being a woman in what was still – at least on the surface – a man's world. She'd come as my sister so that she could have a separate room and not have to wear a ring – but that had a serious downside in that she immediately became a target for every bachelor (and not a few married men) within a fifty mile radius.

We knew Pitt would be returning to the country for Christmas in a week's time, so we got straight to work. Mac split us up in the standard way and I took the first stint, following Pitt's carriage from his town house to Westminster. It was surprisingly easy to do this on foot. The weather was quite cold so the ground was hard. Not something to do in Spring when the streets were filled with mud. In spite of the cold, carriages still got bogged down or trapped by other vehicles every few minutes and I was able to jog along gently to keep up with Pitt. When they were getting the carriage unblocked or out of some ruts I waited, cosy in my special thermal under-clothes and gloves, in a convenient doorway. We'd deliberately chosen to look like an upper-class brother and sister but that had certain downsides. My sword kept getting between my legs. There was the time that I almost tripped over it and some ladies of ill-repute had the giggle of their lives. We were also the natural prey of the pickpocketing species.

The team back at base had thought of this. Similar problems arose in all eras. They supplied us with small tasers, each with two extra batteries. They could be set to three different levels: sting, zap, and stun. Mac refused to take hers – saying that it was a 'girly' weapon and beneath her dignity. She encountered one ne'er-do-well in Oxford Street while following the Pitts in their carriage. The man tried to use a very sharp knife to cut away her purse. Mac broke his wrist and confiscated the knife. There were two attempts on my own purse. One villain almost got it free after his colleague - a woman - had barged into me. The taser was set to minimum but 'sting' was a mild word for what it delivered. The techies said it was akin to having boiling water poured over you. The pickpocket screamed and staggered backwards, down some steps to the tradesman's entrance of a house. He'd have broken bones as well as a seared hand.

Pitt did exactly what the briefers had anticipated. Following him and getting times, places and video evidence was pretty simple. We had a problem with recording him in the Commons chamber but that was nothing to do with local conditions. It was mid-morning and Mac had stipulated that we would both attend. Quite rightly she thought a couple would attract much less attention than a single male or female - especially the latter. So, we walked in stiff silence to Westminster and paused on the steps of St Stephen's Chapel. The whole area looked so different without the modern building and the height of the Elizabeth Tower. Everything was low-rise and haphazard. In modern times St Stephens Chapel is a small part of the inside of the Parliament. At that time it *was* the Parliament.

There were hundreds of people milling around and it

didn't take a genius to see that inside would be like Wembley Stadium hosting a Rolling Stones' Concert. I grasped Mac's arm and threaded it through my own and made to walk up the steps. She removed her arm with a sharp jerk.

'I've already endured you on the way here. I'm not going arm in arm with you any more, Ward.' I was stunned and puzzled.

'You may not like me, Mac, but it's just not done for a woman to walk any distance by herself when accompanied by a man. Plus, it's going to be a bit hectic in there and these blokes will not give way to a female.' She shook her head emphatically,

'I can manage.'

I took a deep breath. 'Yes, you will if you maim one of two chaps first, but isn't that going to make us stand out a bit and defeat our purpose?' She'd put her arms across her chest. It was clear she'd not give in. 'Okay. Could you bring yourself to place your hand lightly on top of my arm? I'm not coming on to you. We must appear natural and we probably need to keep in physical touch in the crowd.'

McKenzie frowned to herself and clenched her hands. The internal conflict was fierce but eventually she agreed. If I'd been an unexploded bomb she could not have laid her hand more lightly on my arm. But she did, and we forced ourselves into the crowd and onto one of the rickety sets of tiered benches. At one point a man pushed her and she was obliged to grab my arm to stop herself being separated from me and potentially being trampled underfoot. My face gave nothing away but I gave a little whoop of triumph inside.

She even gave me a tiny smile as she thanked me for the support. It wasn't the end of the ice-age but a trickle of ice-cold water seeped out under the three hundred foot high snout of the glacier. Thanks to her efficiency and focus the rest of the mission went very smoothly. We stuck to the script. No side trips, no socialising with the locals. In the evenings we sat together in the private room that we'd hired at the Inn. We drank Madeira and pretended to read dusty tomes in which we had secreted our e-readers. We spoke hardly at all and then only about the details of the next day's activities. Naturally, the usual facilities were outside, and there were no complaints from Mac. She'd experienced far worse than those dirty, smelly earth closets. I found them unpleasant until I saw a midden that had piled up behind some of the poorer houses further up Piccadilly. Two blokes were relieving themselves on the rear slope as we walked past. Mac snorted, completely unfazed. For my part I was shocked by the size of the mound of excrement that had built up. It was huge. I thanked goodness it was November when the flies buzzed around in the thousands, not millions as they would be in summer. I watched them rise in clouds around the men and head for nearby hovels. Every one of those flies had been up to its knees in human waste.

Mac instructed me to press the return button exactly as the second hand on her controller informed us that it was time. In typical Mac style she insisted that we return from our exact arrival spot in St James' Park. It was secluded but had a good view of the park in its heavily wooded form. Mac kept both our recorders going right to the end of the mission.

We jumped back smartly at 1700 hours, plus a few seconds, on the third day - dirtier and smellier than we'd set off but with all the research material and records we'd been tasked to acquire. No-one in the universities would be left uninformed about the activities of William Pitt the Elder over those three days. Mac was pleased. She even thanked me very formally for a successful mission. I almost blew it by saluting and telling her that it was all down to her decisive leadership. You'll be glad to know that I resisted.

That evening I went for a run. The drizzle helped to clear my mind. It felt good to be away from Mac's over-zealous gaze and prissy attention to detail. London in 1754 was cold, damp, and smelly. Here at the Briggs, the scent of trees and the clean, crisp air coming across the moors to the south, were like a tonic. For once there was no thought of escape in my mind. I had not dropped it, but the next plan would only emerge from my subconscious. I knew better than to force the issue. The hill to the west fence was still not easy but it was getting a fraction less arduous. My head torch picked out the way and occasionally I caught sight of animal eyes in the darkness. How had they found their way into the top security area behind the fences? I suppose they lived here all the time. I went almost to the fence and, even though I wanted to rest, I forced myself to turn around and run straight back down again. My ribs were hurting a bit as I jogged past the first bend. And there they were. Mrs B and Henry pushing their trolley up the path again – just like the first time I'd met them.

'Where on earth are you two going? There's nothing up there.' I was still a little angry at them - especially at Henry.

Mrs Biddle gave me a broad smile and hoped I was well after my trip. Henry was being conciliatory … I think. He actually said 'Hello, how are you.'

I sighed and was secretly glad of the excuse to take a rest. 'I'm okay thanks. McKenzie was her usual self but the trip went well. How did you know I was on a trip, by the way?'

Henry looked at the woman and obviously received her agreement. 'We know a lot more than you think. We know, for example, what your trips are.'

'I suppose it's difficult to keep secrets with so many people chatting in a small base.'

'Yes, said Mrs Biddle, 'but that's not the only way we find out things. We can get information and we can also get … things … if you need them.'

As usual I kept my attention on the wrong thread and waved up the path. 'What's up there that needs cleaning, then?'

'Oh, just the lodge.'

'I haven't seen any lodge and I've run and walked every inch of this place.'

She smiled in the torchlight, her eyes twinkling. 'But that does not mean it is not there, does it, Dr Ward? Sometimes things are there even though we have not seen them.'

That was all too philosophical for me. 'Yes,' I agreed grudgingly, 'Do you have to go far off this path to get to it?'

It was Henry's turn evidently. 'No, not far. It was an old hunting lodge in the old times. Not large but we keep it clean and tidy.'

I looked at both of them in turn. 'You two are the strangest cleaners I've ever met.'

I was amazed to see Henry smile. Probably the first time ever. 'Thank you. And you are one of the strangest … people … we've ever encountered.'

My mind was full of slightly different thoughts on the way back to the flat. Those two were astute and perceptive, and more than slightly mysterious. I wished I could remember everything they'd said to me over the weeks. I had the feeling that what they'd said was important and that I should have provided more incisive responses.

16

Was I listening to the wake up call?

I did a major session in the gym early the next day and Mac had us doing a debrief for the research team in the Black Building at 11:30 am. An interminable two hours during which she insisted on adding detail to what was already a very detailed set of notes and videos. I did get one laugh, however. On the mission, she'd recorded me many times as we were out and about. I looked quite the dandy. The tricorn hat was actually very smart. If I tilted it just a fraction, I looked pretty good in it. Shades of Dick Turpin although not as nasty. Once the meeting ended and I was officially released, I went to one of the other cafés - the one opposite the main admin building in the interior of the base. The food was identical but there were different people to see, different music, and the furniture and wall decorations were different. How sad had I become?

I picked up a copy of a car magazine. I loved fast cars and had planned to buy a small stable of them once established in my new life. And that got me thinking again about how I could get out of here. Old-fashioned methods stood no chance. The Great Escape made good movie material, but Reid had the technology to render all the old tricks useless. I was not going to be digging any tunnels. Any new attempt could also be terminal for me. While not forcing the matter, I began to open my mind to a range of different possibilities. Could I get Reid to release me without having to escape? Could I impersonate someone? Could I immobilise and tie up the driver of the ice cream truck and get out as the driver? He was never scanned as far as I knew. I even contemplated digging under the fences, but only for a few seconds.

My wildest idea was flying out using a self-made hang glider. I'd experienced a hang glider once when Emma and I had been on vacation in Greece. It was an experience I prefer to forget but Emma found it hilarious. I was strapped to the back of an experienced pilot but was so reluctant it took two men to push us off the hilltop. Emma said I'd yelled like a little girl as they did so. My own memory is that I yelled a war-cry, but suit yourself.

Even if I acquired the materials and the skill to build one, an unpowered hang glider would never clear the fences from the low-rise buildings of the base. I told myself that I was disappointed to have to discard the idea. Myself told me back that I was talking nonsense. I left it at that, convinced that my subconscious would not let me down.

Predictably, I ran into Mrs B and Henry later that week. My run was taking me an unusual route through the various buildings and around the perimeter. I'd hoped to avoid them. But there they were. Pushing a waste bin into an alley behind the communications shed. The 'shed' was actually more like a fortress but everyone called it the comms shed. It was the most heavily protected building on the site apart from the Blue Building. The usual sets of high fences, the usual sensors and cameras, and enough armed guards to protect the Tower of London. Mrs B waved to me and - like an idiot - I trotted around the outside of the fences to where they were struggling with a large bin on wonky wheels. From the other side it had looked close to the comms building but it was actually about thirty yards further away. I helped push the bin into position down the alley and then looked at them with what I hoped was ice in my eyes.

'Still thinking about escaping, I see.' Henry crossed his arms across his chest and stared me down. Mrs B was pretending to adjust the position of the utterly immovable bin. I was flabbergasted.

'What? How do you know? … Why do you think that?'

He just kept staring and I realised I could not say more without either denying the accusation or telling them everything. Instead, I opted to change the subject.

'You two are into philosophical mysteries. I had a dream the other day that you might find interesting.'

They waited and I waited in vain for them to show any interest. So, I launched into the story of the daydream and the inside of the Blue Building. While I was speaking Henry squatted on the ground and Mrs Biddle sat herself comfortably on an electricity circuit box. When I finished, they did not speak. It was exasperating.

'Well? What do you think?'

Mrs Biddle stood and came closer to me than she'd ever done - about four feet. She was studying my eyes.

'Dr Ward, none of us believes that what you experienced was a waking dream. The important thing is for you to work it out for yourself.'

They were impossible. Ask them a simple question and you got convoluted rationales and little in the way of answers. I sighed. 'It doesn't matter. I need to get out of this place.'

Henry perked up at that. 'You're still on that bandwagon? Still following that ridiculous star?'

I nodded. 'You have no idea how much I yearn to be free.'

'Yes, we do,' said Mrs B quietly. 'We can see how tortured you are. But you have work to do and it is very, very important.'

'Reid's projects may be important but they don't mean as much to me as getting shot of this place and him … and his work. Anyway,' I suddenly thought, 'who exactly are you two?'

'We're friends. Probably the only ones you have inside these fences.'

I studied them back. Their faces were serious and calm.

'You say things and do things that make me think you're … well … psychic. But that's crazy. There's no such thing as telepathy or witches.'

Mrs B nodded. 'That's good. You are getting close to the right track. You have powers that you have not yet acknowledged, young man. We need those powers and so do you.'

She stopped and looked at Henry, who nodded. 'In spades.'

'What are you talking about?'

'We need you because you can stop Reid and his cronies. If they succeed in their plot the world you know will be no more.'

I was getting absolutely nowhere.

'This is plain madness. You are both out of your heads. Reid is making himself rich selling information to universities. And I'm on the right track because I'm determined to get out of here and I'll do it soon.'

To my surprise Henry slapped the top of the trolley with a loud bang.

'For heaven's sake Ward, open your eyes. Get your head out of your arse and start thinking of others rather than yourself.'

17

Whip-back anyone?

I was shocked by the aggression from an apparently gentle sort of chap. It goes without saying that we parted company very soon that evening, but I couldn't get his face out of my mind. I was used to scorn and grumpiness, disdain, and disbelief. That night all I saw was anger and even a tinge of disgust from the tall cleaner.

That was two days before the third mission. The general busy-ness of Mac's 'team meetings' and the lengthy briefing and clothing meetings, plus the novelty and excitement attached to the planned mission, drove Henry's outburst out of mind. I did, however, think a novel thought of my own. I have them sometimes. The day after my encounter with the cleaners I was running in the gym. I almost got swept off the running machine with the shock realisation that, by stopping whatever Reid was planning - assuming that Mrs B and Henry were right - but why on earth would they be? - I would escape and get back to my money and a well-deserved life of luxury. I had not thought of it that way before. Probably because I assumed that Reid's was the usual type of shady-business and that stopping such things meant unravelling a large criminal gang with tentacles in many cities and possibly many countries. Mrs B and Henry seemed to think that I could be instrumental in stopping him and, if they were right - big if, I know - I could escape by simply throwing a few spanners into the works. His plan, whatever it was, would fail, the staff would have to be laid off, the base would close, and little old me would be free to resume normal service. No need for feats of derring-do. I would not need to burrow under fences or shoot my way out through ranks of security guards. It was quite a revelation to say the least. But I had little time to think about it as the new mission was filling my every waking hour.

You may have heard of a chap named Winston Churchill. No? Well, his widespread fame derives mainly from his spell as Prime Minister during that little fracas known as World War Two. You've seen the pictures - overweight old man in a grey hat and well-made suits usually using his walking cane to get around and fend off insolent journalists, holding two fingers up to any camera within range. I think he knew very well what that sign represented but took immense secret pleasure in pretending ignorance.

Yet Winston was a firebrand. He was a bit of a rebel who, in his youth, used any excuse to get where the action was. And I don't necessarily mean women. He liked them of course but his focus when younger was always danger. He found any excuse to put himself in harm's way whenever anyone mentioned action. Our mission concerned the second Boer War. There'd been an earlier scrap between British and Dutch settlers in South Africa back in the 1880s. Long story short the Boers wanted independence from Britain in an area called the Transvaal, and Britain thought that was a bad idea which should be discouraged at every turn. In 1899 the fighting flared up again and Churchill was out there on the next steam ship. Officially he was a war correspondent but he was never shy of picking up a gun and putting on a uniform. You'll get the idea from one of his most famous quotes 'Existence is never so sweet as when it is at hazard.' Within two weeks of landing in South Africa the armoured train he was on was ambushed and he was made a prisoner of war. Being Winston, he escaped and went on the run with a 'dead or alive' price on his head, made it back to British South Africa and went on to see action at quite a few battles.

It was this aspect of Churchill's life that the academics had selected for our research. We'd been tasked to go back to late February 1900 to a place called Colenso. The British had been badly mauled by the Boers at a series of engagements following earlier defeats at Colenso and Spion Kop in early February. The Boers had besieged a town called 'Ladysmith' and the British commander, Sir Redvers Buller was determined to avenge recent embarrassments and relieve the Boer siege of eight thousand British troops in that town. They were dark days for the British.

Mac and I had, respectively, been provided with a modern automatic pistol and an upgraded version of the stun gun - this one had four power levels - wasn't I the lucky one! Complain as I might, they refused to give me an automatic. So, I was sent into one of the fiercest and bloodiest of Britain's colonial wars with an electric taser whose highest setting was 'stun with prejudice'.

Our cover story was that we were sister and brother from Ladysmith. We'd been to Durban to visit relatives and were now desperate to get back to see if our family was safe. We were dressed in heavy, trekking clothes which had been carefully stained and covered in dust and mud. Our boots were old leather clod-hoppers that could fall apart at any moment. We carried - I carried - a worn carpet bag with the usual changes of clothes. Our weapons were well concealed under the threadbare canvas jackets and, in Mac's case, her voluminous canvas skirts. After the frantic preparations of the past few days we did not need to pretend to be dog tired.

The jump was effortless. I wish I could say the same about the rest of the mission. As planned, we walked a couple of miles north and ran into British pickets who, after careful questioning, eventually took us to a major who reluctantly introduced us to General Sir Redvers-Buller. Their thoughts were that, with our local knowledge, we might be of assistance during the approaches to Ladysmith. We had no intention of still being around at that point so that was not going to be a problem.

More to the point, seated at Buller's map table was a young officer who was introduced to us as Lieutenant Churchill of the African Light Horse. As we'd hoped, the young Winston was interested in our story for his newspaper dispatches. We therefore got to know him quite well over the next twenty-four hours and everything seemed to be going well, until Buller decided, on the basis of fresh intelligence, that his whole force would move immediately up closer to the river Tugela. He assigned Churchill to the task of scouting the approaches. So that's how we ended up accompanying Winston with an advance party of two columns of British cavalry east of Colenso. It was an uneventful afternoon but I found the heat and dust difficult to cope with. The land was parched and it totally baffled me as to how trees and bushes, even small ones, managed to survive. The constant strong breeze picked up tons of grit and flung it straight into our faces. By the time Churchill ordered a halt for the night my face felt like I'd been rubbing it with sandpaper all day.

Over a meagre supper of dried meat and even drier bread, Churchill was full of eager anticipation of a big fight to come. The Boers were north of the river and they were also on this side, to the west of us, in Colenso itself. He absolutely loved the fact that we were outflanked and outnumbered!

That evening I lay on a blanket on what they said was grass but was actually a mass of sharp stones with a few blades of yellow vegetation between them. Never before had I truly appreciated how harsh campaigning had been in those days. Even Mac passed a brief comment that her SBS backpack with its waterproof memory foam ground sheet was infinitely preferable.

I was unable to get to sleep. The briefing had included very graphic and highly complimentary descriptions of the skills and tenacity of the Boers. The briefers explained Boer ambushes and lightning raids in great detail. The cavalrymen around me seemed to be able to sleep anywhere at any time but, amid their snores and farts, sleep was a distant prospect for me. I'd held the equivalent rank to Captain in the British Army but my weapon skills were managing a computer in an air-conditioned bunker. Trekking through the South African bush had not been part of my training.

The thing that astounded me was the sky. It was a blaze of light, crammed with more stars than I'd ever thought existed. They provided enough light to see by but mostly they reminded me of the immensity of the universe and the total insignificance of humans. And those thoughts led me inevitably back to my own predicament. I was confused and conflicted. Were the cleaners - the *cleaners* for goodness sake - right? Did they know something that I did not? Why had I not thought that Reid would have much more layered security? Why was Mac so set against me? The questions went on and they mostly reminded me of my incompetence and impotence, and that made me very angry indeed. I knew I could be a wally, but I was also intelligent and competent. How had I got myself into this mess? Even when I tried to focus on the problem of trying to escape versus trying to 'stop' Reid, the maze of options just got more complex. The exasperation was building within me into something close to pure rage.

Then, without preamble, I was having a dream. I was in a shallow ditch and bullets were flying all around. Mac and Churchill were with me. He was shouting something like 'they are all around us,' and I was thinking that this was it. We were going to be killed in a Boer raid in the year 1900. Stupid isn't it. What does it matter what year you die? Mac was telling us to keep down because she could hear British voices shouting and then the bullets were not pinging viciously off the rocks any longer and it seemed we'd been rescued. But that was not the end of my dream. The ditch turned into a street, quite a modern street but definitely old-fashioned by twenty-first century standards. I was standing by the side of the road and some pedestrians were stopping and pointing, saying that the President was coming. I watched as several huge limousines turned into the narrow street from a wider boulevard. There were three of them; all highly polished black limos with white-wall tyres. It's the President, my neighbours on the sidewalk were saying as they began to applaud. I recognised the man immediately as he passed. His rear window was down and he was waving to the people. It was Franklin Delano Roosevelt. I was dumbfounded. Why was I watching FDR? And then it became clear. A man about twenty feet to my left stepped towards the car and opened fire. My mind registered immedi-ately that it was a modern automatic because he must have fired twelve shots, in machine gun style, through the car's open window. Then the assassin just disappeared. Literally disap-peared. Even though it all happened in a few short seconds, it was something that only Reid's time-travel system could organise.

I remember feeling mortified, but the dream was getting highly confused. Churchill as a young man overlapped FDR's face smiling out of the car. The roadway became the ditch. Bullets whining off rocks were interspersed with bullets slam-ming into flesh. I was beginning to panic and my next clear recollection was of lying on the floor of the Black building surrounded by staffers who were in obvious alarm. Mac and I had returned early and at first they thought we were injured. We were stretchered immediately to sick bay but we were both unharmed. Mac was very restrained. She left it until we were on our way to Reid's office, still in our South African clothes, before rounding furiously on me.

'What the frigging hell happened Ward? Why did you drag us back? We hadn't finished half the mission.' She was actually shaking with anger and a careless word from me would have been my last.

'I don't know,' I replied truthfully. 'I really don't know.' She harrumphed her disbelief and strode off with me following lamely in her wake. To be fair to him, Reid was not angry. Puzzled yes, but not in the same fury as Mac. He sat us down, oblivious to the dust invading his upholstery and carpets. His first question was the obvious one.

'I honestly don't know,' I replied. 'One minute we were trying to get to sleep somewhere near Colenso in South Africa in 1900, the next we were here again.' Reid examined us both carefully.

'Did Ward do anything?' he asked Mac.

'Unless he pressed the return button, I don't see what he could have done.'

'No. We checked the software. The return button was not used. It seems that the 'whip-back' glitch has struck this mission. The system, as I told you at the start, is temperamental and sometimes causes a return without warning. It baffles the engineers.' He sighed and motioned us to leave. 'Turn over what records you were able to get and then go and have a shower. We'll have to return to this unfinished business, but the schedule is tight.'

Lying in my much more comfortable bed that night I reviewed the events of the day. I'd been lucky that our 'whip-back' could be blamed on the system. Reid had warned us that the tech could be unreliable and capricious. But I knew that that was not what had happened. Somehow, it had been me who caused the return. That dream had somehow broken the time-link and dragged us back. That was one aspect of the affair. The other, potentially far more serious, was the dream itself. I did not need Mrs Biddle and Henry to tell me that it was, somehow, real. I had seen us in a very dangerous situation and I'd seen someone, with or without Reid's knowledge, assassinating FDR.

Something was terribly wrong here and it was not just my kidnapping and incarceration. The targets we were investigating were all key historical figures. I didn't know who else was on the lists. The London teams would have far more than we did. But, if the ones slated for Mac's team were anything to go by, they would be similar, eminent figures from around the world and around history. My vision of the killing of FDR gave me the answer. Reid was almost certainly trying to change history to stop effective leaders from doing certain things. I also realised why the dates were strange. They were all earlier dates in the lives of the historical figures. If I had access to a laptop I am sure I'd find that those dates were very close to the dates at which the figures became powerful or did history-changing things. How that would help Reid I couldn't see but that was the only explanation that fitted all the facts.

Perhaps Reid was trying to change specific bits of history to please certain powerful clients. My stomach contracted at the thought but Mrs Biddle and Henry were totally right. Reid had to be stopped at all costs.

18

The mists clear ... a bit

My next meeting with the two cleaners was very different to the previous ones. As required by time travel protocol, Mac and I had been given the week to recover, but Reid made it very clear that he wanted the fourth mission completed successfully as soon as possible. Our briefing and planning must take place during the week, he insisted. Two days was all he really gave us, and on the second night, after I had returned from my run, I emerged from my shower in a bathrobe to find Mrs Biddle and Henry standing square in the centre of my sitting room. The fact that I did not have a heart attack is ample proof of how inured I'd become to weird happening.

I put my finger over my lips, pointed at the room in general, and then held my hand to my ear. I was certain the place had more bugs than an anthill. Mrs Biddle smiled.

'Don't be concerned Dr Ward. We have suppressed the microphones and the three cameras. They are now playing the sounds and sights of you having a snack and a drink and watching a DVD film. This will go on for two hours, easily long enough for us to speak.'

And speak we did. I told them about South Africa, about

the dream, about FDR and my suspicions. They just nodded throughout, and Henry only interrupted once to tell me that he'd been sure I would eventually reach the right conclusions. I chose to believe that he wasn't intending to be patronising, so I let it go.

'If my dream about the Blue Building was correct, that wall contains all the information we'll need to put this all together. Could you get me a blue jumpsuit?'

'No,' said Henry. 'We've told you before. Even if we could, you'd never get through security.'

'And anyway,' added Mrs B, 'your idea of stealing and using a blue jumpsuit is evidence that you are still thinking in the wrong way. Henry and I know what Mr Reid is planning and we assure you with all our hearts that he has to be stopped.'

'Why can't you tell me then? It would save a lot of time.'

'No,' said Henry again. His penchant for negative responses was getting annoying. 'We can't tell you why, but you need to understand this by yourself.'

Mrs B stepped in before I could properly show my disgust for all that. She came a little closer. 'There are two sorts of people in this world, Dr Ward. We call them the 'mechanics' and the 'believers'. The human race has been conditioned for hundreds of years to think of the world as a mechanical contrivance. First Galileo, then Newton, then Einstein, they all saw the universe as a thing that can only be described in mechanical terms. Even doctors see the human body as a machine. I could say more but you will get my drift. A believer on the other hand is someone who stands outside that whole mechanical nonsense. They know that the universe is not a machine, that the Earth does not operate to mechanical principles, and that human beings are far more than just electro-biological constructs.'

I raised my eyebrows. 'That all sounds terribly philosophical or religious but where does it get us?'

She shook her head. It was the nearest I'd seen her get to an expression of frustration. 'This is not religion. Although some - a very few - use religion to get to the point I'm speaking about.' Showing surprising strength for a little old lady, she pushed me onto the sofa and sat down heavily beside me.

'Haven't you ever wondered what the difference is between knowledge and belief?' My face gave her the answer and it elicited a huge sigh before she went on. 'We have become so used to the scientific method and 'proof' that very few of us can tell the difference. If a scientist tells you he has proof of something, that usually becomes something you 'believe'. The Earth is a sphere, electricity works through electrons, a certain amount of petroleum will cause an engine to start. Very, very few understand that all that mechanical stuff is only a part of reality - that the universe is far more complicated and that mind,' she tapped her forehead, 'is the most important aspect.'

'You mentioned Einstein but not quantum physics, which I think is much less mechanical.'

Henry gave his friend a break. 'True, Dr Ward. It is the beginning of uncertainty in physics and possibly the beginning of a new era in which people begin to believe.'

'Belief is not just important, Tim, it is everything. But, and this is the point I have been trying to make, believers have to believe with their minds, not their brains. The brain might tell you that science knows an answer and that magic does not exist, for example, but if the *mind* believes in magic, it exists.' She held up a finger to stop me butting in. 'You must first believe and only then will your mind fully accept what is happening to you. Henry and I cannot simply tell you.'

'That's all very well but how can I believe if I haven't been told what to believe in and how it works?'

There was a sad little smile at the corners of those inscrutable eyes. 'You will understand when it happens, but essentially you have to stop thinking with your brain and allow your mind to take over.'

'All very Zen, but not helping,' I said. 'I have never been as confused in all my life and you two are like the proverbial fireguard.'

'What fireguard?' Henry didn't do ignorance very comfortably but it gave me a tiny thrill to have flummoxed him.

'The chocolate fireguard,' I explained. He gave his colleague a question-mark look.

'Dr Ward is being facetious, Henry. He is saying that the two of us are being of little use.' She must have recognised that her colleague still did not get it. 'Like a fireguard made out of chocolate.' Henry was not pleased at being bamboozled by such a silly simile. He glared at me even as he nodded his understanding to Mrs B.

And then his patrician features swivelled towards me; the eyes boring into mine. 'You will find that we are actually of great use. But first you must begin to use that mind of yours. If, of course, it has not completely atrophied with your brain feeding it all this nonsense about escape plans and blue jumpsuits. I suggested to you a while ago that you start to think. That is still my advice, but you also need to let your mind do the thinking not your brain.'

'Okay. I think that's enough philosophy for now. If we are going to stop Reid we can't wave a wand at him. We must take concrete action. Would you be able to get me a laptop?'

The exasperation was almost a fourth physical presence as they looked at each other.

'You do not need it, you know,' tried Mrs B.

'Uh, yes I do if I am to find out Reid's plan.' Henry was shaking his head vehemently in the background.

'Alright,' she sighed, 'we will do that.' Henry stalked across the room to the door and stood there, fury radiating from him in invisible but potent waves.

'It will need to be a powerful one,' I added.

Henry shot me a look that would have melted steel.

Somehow the next target did not surprise me. JFK was one of the most important US Presidents of the twentieth century. I'd already guessed that he would be on the list. True to form the research dates were three days in early May 1958. Kennedy went reluctantly into politics. The death of his older brother pushed him to the forefront of his father's ambitions. JFK made the big leap in 1952 by winning a Senate seat. We were to investigate him over three days on one of his political trips six years later. When I thought about it later, the implications of an early demise for the young Kennedy were quite scary. If he were to die in 1958 he would not be around to defeat Nixon in the 1960 Presidential race. What would happen to the USA under Nixon facing the threats of the Soviet Union was anybody's guess. And he would not be around to take that brave leap into the space race by promising an American astronaut on the Moon by the end of the 1960s.

Reid began the briefing by saying that Kennedy in 1958 was a fascinating study for our academic clients. Still in the heyday of his Senate career, still trying to push a socially-oriented agenda, still fighting the Republicans tooth and nail. The briefing from two staffers was detailed and fascinating. I say that because I was drawn into the period in spite of myself. JFK had been the subject of many university seminars for me, but the focus had always been on the assassination and the conspiracy theories. Now the briefers were giving me a much deeper, all-round picture of the man. They spoke about his relationship with his father - fraught to the end - his secret wish not to be in politics at all, his controversial alleged attraction to just about anyone in a skirt, and his rigid focus on doing his duty. Mac and I also learned about late 1950s American society. We were warned about race relations, rock and roll, and the teenage revolution, and we were particularly advised not to underestimate the sexism of the times. Females might seem free but this was still a male dominated society. Women were expected to tend to house and family while their menfolk brought home the bacon. Black people were confidently relied upon to know their place, especially in the southern States. There were tiny tremors from the social earthquake that was coming later in the century but they were easily ignored.

The briefers anticipated no violence during the mission. The team was there to follow and record. We were, however, issued with stun guns 'just in case'. I loved the cash we were given. It even smelled like real greenbacks and looked suitably worn and dirty. The clothes were a bit of a two-edged sword. I was trussed up in a dark suit, button-down shirt, polished black brogues and a stylish grey tie. The hat I was issued was something I had to get used to. Most smart men wore the same sort of Trilby those days. To get used to it, I wore it all day long for almost three full days at the base. It went great with my yellow jumpsuit! The socks were long, knee-length monstrosities that needed suspenders to hold them up. I begged to be allowed to wear ordinary modern elasticated socks instead. After twenty minutes of argument the wardrobe department gave in but insisted on them being long and dark. Showing the top of a sock would brand me as a commoner.

Mac was fully dolled up. Apart from the hair colour she could be mistaken for the young Jackie Kennedy. Pencil skirt, tight white blouse, smart but understated high heels, and accessories to match. Quality for 1960s American women was in the cut and material of what you might call office day-wear, not in showiness. For Mac, the hat was also a problem - a small one with a frill of lace which she rejected out of hand until wardrobe showed her the alternatives. Her biggest complaint was with the nylons, and the suspenders they needed. It was a losing battle with wardrobe. She said she hated tights but would certainly not wear the belt and suspenders necessary for nylons. Tights were ruled out in case she had to get changed in front of other women, so nylons were the winners. She was lucky she didn't need a corset but, if those nylons had been human, they'd have cut their own throats to avoid the retribution she threatened for them when she got back.

19

Seducing Mac (don't get excited, it wasn't me)

The place to which we jumped was the then municipal airport for Atlanta, Georgia. It was 0700 local time and the air was already stiflingly hot and humid. Worse, I felt like I was breathing solid aviation fuel mixed with old-fashioned leaded petrol fumes. We carried our small suitcases to the airport restaurant, the Dobb's House, to have some breakfast and get acclimatised. The idea was that everyone would think we were there for an early plane. In fact we were waiting for a couple of early arrivals so that we did not draw attention to ourselves as we travelled into town. I argued, successfully, to be allowed to go up to the rooftop terrace on the basis that, from there, I'd be able to see how long the taxi queue was. I pleaded with Mac over a quick breakfast and she eventually surrendered. Up there it was already uncomfortably hot and humid, but there was the slightest of breezes and it was the chance of a lifetime for me. I'd known Atlanta-Hartsfield in our own time, a vast sprawling modern airport bigger than most decent-sized towns and not a few British cities. Atlanta Municipal in 1958 was big, I counted five runways, but the terminals were still old-fashioned and civilised. I watched the ground crews getting an Eastern DC-

7 and a Delta Constellation ready for engine start. The passengers were already lining up outside the terminal, waiting to be told to walk across and board. In the distance I spotted an incoming Constellation floating in over the trees. It would be landing in a couple of minutes and at the terminal in ten more. We had fifteen minutes or so to get to the head of the taxi queue and pretend to have come in on that aircraft. On the way down the stairs I checked the boards. Delta from Washington DC and a Convair following on close behind from Miami, so our story was that we had flown in from the capital.

In Atlanta, after a stifling ride in a smelly Ford, we checked into the Biltmore. The briefers had specified this hotel because JFK would be flying in later to take one of the Penthouse Suites plus a few more rooms for his staff. That would be at about 3 pm. The Biltmore was smart. We took middle of the range rooms and made ourselves comfortable while waiting for Kennedy to arrive. Mac took us for a light lunch downstairs to suss the place out, and afterwards I volunteered to sit in the lobby to record the great man's arrival. Mac was having none of it. She was so excited, she even twitched an eyebrow slightly at one point, that she insisted we would both do that bit. Her argument was that she wanted to see how tight his security was. And I believed her of course. The arrival was quite a show. Mac seemed to take it in her stride, commenting under her breath about the mistakes the two security guys were making. I just watched the histrionics of the grand entrance of a Senator and his entourage to a top Atlanta hotel. It did not take long. The manager and his assistant swept the entire group out of the lobby and into the lifts within two minutes. Interestingly no-one remained to watch their luggage. A massive black mark against security for Mac. It was left piled on the floor for anyone to trip over or plant a bomb until a gang of four bell-boys whisked it off on four brass trolleys. I looked at Mac.

'How are we going to get close to them without the security chaps spotting us?'

'I've brought special equipment so that we can do most of it at a distance. The tech team gave me two long distance microphones disguised as portable radios from this era. As long as we can sit ourselves somewhere within about twenty yards, the mics will pick up their conversations. We have the telephoto lens on the hand recorders as well as our lapel equipment. It shouldn't be difficult.'

'What about private conversations. This era is already quite security conscious and we'll struggle to get sight of the sort of documents we did during the Lloyd George mission.'

Two small lines appeared in her lovely forehead. 'We'll have to make it up as we go along.' And those eyes …

The first day went pretty well. We hired a cab for the day and it took us everywhere that Kennedy went. The cabbie was curious but we'd got pretty convincing police IDs and Mac told him we were undercover, shadowing the Senator's security team. He was so excited he spat out his gum and opened another stick.

One of us was on duty at all times while the other rested in a café or hotel lobby. His schedule was packed tighter than a doctor's appointment list. He met local politicians and Democratic party workers, he shook hands with bystanders to the joy of the attendant press photographers, he even shook the hand of a little girl which sent them into raptures and which then required several shots from different angles. This being Atlanta he made sure it was a white girl. Most of it was straightforward but Mac also decided we should get an idea of what was going on in the closed rooms in which Kennedy was holding meetings. One such meeting was with a Democratic member of the House of Representatives at another swanky hotel in downtown Atlanta. We saw Kennedy meet him downstairs. Mac told me to take the contact mic and try to place it against the meeting room door. There were so many flaws in that plan that I didn't know where to begin. I tried, but she insisted and that was how I found myself outside hotel room 3144.

The corridor, which I had told Mac would be lined with security guards with large guns, was empty. All I had to do was to insert the almost invisible mic into the gap between the door and the hinges and then I could leave and let it do its job. I walked confidently down the corridor and stopped briefly outside 3144 leaning against the door to check my shoelaces. The bug was easily placed but as I stood upright I found a black-suited security man behind me.

'What are you doing,' he asked while examining the door and its surrounds. He would not be used to such small electronic equipment so I doubted he'd spot anything. Apparently satisfied, he gave me an up and down look.

'You'd better come with me while we check you out.'

I shrugged and made to follow him as he turned but he simply spiralled to the floor.

'Quick,' said Mac. 'He won't be out for long and his mate might be nearby.'

We scooted and I was told to keep a very low profile for the next day while we finished the work. When we got back to the Biltmore, Mac motioned me to a secluded corner table in the lobby.

'The bug is picking up signs of discord in the Democratic party and Kennedy is playing all his cards, especially his father. The Representative has told him he must sign the documents by tomorrow lunch time or the money from Georgia will be almost impossible to release in his favour.'

'What documents?'

She stared into space. 'I'm just a simple soldier. You're the worldly-wise, devious one. You tell me. Can't you make a stab?'

I thought carefully about what I knew about US Presidential campaigns. They relied on copious and continuous dollops of cash and those generally had to be secured over several previous years from a variety of sources. A US Presidential campaign was very similar to a car crash victim, without constant transfusion of life giving blood in the form of green-backs the campaign would wither and die. No mazuma, no victory. The only standard in campaigns was that nothing ever came free - there was always a price for support. What price would JFK be paying? When I gave Mac this conclusion she was quiet for a long time.

'We need to get sight of the documents somehow. Could you steal them from his room?'

I snorted. 'I'm a virtual thief and I can do a bit of the physical stuff at times, but I've been made by the security guy and Kennedy won't leave documents around while he's out. If there's a wall safe I might be able to crack it but I'd need to be inside first. Even then, the odds are that I wouldn't be able to get it open.' Another thought came to mind. 'He might also not trust wall safes and opt to have the documents and any other valuables stored in the hotel strongroom.'

She nodded. 'So, there's only one way. I will have to get to the documents while he is in the room.'

'How on earth are you going to manage that? I think he or the security people will notice a strange third party in the room?'

'You're a twit, Ward. How would a woman get into the handsome Senator's hotel room?'

'Oh.'

This was proving to be the most difficult mission so far. Mac disappeared for an hour or so and when she knocked on my door later I staggered back in surprise and admiration. She looked like the proverbial million dollars. To be honest, if I'd had more, I'd certainly offer two million. The nice but ordinary pencil skirt which had seen much activity that day had been replaced with something that looked very sleek and expensive. Silk? The shoes were about five levels up from the ones she'd been given by the Black department, her hair was now in a highly fashionable bun-like thing. The jewellery and accessories were probably worth more than I'd have earned in a lifetime in the RAF. I told her she looked stunning. She shrugged it off.

'Thanks to fake cheque books. Help me work out how I am going to get hooked up.'

You'll see how my mind was working in the presence of such mind-boggling female temptation, when I say my heart skipped a beat. I had visions of her taking the new clothes off and needing me for hooks and eyes later. In split-seconds I'd created the most wonderful scenarios. Predictably, the thoughts appeared on my face and she grabbed my collars.

'Don't even dream about it you foul-minded bastard. I meant hooking me up with Kennedy. I can't just pick him up in the street.' She let me go and I tried to put those lovely visions aside.

Focus, Ward, focus. 'He's downstairs at the moment having dinner with a bunch of Democrats in the hotel restaurant. He'll not be finished for an hour or so but you could literally bump into him on his way back from a bathroom break. After that it's up to you I'm afraid.'

'You've done this before I can see.' I grinned and she scowled and moved on.

'We must get down there now with the listening gear. You can do the surveillance while I wait near the entrance to the bathroom having a cocktail and being engrossed in a woman's magazine. I need some more time to get my story straight.'

Towards the end of the meal when all the business was over and everyone was talking about the next football season, JFK excused himself and headed to the bathroom. I saw Mac bury her head in the magazine. The Senator breezed by her and she got up and followed him into the plush corridor leading to the ladies and gents facilities. Accidentally dropping the magazine would be her excuse for bumping into him. And she clearly did a good job. They emerged together, Kennedy looking down into those beautiful green eyes, obviously entranced by the package and by her British accent. It was a done deal. He went back to his friends for fifteen minutes and then headed for the lifts. On the way he collected Mac, who slinked into position by his side as though she'd always been there. The security guards kept their faces straight and ignoring Mac entirely.

I returned to my room and listened in. The voices were loud with drink (or in Mac's case because she knew I'd be listening and recording).

I caught up as he handed her a Martini.

'Thank you, that's very kind,' Mac said demurely.

He laughed. 'Kindness has nothing to do with it. Tell me about yourself.' I heard a seat being patted. He was inviting her to sit beside him.

'There's not much to know really. My name is Macie Bloomfield. I'm widowed now but I was married to Herbert Bloomfield III. He left me a lot of money and three plantations.'

In his slightly slurred New England drawl Kennedy carried on the interrogation. 'You must be a busy business-lady then Macie … no? Why not?'

'Bert stitched it all up and made sure the companies would carry on as always. I was excluded from all but the Democratic party activities. That's why I'm here tonight. I'm dating one of the chaps you were speaking to this evening.'

She was very, very good. I did not need to be there to see JFK prick up his ears.

'You have a role in Democratic money? I had no idea.'

'The money Bert left was divided into three parts: the majority went to the plantations and companies. There was a very substantial amount for me personally and another larger pile for the party. He thought he was being kind to me when he made me the sole decision maker for the party money.'

There was a silence while Kennedy digested the implications of this news. I could hear his mind ticking over from here. 'So, it was you who set the conditions for my funding?'

'Well no. And yes. There are strict stipulations from my side, but I think the party has added a few. Don't know what though.'

I heard someone get up. 'I have the document in my folder here. Would you take a look and tell me which are your requirements and which have been added by the party?'

Another long pause with the sound of pages being turned. 'Yes. These five at the top are mine but the other six have been added by those bastards downstairs.'

That was what we needed. Mac's recorder will have taken photos of every page. She could make her excuses and leave whenever she wanted. I was conscious of a pang of jealousy as I wondered what would happen next. With Kennedy and a beautiful woman alone in an hotel room the imagination did not have to over-exert itself.

'Thank you very much Macie.' I heard him say. 'Now have another drink and we can talk about what we can do with the rest of the evening.' The ensuing silence was eloquent. I heard a shuffle, presumably Kennedy moving in, and material rustling. There was the sound of glasses being dropped, then a yelp from Mac, and finally a dull thump and something crashing to the floor.

~

'I don't believe it! You laid out John F Kennedy?' Mac had returned to my room looking a little flushed.

'Well, he was getting very frisky, what they apparently call 'fresh' in this era.' She took another look at my shocked face. 'Don't be an ass. I didn't kill him - he'll just have a headache for a while.' She, at least, knew where the pressure points were.

She showed me the photos of what was an important election plan and an agreement by Kennedy to do certain things in return for a very respectable amount of funding.

She smiled. Her smiles were extremely rare and when they came it was like a searchlight being turned on in a dark room. In this case, in that million-dollar outfit, it was almost life-changing. I clung to the practicalities so that my face would not betray my thoughts.

'He'll set the security people to track-down you, us.'

She snorted. 'He won't even mention my presence. He'll be too embarrassed.'

'But he'll be suspicious about the documents and you.'

'So what? We'll be long gone, and I'd put a huge bet on it remaining a quiet, very personal and embarrassing mystery in his secret diaries.'

When we returned to base the next afternoon Mac was as close to ecstatic as I ever saw her. It had been a supremely successful mission. We'd got everything the researchers could want and quite a bit more. Mac even praised me in front of Reid for planting the bug and supporting her during the 'hooking up with JFK' episode.

I was personally pleased because Reid's face during the debrief was not hostile. I'd learned to read his almost imperceptible facial tells. I was still not flavour of the month, but the success of the JFK mission had taken just a little of the heat off me. A debrief with Mac followed the one with Reid and Marshall. Would you believe, coffee and pastries in Briefing Room 7? I kept looking around in case she thought someone important was going to be attending. I had never seen her so relaxed and content. We went through the mission in her usual professional style. There were a few things that we could have done better and those were duly noted, but, on the whole, she was happy.

Once the main business was complete, Mac leaned back in her chair. I was used to her departing immediately. I tried not to show my surprise when she poured herself another coffee and indicated that I should do the same. To be honest I became suspicious that something was not right and she was going to lambaste me for an error I'd completely over-looked. No. She just wanted to talk. I learned a bit about her stint in the SBS and she asked me about mine in the RAF. Chalk and cheese. She knew what was in Reid's file about me so she also asked why I had taken the criminal path. I remember grinning and saying that it was a way of easing the boredom.

'I can see you would easily get bored with humdrum service life. Perhaps Mr Reid did you a favour by making you apply yourself to something else?'

I was emphatic. 'Not at all. I can't wait to be set free again.'

'Aren't you even a little fascinated by this work?'

'Uh, huh, but Reid is just using me while he can. When he's finished I'm not at all sure he'll really let me go.'

'You don't know that. His is a well-run outfit and the boss knows good people when he sees them.'

'And that's the strangest thing. How did Reid know that I was 'good people'? You know what happened. He went to extraordinary trouble to stage that fake arrest. He'd already done deep background checks. Why me?'

She leaned over the table and pushed her debrief notes to one side. 'I can only tell you what Mr Marshall told me. It seems the original government experiments on time travel did not go well. They found out that the technological bits worked haphazardly, even fatally. Gradually they became aware that certain teams could do it reasonably well and others failed hopelessly and sometimes terminally. They tested and tested all the teams, good and bad, but could find nothing that distinguished them. It wasn't about gender, age, race, intelli-gence, fitness, or any other scientific variable. Towards the end someone thought to test mental powers. They put everyone through a range of psychological and psychic tests including coin-guessing experiments.' She raised her eyebrows. 'Could you believe it?'

'They were testing for psychic skills?'

'Well, as far as I could see they just did the precognition tests on the ability of people to guess the fall of a coin above pure chance.'

'With what results?'

'Marshall said they were not good. Averaged about 53% if I remember right.'

'It's always baffled me that I get the controller with the out-and-return switch but you're the team leader.'

Mac got up and walked to the tray of snacks. She took one and offered me the tray. 'I realised from the start that you are the one with the mind skills. Every team has one member with something, who knows what, in the way of psychic skills.'

'That sounds like something out of a Harry Potter book. And anyway, it's crazy. How would Reid know that I'd got those abilities? I was not tested when he kidnapped me and never since. I don't even know if I have them myself.'

'Marshall told me that you have a 68% score so they must have got that from somewhere. All Reid's teams operate with one person with above average precognition. Our average seems to be around the 57% mark.'

'So, if precognition skills are essential to time travel and the government knew that fact, why did they end the experiments?'

'A few fatalities, one or two total losses for unknown reasons, and a lot of money down the drain. Mr Reid thought he could do better and obtained the rights to the tech.'

'Wow.'

'Yes, wow, but it doesn't explain how he found you.'

My suspicions suddenly coalesced. 'I think I know why. When I was at university, second year I think, the psychology department offered a few quid for volunteers for something which began with 'G', Grassfield … Ganderwell … Grandfell, something like that.'

'A Ganzfeld Experiment? I saw the title on Marshall's personnel lists.'

'That's it. It was a laugh. Me and a bloke named Tommy Arnott together with a few others were dumped in separate rooms. We had to guess whether a computer would give us a heads or tails emblem on the screen. The guesses had to be made before the screens showed what the computer had decided. We had a couple of hours' fun and then went to spend the fee in the university bar. I remember we got well pissed trying to debate why the rooms were lit by red light and why we had to wear earphones with the muzak playing through them.'

'If that had been government funded, the results would have found their way onto a government database and Reid would have had you on a list.'

'Crafty buggers. Tracked me down, probably used the time-travel teams to investigate me, and stumbled onto the little games I was playing.' It was annoying but too late to do anything. 'So, every team has to have someone like me?'

'Marshall says that they do but your score was the highest that he and Reid had seen.' She actually grinned. 'Told me never to decide anything with you on a coin toss.'

20

The Great Hack

The atmosphere during the ensuing rest week between missions was very different. Mac organised her debrief meetings for us in the café near the gates. She explained that it allowed her to be much closer to her normal place of work. I didn't argue. Having tea and pastries in the café at a secluded table was much nicer than being berated in one of the formal meeting rooms. Nevertheless, she went through everything, yet again. The many things that I'd done wrong, and a few she felt she had not done well, and the things that might possibly offer lessons for the future. All were thoroughly discussed and noted.

While being professional at all times I also watched her carefully during those little tea parties. I tried very hard but I could see no signs that she knew what Reid was up to. I even dropped a few hints that I thought there was more to this than just some well-paid academic research. But, for her, this was a tremendously exciting new venture, helping the world by delivering accurate details to high level historical research.

'I wonder what's next?' she'd said. 'Could we be offering school children the chance to see the Armada or attend

Martin Luther King's most famous speeches or watch the Blitz from a safe place?'

I shrugged. 'Above my paygrade I'm afraid.' She slapped my hand.

'Come on, Ward. Aren't you just a little bit enthused by what we're building here? It could even mean your freedom and a new life.' My comment about pigs flying stopped her in her tracks but she was still bouncing as she left the café.

During that time we saw Reid together for a catch-up and, I suspect, a 'get on with it' reminder. He was anxious to get the third, aborted mission completed. Waiting for the regulation week of rest to be over was a trial for him.

How the two cleaners got hold of a brand new, high spec laptop was a complete mystery, but they appeared one night at my door, handed it over and told me I had twenty-four hours. As usual they told me that they had disabled the security for a few minutes but that I should hurry. I covered it with a magazine and took it straight into the bathroom to avoid the cameras. There was no way I could plug it into a mains socket, they were all in camera view, so it had to be battery power only. When that ran out I was stymied. I had perhaps two or three hours.

I laid the machine reverently on the shelf and gazed at it for a few seconds. It was like being reunited with one's best friend after a long trip abroad. The smell and feel of the machine was intoxicating. The smooth, cool exterior was a sensual delight and the little thrill that came from firing it up was what I expect a junkie gets from seeing the next fix lying waiting for them. I sat on the little stool and rested the machine on the side of the sink. The software did not, as I had feared, try to connect automatically to one of the base networks. I won't lie to you, I was as nervous as a kitten as I tentatively explored the embedded software. I was searching for little trackers and bots that would alert a central IT department to the laptop's presence or to someone using specific routines and sub-routines, but there were none. It took me fifty minutes to be certain that the machine was clean and not yet visible on a network.

It was a bind, but I had to leave the bathroom and make a show of having a sore stomach. I sat down for a while and picked up a magazine, all the time rubbing my stomach and making small groaning noises. After about ten minutes I gave a louder groan and rushed back into the bathroom.

It was time to put my money where my mouth is. The wifi networks were listed for me. All were secured and internal to the base as far as I could tell. Most were lightweight, probably for staff use for internal emails and entertainment from the base servers. They were not going to have anything on them that I really needed but they did give me a way of getting onto the wider internal network without attracting attention. It was child's-play to get onto it. The laptop was now one of several from this building showing on the central monitors. I was banking on the fact that no-one would be paying any attention to this network because it was for local comms and entertain-ment. The external Internet was blocked. That block fell after ten minutes' work and I was then able to access the dark web and disguise this machine. I quickly gave it several layers of obscurity. It was not my usual meticulous job but I did not have much time. The new identity and an apparent location in Russia gave me a way of hacking into one of the internal networks named OSR1. The name had attracted my attention.

I took a deep breath and took the plunge. It was a hairy ride. Whoever had set the network up had top level skills. Some of the code and the structures reminded me of the work I'd seen around high-security government establish-ments. Reid had employed the very best by the look of it. There were passwords and biometrics and layers of comple-mentary handshakes. I reached a couple of pages headed 'Orwell' with innocuous instructions, I tried hard but could not break through. I thought afterwards that I must have been very close, but as my maths teacher used to say - close is not good enough. I had already used up over two hours and the battery was down to seventeen percent. I tried one more approach. This time through what I hoped would be Reid's personal access. I hoped he would have no patience with complex passwords and I was right. He'd changed a twenty-digit, mixed symbol password for the word Barrow-Briggs with two ampersands. My triumph was short-lived though. It led me to another security page requiring an iris scan and I had no doubt there'd be another couple after that.

Giving up was not easy but I could read the writing on the wall. I did as good a job as I could to cover my tracks and logged off. I scrubbed all activity, rebooted the laptop, and checked for tell-tale signs. There were none but I knew that, being hurried, I would have left multiple loose ends. No-one would be on the trail straight away, but in a month a routine check of activity on the staff network would reveal some small inconsistencies and then one of the top people would eventually track the whole thing down to my floor in the residential buildings. That job would take a long time because the dark web does not give up its secrets to just anyone who asks. My guess was that I had between six and ten weeks, no more. Then Reid would run out of whatever reserves of patience he had and he'd decide to cut his losses. Which meant curtains for little old me. I could see the triumph on Marshall's face as he pulled the trigger.

When I handed over the machine the next day I quickly told Mrs B of my fears. Henry said they'd destroy the laptop.

'Thanks for the offer but that won't do any good. There are no traces on the machine. It's the hacking attempts that will be spotted and they'll trace it to the wifi extender or router on this floor. Reid is no fool, he knows my background and will immediately tie any superbly covered up hacking attempt to the only person on the base who could have done it.' They were listening closely as usual and Henry spoke first.

'Time is now critical.' It was a rare occasion for Henry to make a statement without a negative opening. I grinned at him.

'You're not kidding but it won't be cleaners they'll be coming for. Look, from what I've seen recently you two are something special. Why can't you stop Reid yourselves?'

'Do you not think we'd have done it already if we could?' Henry's voice carried more than a hint of regret. 'We're not strong enough to succeed. Call it what you will, metaphysical or psychic, it is too hot for the two of us. We can do a lot of things but we need you. Your role is crucial. It is you who has to stop Reid.'

That sounded more than a little daunting. 'You'll help me, yes?' They both nodded vigorously. 'Good. Stopping Reid would also give me a route out of here and get me back to the life I'd planned.'

I became conscious of the two of them looking at me pityingly.

Mrs B placed her hand on my arm. 'Dr Ward, there can never be a return to your old self. You have changed even though you haven't yet realised how much. You can carry on planning an escape and a return to your original plans but I doubt that is what you really want.'

I said nothing but my first thoughts were … think what you like, my stash of cash has taken a long time to accumulate. My arrangements have been painstaking and detailed. There's no way I'd just dump them.

I just need to get away from all this nonsense. I'd help to bring an end to Reid's little plot if I could but, after that, I would be in First Class on the first widebody out of Heathrow bound for Brazil. Do you have any idea what a hundred million can do for your life? Sun, sea and women beckoned like a field of lavender to a bee.

21

Me, panic? Never

It was time to complete the third mission, the disaster that had been attempting to track the young Winston in South Africa. Reid had been nagging and fretting all week and he left us in no doubt how important it was.

'We have almost completed all missions. This one is among the very last on the planning board. It is also one of the most important.' I was feeling mischievous.

'Why it is so important? I thought all the missions were being paid for. So, if we're being paid the same amount for the data, why is this one so vital?' He was quick, I'll give the bastard that.

'It's important because this one is being priced at far more than other missions. I need it finished so that we get paid, but also so that we can wind up all the missions.'

Mac seemed a bit puzzled. 'I'm hoping there will be more to follow, sir?' He looked at her as if she'd spoken Swahili and then his brain gave him the answer.

'Of course, Major. There will be many more as we build the business. I just meant that this first contract is coming to an end.' She seemed satisfied and he continued. 'This particular mission is one of the key ones. We marked them with a gold star on the contract, the universities consider it a jewel in the crown.'

I laughed. The man could bullshit with the best. Luckily he assumed I'd laughed at the universities. He asked whether we could take it up from the point we left.

'I guess so,' I said. 'We'd have to time it to the second, or at least to within a few minutes of when we flipped back. Everyone was in their sleeping blankets so it is unlikely that anyone would have noticed our absence. And if they did they might think they were dreaming or that we were answering calls of nature. We've got a little short of thirty-six hours of the mission to complete. I suggest we finish the day here and leave just before our normal bedtimes - that way we'll be wanting to sleep when we get there.'

Mac agreed. 'We'll need a decent weapon each though.' Was I hearing right? 'The Boers are excellent fighters and great shots. Our automatics would be a bit of a balancer.'

Reid looked at me for a while and then nodded. 'Alright, it is your call, Major. But be aware Mr Ward that there will be armed guards pointing powerful weapons at you when you return. You will need to be ready to immediately hand over your weapon.'

'I wouldn't have it any other way,' I lied. 'I think we should also carry stuns guns for any occasions when we do not want to draw attention to ourselves.'

'Goes without saying,' Mac added.

That night we dressed in our bush clothes, checked our weapons and supplies, and had the coordinates triple checked. At about 10:30 pm we did the final checks of hats, bags, clothes etc. I exchanged a glance with Mac. She nodded and I pressed the red button. My last thought before I pressed the button was that this had to go well. With the impending threat of discovery of my hacking efforts I did not need any other problems.

Why anyone would want to do this voluntarily I could not

imagine. We materialised standing but quickly got down onto the blankets which still lay as we'd left them. I lay awake on the stony ground most of the rest of the night. I may have slept for a total of an hour or so. Infuriatingly, every time I looked across at Mac she was wheezing gently in a deep slumber. The soldiers had shown us how to surround ourselves with a hemp rope and make sure there were no gaps. The rationale was that snakes hated the roughness of the hemp and would not cross it. Sounded a bit thin to me but any protection was good protection and we were not disturbed and neither were any of the cavalrymen.

I was exhausted at dawn. I lay trying to keep my eyes open. Why is it that the body can stop you sleeping for hours and hours but, as soon as dawn arrives, it wants to sleep for England? I listened to the troops fixing their breakfasts and feeding the horses. Mac and I gratefully took a couple of small nose bags for our own mounts and then saddled them. Within an hour we were on our dusty way north towards the river. Churchill was having the time of his life and he'd taken a decided shine to Mac. His horse got to know hers very well during that morning. Churchill had taken the decision to split his force. A Sergeant Major led one half and Churchill, as a Lieutenant in the African Light Horse, led the other. That did not stop him chatting away merrily to Mac for almost the entire ride, though.

Churchill had scouts out ahead and suddenly one of them sped into view shouting. From where I was riding I could not make out what he was saying but the import was clear. He had not even reached us when his mount was shot from under him and we were under heavy rifle fire. A trooper got a round in the shoulder beside me and fell to the ground, Mac and I were right beside him within a split second and we dragged him to a shallow ditch. Mac grabbed his carbine and started firing at the muzzle smoke. The Boers were only seventy yards away. Meanwhile I got the trooper to press a pad of his shirt to the wound. It did not look too bad, the round had clipped him rather than penetrated. He'd be fine as long as he did not contract gangrene.

Horses were screaming all around us. I don't think the Boers were deliberately targeting them. Ricochets and stone splinter were doing the damage. People say that battles are confused and that you hardly know what is happening from minute to minute. They're spot on. Mac was firing steadily and she was clearly having some success because I heard a distant scream immediately after one of her efforts. I got the occasional view of the proceedings by quickly raising my head, but it was not terribly informative.

A horse had been killed near us. I crawled to it and retrieved a carbine and ammo pouch for myself. Using the horse for cover I tried to emulate Mac, watching for the smoke and then aiming as close as possible to the source. The range was so close that I did not have to allow for distance or wind. Suddenly Churchill crashed to the ground alongside me.

'Splendid,' he shouted. 'You two are worth three or my men.' He used his own carbine, his revolver out of its holster and on its lanyard beside him. 'We'll beat these bastards. We just need to outflank them.' No sooner were the words out of his mouth than he began to stuff his revolver into its holster. 'Come on.' He waved both of us to follow him and began to run in a crouch. It was the hairiest time of my life. I followed Winston's backside and I think Mac followed mine. Bullets were literally flying all around us making that nasty zipping sound as they flew by. I think the Boers thought we were trying to escape. After about a hundred yards Churchill threw himself behind a small knoll, more like a large bump in the ground than a hill. We followed him the few yards to the top and peaked over. We were no more than about fifteen or twenty feet above the surrounding terrain but it gave us a much better view of the Boer flank. I could instantly see three men firing efficiently at the cavalry squadron.

'Targets ahead. Rapid fire,' shouted Churchill, and without waiting for acknowledgements he took careful aim, his carbine resting on a small flat rock. His first shot killed one of the men and our combined fire wounded another and both he and his comrade scrambled awkwardly for their horses, shouting to the others. Churchill's men got two more on the Boers' retreat but I counted six who mounted their horses and hightailed it for the denser bush towards the river.

We had two British soldiers dead and two wounded. Five Boers did not make it. My experience of battle was limited to mock ones staged at Officer College. My involvement in real battles had started here. I was in shock, trying to stop trembling while I watched three troopers digging a grave for the Boers. We had enough horses, but our speed was now limited by the wounded and the need for two horses to carry a trooper as well as a body. I heard Mac talking to Churchill. She was advising that the squadron should camp and send a couple of riders for help. Getting field advice from a woman was clearly not what Churchill was used to but he saw the sense in it and accepted the advice. While the Lieutenant arranged his pickets and spoke words of encouragement to his men, Mac and I tried to make the wounded comfortable. One of them was in a very bad way. Mac whispered to me that he would not make it. I saw her slip him a dose of our own morphine. It would not be around for decades but it eased the passing of a brave soldier back in 1900.

What surprised me to hell was our subsequent whispered conversation. She as much as accused me of sabotaging the mission.

'Reid told me that you might try to sabotage this mission as well as the previous one. Did you deliberately advise the best route to the river knowing that it was very likely the Boers would have crossed and be waiting for us?'

I'd had enough of this. 'If I did I'd be doing Reid a favour. He clearly wants Churchill dead.' I thought some more. 'And why would I do that? I was in as much danger as Churchill and you.'

The silence was lengthy. 'Why do you say you'd have been doing Reid a favour?'

'Look, Mac, I'm not a complete idiot. His intentions are clear from the sort of targets we're gathering data on. Think about it. Every one of them is a pivotal figure in history and for every one of them we are researching the most important turning points in their lives.' She remained quiet. 'I've picked up, just from loose café gossip, that the London teams have had targets in China, India, Russia, Germany, and the USA. Reid's list is weird. Not the stages of people's lives in which they were famous and powerful, but the vital early stages, those just before they became famous.'

'You're making a lot out of a little,' was her quiet response.

'Isn't that the way good detectives work? Even our own little set of missions is convincing, don't you think? Lloyd George was not far from leading Britain through the terrible last years of World War One and setting up the society that followed. Almost immediately after we saw Pitt the Elder he became Prime Minister and started on his drive to establish the British Empire. Not long after this episode in Churchill's life he wins his first by-election to become a Member of Parliament. And we all know where that led. JFK was a couple of years from becoming America's youngest-ever President. A brief but pivotal Presidency.'

'Yes. But those things could also just as easily explain why the universities want the detail.'

I sighed. 'But which explanation is more plausible in the circumstances? Reid's only plausible goal is to change history, presumably to his own benefit.'

She was very still. 'I still can't see yours as being the most plausible outcome.'

'Oh, come on Mac, get your head in the game. You seem

to be so focused on hating me that you can't see the brick wall facing you.'

'Don't be stupid, Ward. Your dislike of Reid and your past history with him are driving you into wild conspiracy theories. Why wouldn't universities want all this wonderful detail?'

'They would … but could they really afford it? And why don't they want social information?' That must be the clincher I thought.

She gazed around for a moment. 'No. Reid is a business-man. His only goal is money.'

I was so infuriated I could hardly speak. My anger almost boiled over but, all at once, we were back in the Black building at the base. The whip-back felt like every bone in my body had been broken before my pain-riddled body had been dragged through a gravel quarry and dumped on shards of glass. It was a bad one. We'd had another involuntary return with the mission still incomplete. Goodness knows what Mac must have felt like. I sensed her lying beside me and heard her moaning pitifully to herself. Or was that me?

Reid was not going to believe this was a system fault again. We slowly came to our senses and, before Mac could kill me, I guess I panicked. Under the pretence of having to use the bathroom, I spent ten minutes pulling myself together and checking that all my appendages were still properly connected. Then I slinked out of the building and ran for the west fence. The whip-back must have addled my brains because I was not thinking at all. I could only remember that Mrs B and Henry had mentioned a lodge in the woods somewhere. Perhaps Reid did not know of it. He'd certainly not mentioned it.

22

Running to nowhere

If you think what I'd done hitherto was weird, it now got much, much worse. Ward excelled himself on the scale of idiocy. I recognised the stupidity of what I was doing almost before I got to the end of the built-up section of the base. But I'd run and that was as good as a confession of guilt. I was still in my 1900 bush clothes, and the heavy things bashing against my thighs and body reminded me that I had not handed in my automatic or the stun gun. Things just kept getting better. Reid would be sure I was trying to get away again and that, this time, I would use deadly force to do so. His men would be told to shoot on sight.

And with that thought, a siren started up down near the gates. They were already on their way and were using the siren to alert any other guards who were not on their radios. I immediately ran off the pathway and into the woods. The wooded area of the base was not that extensive but at least the trees would preclude vehicle access. Soon I was deep into the small forest that bordered the fence to the west and north and extended to the other side of the fence. Probably about a hundred acres of forested land but most of it was on the other side of the broad, cleared strip on which the fences sat.

I tried to head north. The sound of SUVs skidding to a halt on the rough trackway echoed through the gathering darkness. They'd have watched my escape on the cameras and probably wondered what I'd done with my brains. Shouts followed me as I stumbled through the brush. For once I was grateful for the mission clothing. It had been made for just these conditions. When I turned my head I could see the flashes from heavy duty lanterns not too far away. They'd have infra-red night vision goggles as well. Oh, happy days.

The problem was that I'd run in a loop and reached the clearing in front of the west fence. There'd been no sign of the lodge. I turned and ran in a different direction into the trees knowing that the cameras would have picked me up as I broke cover below the west fence. Where was the lodge? Did Mrs B and Henry lie to me? My breath was coming in ragged gasps and not all of it was about exhaustion. I could hear the chasing group getting closer and could feel the fear and panic of a hunted animal surging in my gut. I had perhaps a couple of minutes after which I'd be dead. I stopped by a tree and looked frantically around. Nothing. Not a damned thing. I almost yelled out loud when I felt a hand on my shoulder. Henry was dragging me towards the steps of a neat little one and a half storey lodge. Why hadn't I noticed it? The wooden walls were neatly stained, it had three or four windows across the front and a couple of small gabled windows in the roof. He almost lifted me up the steps, pushed the door open, and shoved me inside so forcibly that I fell over.

I lay there panting and almost crying with frustration. 'Thanks Henry but they'll be here in a few moments and I don't want you and Mrs B to get into trouble.'

He sat down on a wooden chair at a small dining table. 'They will not find us here.'

Mrs Biddle was coming down the stairs wearing her usual benign smile. 'This lodge is not really here, Dr Ward.' It is located about fifteen miles away in quite another wood. We set up a link between this wood on the base and our real one. As far as Reid's men are concerned the wood is empty of you and the lodge. We are actually fifteen miles away and well outside the base.'

I did a double-take and didn't know whether to be relieved or livid with rage.

'You're telling me that you have had a way of getting out of the base all this time and have not told me?'

'Afraid so,' said Henry smugly. 'We could not allow you to escape Dr Ward. We need you too much. The world needs you too much.'

'The world? Isn't that a bit of an exaggeration?'

'No. There are doubtless many others with your level of power but they are not here. You are our only hope.'

My relief at getting away didn't last long. 'So, you aren't going to let me go from here to resume my life.' He just continued to glare at me. 'You're telling me that I'm still a prisoner. I either stay in this lodge for the rest of my life or I have to go back to Reid who will end it pretty damned soon.' I thought about that. 'As long as it is not Marshall. He'll be only too pleased to make my death a long drawn-out affair.'

Mrs B gave a small cough to remind us she was still there. 'You'll be in trouble, yes, but I think you'll be able to get out of it with that smooth tongue of yours, Dr Ward. Mr Reid needs you more than you think.'

Henry snorted. 'That won't last long of course but, yes, he needs you at present.'

'Aren't you two just a huge bundle of fun. Your optimism gives me tremendous confidence.'

'I am very pleased to hear you say that,' said Henry.

'I think he was being sarcastic,' murmured Mrs B. 'Dr Ward, you can have a brief rest here. A meal and a nice comfortable bed for the night, but tomorrow you must give yourself up.'

'If it's not too much trouble, what's the rush? Could I not have a couple of weeks' rest here? I've certainly earned them.'

'No,' said Henry in boringly familiar style. 'You haven't earned anything yet. The missions are almost at an end. Reid will be moving to the critical stage next and you must be there to stop him.'

I got up and drifted to the kitchen area. 'You're hard task-masters. I've been almost killed fighting in Natal today and I need a good solid meal.'

Suddenly Henry was in my face. 'Fighting who?' I was surprised at his vehemence.

'The Boers of course, and great fighters they are … were.'

Henry visibly relaxed and I frowned at Mrs B.

'Henry is of Zulu extraction,' she explained. 'He would have been … somewhat miffed … if you had been fighting his ancestors.'

The next morning I was virtually force-fed with an early fried breakfast and then tossed out of whatever magical bit of the lodge could manifest itself in the forest on the base. I felt like a child that had been given an errand and forced to fulfil it come what may. It had been raining overnight so I rolled in some very wet bracken, smeared my face and hands with mud, and soaked my trousers in a small brook. Then I took a roundabout way out of the area and walked wearily down the hill. I'd been in a beautifully cosy bed just an hour or so ago. This was utter madness. Everyone I passed gave me puzzled looks. What was Ward up to now? A few even turned around and followed me to the Black Building where I formally handed myself in. In true security style I was forced to the ground, spreadeagled, and my weapons confiscated. Two of that honourable profession managed to accidentally stand on my hands. Par for the course but bloody painful all the same.

I was handcuffed and marched to Reid's office where they took great pleasure in making me lie face down on the floor while we awaited the boss's pleasure. Lying there on the plush carpet, my hands throbbing with pain, gave me time to appreciate the fried breakfast that Henry had made for me. The two cleaners might be careless of my safety but they ran a good boarding house.

I must have lain on Reid's soft carpet for a good forty minutes with people coming and going. I could not see their faces but I was sure I recognised Mac's well-cleaned military boots.

Reid's orders were filtering through even though he was not present in person. The guards took me into one of the bathrooms and stripped me of the South African clothing and allowed me to avail myself of the chance to take a pee. I was back looking like a very large canary again. The man himself returned while I was being changed. The handcuffs were replaced before I was led into the presence. Mac and Marshall were standing to one side. Mac looked quietly pleased. Marshall looked like he'd tear me limb from limb if I so much as breathed wrong. Reid sighed, long and loud.

'Tell us about it, Ward and make it good.'

I glanced at Mac but there was no help there. I had decided to stick as close to the truth as possible. 'I was sure you'd accuse me of sabotaging the mission again, so I panicked and ran.'

'You went to the woods where, somehow, Mr Marshall's men, with the latest technology, could not locate you. Their search with night vision and torches was very thorough but they could not find you. Why was that Mr Ward?'

I'd thought of that one. 'You would be surprised how little heat escapes from three feet of brush and bracken. I burrowed into a tributary of the brook - something I would not recommend. When I heard Marshall's men coming I tried to hide most of my head and body under the water. It was only about a foot deep so that was a major achievement I think.'

Reid glanced at his two security chiefs and received shrugs in reply. 'Mr Marshall, what do you say to that explanation? Is it possible that Ward could have evaded your men using that ploy?'

'No,' stuttered Marshall, 'there's no way they'd have missed him. My guess is that someone helped him and he's been somewhere else on the base.'

Reid was being very reasonable. 'None of our security sensors or cameras spotted him until he exited the woods two hours ago. Where could he have been? If someone had helped him to leave the woods and sheltered him in the main part of the base we would have seen them last night. If, by some miracle, they managed to evade us last night, he would have had to return to the woods this morning and we'd have spotted him. We have him on camera a couple of hours ago emerging from the woods and walking down here. Not a single sign of him or an accomplice prior to that.'

The Security Chief had no answer to that. He was saved from further embarrassment by Mac.

'Sir, if I may, I think Mr Marshall is absolutely correct. There is no reasonable explanation for the men missing Ward in the woods.' Marshall began to smirk a little. 'My feeling is that Ward was extremely lucky. That the combination of cold, wet bracken and partial immersion was just about sufficient to conceal him. The woods are quite an area to search in the dark and, even with ten men, it would have been all too easy to miss a very, very small heat signature.'

'Thank you Major. So, to the most important part. Why did this fated mission once again get terminated early?'

Again, I relied on something close to the truth. 'I genuinely have no idea, but I was sure you'd blame me anyway. As Mac, the Major, will explain, we were talking about things and suddenly we were back here. I knew at once that I'd be the prime suspect.'

He inclined his head and I noticed him press the desk button. 'Two premature returns from the same mission is very unusual. In fact unique. Ah, Dr Tran,' he addressed a black clad, Asian individual who had just entered. 'We spoke about the subject of a second unrequested return earlier and you said that you would look into it. What have you found?'

The man was short and wiry. His intelligent eyes were almost hidden behind tinted, rimless spectacles. He sported a tiny moustache. Clearly nervous at having his presence demanded by His Eminence, his eyes were all over the place, his hands rapidly clasping and unclasping each other against his stomach. He licked thin lips.

'Er, yes, sir. I have not had long, but I have consulted with my colleagues and with London. It seems that this is not, in fact, a unique episode. One of the missions from London to …'

'Those details are not necessary Doctor please just give us the conclusions.'

'Ah, yes, sir. Er … one of the London missions experienced two such returns very close together on days one and two of the mission. In one case there was an unfortunate casualty …'

'That will be sufficient Doctor. Is there any indication of why such things occur?'

Tran was glancing about anxiously. I got the impression that the two Security chiefs were making him very nervous indeed. 'Not really, sir. There are a couple of theories but only one seems to hold any scientific weight.' He stopped until Reid motioned him to continue. 'There is a theory, although no more than that, that certain locations on the planet focus electromagnetic energy and that it is the fluctuations in that energy in that specific location that override the time travel controllers and prompt the unexpected returns.'

'And why would there be such locations?'

'We have no definitive evidence that they exist but we do know that substantial masses of iron in the Earth's crust can cause magnetic anomalies and perhaps bend wireless signals.'

Reid gazed at him for a few seconds. I think he enjoyed

prolonging the man's terror. 'Thank you Doctor Tran. That will be all.' The man flung himself at the door and staggered out into the anteroom followed all the way by Reid's penetrating gaze, which quickly resumed normal service by fixing on me.

'Once more Ward it appears as though you are exonerated.' I sucked in a long delayed breath. 'But do not get comfortable. I have lost patience with this mission and am, therefore, abandoning the regulation week of rest between missions. Tomorrow morning you and the Major will set off to complete that Churchill job if it is the very last thing you do. You may go.' I gave him a quick nod and turned for the door. I'd reached it when he called to me.

'Mr Ward.' I turned and felt a pang of dread for whatever was coming next. 'If it is any motivation, you are in line, in spite of your stupid antics, for a permanent role with Reid Research. We may or may not speak of this again but I need, first, to see that you can be serious and work with the system.'

I pinched myself as I walked down the plush executive corridor.

23

Enter Nurse Ward

I was not surprised the next morning when I reported to the Black Building to find that Reid had extended the mission. He now wanted two extra days, to cover the British advance towards Ladysmith. I was not allowed to carry an automatic this time.

The British Army eventually relieved the besieged garrison but, for these two days, Churchill was still closely involved in the fighting as the British took well-defended hills and punched through the Boer lines. On our third jump, we found Churchill in a small town just north of the river. The town lodging house was also its bar. To my eyes it looked like those shanty towns that grew up rapidly during the 1849 California Gold Rush. There were a few crude homes with corrugated iron roofs, quite a few without the luxury of corrugated iron, and only two, two-storey buildings, both only half-brick. One seemed to be a bank, post office, and general store. The other was the bar and lodging house. We trudged up to the latter building having thrown many handfuls of dirt at each other to simulate a long walk. We stepped wearily up onto the wooden porch. The interior of the bar was dim but there he was, sitting with a Scotch, or whatever passed for it in these parts, writing a dispatch presumably for his newspaper.

'Ah,' he exclaimed with a chuckle. 'There you are. Very pleased to see you. You seemed to disappear on the way here.'

'We were helping with the wounded,' Mac said, and it seemed credible. He was far too engrossed in the dispatch to think about two locals who were trying to get back to their family in Ladysmith.

'Have you and your sister ever been to England?' he asked. Subtlety was not one of Churchill's strengths where women were concerned. I told him no, never, and the obvious invite followed close behind. We agreed that we would certainly think about his kind offer and, to make it more interesting for him, added that we would dearly love to see the old country, especially with such a distinguished soldier. We gave him a few seconds to preen himself and then asked him what was going on.

'I've been interviewing some senior chaps for my dispatches. This one will go back to Durban tomorrow with the dispatch rider and then we'll be off again. My orders are to scout the next few miles towards Ladysmith and get intelligence on Boer positions. My objective will be to find some local farmers and see what they know.'

'Will you take the squadron?'

'Good heavens, no. Tomorrow will be a very small party. We will only be talking to locals and you might actually know them. Why don't you tag along.'

Our agreement was not in question. With the prospect of Mac riding alongside him he'd not have taken no for an answer anyway. We spent the rest of a very interesting day watching him interview more officers and non-commissioned officers. He was a real worker. Never stopped for more than a few minutes all day and then carried on questioning all of us, but especially Mac, over a simple dinner. As the rooms were all occupied by officers, we newcomers slept on the floor of the bar. Mac found herself able to whisper her thanks for my help during the day in recording different aspects of the camp outside the town while she was buttering up Winston.

I was, however, growing to hate South Africa. The heat and the dust even at this time of the year were not to my liking and I was still saddle-sore and tired from previous days. Another night of sleeplessness did not help. I needed to send my mental thanks to Mrs B and Henry for the night in that lovely bed at the lodge. If psychic powers were real, as they insisted, they should receive them telepathically.

Churchill was overflowing with energy the next morning. At his age he should have been, but I could have done with less hurry on horseback and more sitting and talking.

We rode gently northwest into the country for about fifteen or twenty miles. It was just Churchill, a couple of his men, and a servant, plus us two. After a long time seeing nothing, our outrider spotted a homestead. Churchill spurred towards it and began closely questioning two men who looked like farmers. They were probably Boers or Boer sympathisers and I hoped Winston knew what he was doing.

We watched and recorded as the afternoon wore on. Eventually Winston had learned enough and we set off back towards the river.

'We'll double back in a moment,' he announced. 'If those were sympathisers, the Boers will be looking for us near the river tonight. They won't expect us up here in the bush.'

I had to admit that it sounded sensible and I saw Mac nodding.

'No fire tonight I'm afraid. Bread, cold meat and water is all. Tomorrow in the daylight we'll head back. But carefully.'

After about half an hour he turned around and headed west into the bush. After another half hour he turned back north. Eventually we reached a place where he calculated we'd be about two miles from the homestead and that's where we camped. A guard schedule was agreed with each of the four men, excluding the servant who looked as if a stiff breeze would finish him off, taking a two-hour slot. Typically, mine was in the middle of the night, 1 am to 3 am. I never seemed to catch a break. Churchill was my relief. We ate as a group and, as it got dark, laid out our blankets. Somehow Winston managed to be on one side of Mac. I was on the other. I was so tired that I actually slept until I was woken by Mac at just before one. It was good of her to do that and I thanked her.

'Don't forget the password is Harriet.' I grinned at her and whispered 'Trust Winston'.

The place chosen for the watch was on a small hill nearby. From its top the watchkeeper had a full circle of visibility for at least a couple of miles. As long as the guard stayed awake the small group could sleep in peace. My own spell on watch was totally uneventful. There was no chance of me falling asleep. I was constantly circling to ensure that no-one could creep up on us. I also jumped at every noise, of which there were thousands. All the animals were unfamiliar to me so every shuffle, bark, whistle, scream, or groan was a shock to the system. Churchill tapped me on the shoulder at dead on three. I was proud of myself. I'd heard him coming so it did not make me jump out of my skin. I think he meant to shock me though, naughty character. I can call the great Churchill a naughty character because I was there, I saw the way he looked at Mac, I saw his cheeky grin when he was planning an unexpected raid, I saw his incredible bravery when faced by the enemy. He was naughty at times but he was also a real character, a man you'd be honoured to call a friend. Someone you would want on your side.

After I'd told Churchill about the uneventful watch, I walked back to the camp, stepped carefully over Mac, and laid back on my blanket. I was nowhere near being able to sleep. I was still alert and the constant racket from insects and animals was not easy to ignore. But Mac and the other men seemed to be fast asleep. The night was drawing to a close. It would not be too long before everyone would be awake. So I closed my eyes and let my mind take me wherever it chose. It dithered a bit but eventually selected the two mysterious cleaners. So, I thought about the cleaners, just a little incongruous when camping in the Natal bush in the year 1900. I recalled what they had said about me being able to stop Reid and me not needing computers or whatever. I chuckled to myself. Yet I was somehow convinced that Mrs B and Henry were right. The dreams and especially the vision of FDR being assassinated were weirdly persuasive. Something was very wrong with this whole thing but I had no doubt that only guns would stop Reid. I'd had too many dreams for me to dismiss what they'd showed me. Was I what Mrs B said I was, some sort of special person who could bring Reid's plans to an end?

A distant bark brought my mind back to the here and now. Too many animals out here. I could hear an owl, somewhere, a wild dog barking, and a slithering sound. I sat bolt upright. A slither?

Suddenly, I heard Mac yelp. I turned to look at her and was in time to see something light coloured slithering into a nearby bush. It seemed shiny in the moonlight. Mac sat up, holding her left thigh.

'I've been bitten by something.' I looked around uselessly. Luckily one of the troopers had been awake and had seen what happened.

'Cape Cobra.' He said and began to move himself and the horses away from the bushes. There were a few minutes of frantic re-arrangement but then the two of them lay down on their blankets again.

Mac had gone white and I pushed her gently back onto her blanket.

'I thought it was a stick. I was half asleep and pushed it away from me. Then something bit my leg.'

I watched her face. She was worried. What the hell, I was worried too. 'What should I do?' I asked quietly.

'Some water, please.'

The two troopers had given up trying to sleep. They were having a cold breakfast. One of them, a Sergeant, turned his head and spoke quietly as I picked up a water bottle. He pitched his voice so that it would not carry to Mac where she lay. 'I'm really sorry mate. Your sister's a nice lady.' I frowned at him. 'Well, you know,' he grimaced, 'bite from one of them yellow bastards. You've got an hour or so to live. Nothing to be done 'cept get lots of whisky down 'em.' I nodded vacantly and took the water back to Mac.

'They say this is serious.'

She was looking paler by the minute but gave me a little smile. 'Yes. Even with the antivenom in my MedKit it will be touch and go. You must listen carefully before I lose focus. We've got modern antivenom but it can often cause severe allergic reactions. We have some adrenaline pens somewhere. We need to balance the chances that the snake was not too serious and only gave me a little venom, against the dangers from the anti-venom itself.'

'I'll pull us out.'

'No,' she said hastily. 'The soldiers will see and I don't want yet another incomplete on my record.' She coughed. 'I'm ordering you not to pull us out until either I say so, or I'm dead. I'll finish this mission even if it's my last.'

I crossed to the soldiers to collect another couple of water bottles.

'Keep her warm and make her comfortable, mate. She'll go unconscious and then slowly lose touch.' I asked him about the snake. 'Deadly as sin,' he replied. 'That one looked to be about four feet so probably young.'

'Could it have been any other type of snake?'

'Nah, mate. Mustardy with brown patches. Cape Cobra, sure as eggs is eggs. Saw one once in a garden. Cape Town just after disembarking from Blighty. Ugly bastards.' He shivered and returned to eating his rations.

When I got back, the symptoms had begun. Her pupils were dilated, sweat was clear on her forehead, her hands were shaking a little.

'Tim,' she whispered, 'the neurotoxins and cardiotoxins kill an adult in around an … hour. My vision is blurring. Get my MedPack quickly. Antivenom. Look for … ones marked 'deadly venom'. Give me now.' Mac's Medpac was secreted around her waist. I found several vials marked 'Deadly'. They were ready to use as soon as opened so I quickly unwrapped one and quickly checked the soldiers and Churchill's servant. They were tending to the horses. I gave her the jab in her bare arm then wrapped the empty hypo in some old newspaper and put it my saddle bag. She was shivering violently now, wheezing, and sweating at the same time. Her lips were swollen. Truth be known I think I was far more terrified that she was. I didn't have a clue what to do. I put a water-soaked rag on her forehead.

'Rest and keep warm,' was my learned advice.

Churchill had come back and had obviously been told the news by the men. He crept up and offered his whispered condolences as well as a hunk of bread for me.

'Bad do, old boy.' He patted me on the shoulder. 'I am very sorry but we'll need to be off soon. Do you want to move her?' I shook my head. 'Can't say I blame you.' He marched off to get the little party ready to return to the town. I considered the options. I could do what Churchill was suggesting, put her on a horse and try to get her back to that little town and its lodging. It wasn't that far but something told me a fifteen-plus mile ride would kill Mac. The exertion would speed up the transfer of venom in her bloodstream and she'd die long before we reached safety. I could pull us out, but she was adamant on that. The only other option was to stay here and that filled me with dread. I was not a doctor … or a nurse … I had no training except basic first aid.

Mac went into and out of relatively lucid moments for a

while as I watched anxiously to see whether the serum was working. After forty minutes she was still shivering and wheezing like an old steam engine so I gave her another shot. Churchill had already made his farewells, promising he'd send another party out to help me if he could. He did warn me however that orders might be waiting for his return. I almost panicked completely as I watched the group ride off.

'Need more antivenom.' Mac slurred. 'Might need several jabs.' I was surprised but gave her another. 'Watch for allergic reaction. If … happens … could be end.' I was mildly pleased by the fact that she'd lasted more than an hour but the first injection had been a bit delayed so I was not getting my hopes up. She was unconscious for pretty much the rest of the day. I wet her lips regularly and replaced the water-soaked rag on her forehead as often as I could. Churchill had left me all their remaining water canteens except two and all their rations. He'd had his men fill all the canteens up from the brook which trickled in a gully about a hundred yards off. It was good of him given that he thought I'd be alone by lunchtime. He was trying to make me feel better but was certain inside that I'd be back in the town by nightfall – alone.

I was totally unsure about the antivenom but I settled on a routine. Between the two MedPacs I had enough, I hoped. I decided that if she was still sweating and wheezing an hour after the last dose I would give her another. I gathered armfuls of twigs and bits of dead branches and built a fire as close to Mac as I could. I was very wary of the bushes the snake disappeared into but I could see no sign of it. Nevertheless, to make me feel better, I turned my stun gun to its highest setting on wide angle and gave the bush a zap. At that range the setting would kill a man so I was hopeful the snake, if it was still there, was now an ex-snake. But there could be others so I laid a length of rope around our sleeping area which included the fire. I'd cadged the rope from Churchill as a spare corral rope for the horses - but he knew why I wanted it and handed it over straight faced. Our Med packs contained plenty of water purification tablets and I used them to purify the water bottles we'd been left. It struck me that, in Mac's condition, she did not need a bacterial or worm infection.

I'd had some long nights recently but the following night was the longest. Technically it was after the original end of our mission but I didn't even think about trying to put Mac through a time jump. I kept the fire burning, dozed a little, gave Mac her antivenom jabs, zapped a few bushes every now and again, and dozed some more.

It was during one of the dozes that I was woken with a start to find that she had vomited with some force. I'd been woken up by bits and pieces that had reached me. There was nothing I could do about it. I made sure her mouth was clear, nasty task, wiped her face as clean as possible, scattered dust over as much of the mess as I could and sat there on my haunches trying to make sense of what she was trying to say. She was barely conscious. Does she want more anti-venom? The last jab had been only half an hour ago and there were only five left. Or is this an allergic reaction setting in? Was she going into shock? For a while I was confused and uncertain but then I thought it through. It had been many hours since the bite and she'd had at least five vials of antiserum. That might indicate that she was perhaps through the worst of the reaction to the bite. But she'd now begun to shake violently and I noticed that blisters were appearing on her bare arms. I lifted the waist of her shirt a little and could see a red rash and similar blisters on her stomach near where her MedPac had been. She was developing an allergic reaction. Dr Ward, in his new identity as super-medic, sucked in a deep breath. I located the allergen pens, we had eight of them between us, and suddenly wondered where I should administer it. In the arm? Possibly but she'd recently had antiserum in there. Would they clash? I hadn't a clue but I thought the safest and perhaps the most appropriate place would be her thigh near the bite. I undid her belt and pulled her heavy skirt down. Only then did I become aware of the smell of urine. It was rank and how I'd missed it before now could only be put down to the fact that there were just so many bad smells around. She'd wet herself during the shock, I suppose. In spite of my wimpy side telling me to leave it to dry by itself I knew I could not. Her skirt was sodden and so was the blanket underneath. If I left her she might catch a chill and, at the very least, her backside and thighs would become chafed. But first things first. I lifted a leg of the long linen drawers she was wearing and almost fainted at the sight of the red swollen bite. I chose a spot higher up, wiped it with an antiseptic pad, and punched her there with the pen. I just hoped the adrenaline would work quickly.

But now I had a real engineering problem. How to get a fever-wracked, marginally-conscious woman out of her skirt and drawers and, more importantly, off that soaked blanket and onto a new dry and comfortable one. It was my sort of problem. Forget all the gooey medical stuff – this was a prac-tical job. I cleared a space closer to my own sleeping place and laid out my own top blanket beside Mac. I then managed the delicate task of getting her skirt and drawers off without damaging the horrible swelling, dried her body off with a piece of blanket that I'd cut off using her knife, wiped her down as best I could with another antiseptic pad and dragged her onto the fresh blanket. At which point I realised she was still a bit wet because I'd stupidly put her back down on her pee-soaked bed! A bit more drying and I was able to cover her properly and leave her be.

I sat back against a rock and exhaled. Job done. It was only then that I thought properly about what I'd done. Believe me there is nothing in the least sexy about a woman lying half naked with her desert boots and knee-length socks on and a red swollen thigh looking like something out a horror film. But, I pondered, is that the way Mac would see it when she came to and realised what had been done to her … by me of all people?

To distract myself from visions of being gutted with a blunt knife by a furious ex-SBS Major I began to read the pen instructions below the emergency bit. Oh dear! The pen can be administered through clothing. Talk about a French farce! Sleepless hours followed. One minute I was worrying that Mac would die, then I worried that she'd wake up in a relatively lucid state and discover herself half naked with her skirt, drawers and original sleeping blanket hanging over a bush. Come what may, I'd done what I thought best at the time and - let's face it - the whole undressing business had meant about as much to me as saddling my horse. But is that the way Mac would see things?

Near dawn I decided to give her another allergy pen. The shaking had subsided but she'd vomited again and the blisters and rash had only partially reduced. After that I managed to get a couple of hours sleep. When I woke, Mac was looking at me with swollen and bloodshot eyes. I gave her small sips of water, mopped her brow, and felt her pulse. I counted as well as I could, watching the controller to measurer fifteen seconds, and estimated the count at 110. Not good but not as bad as it could be. The water sips were gratefully received though and slowly she seemed to become more alert although still very weak.

I busied myself with the fire and purifying more water bottles. I'd refilled all of them the previous afternoon and used unpurified water for cooling her forehead. The purified ones I shared with Mac. Now that she seemed to have finished vomiting I added her own dust-coat to her top blanket. I'd already taken her automatic, stun-gun, and two very nasty-looking knives out of the inside pockets. For good measure I added another horse blanket. With one of the saddle pouches acting as a pillow she was as comfortable as I could make her.

Gradually, over that and the next day her colour began to

return. We were significantly overdue for returning but Mac was still adamant that we should stay and see Churchill again if possible. It was pretty exhausting taking care of a recovering snake-bite victim but, now that she appeared to be on the mend, I slept like a baby. I'd managed to move all the sharp rocks from underneath me and my little pit was now halfway decent. Next morning - I had genuinely lost count of how long this mission had lasted - the rations were running low and I had another go at her to permit me to pull us both out.

'I've stopped shaking, I can see clearly now, my pulse is almost back to normal, and I've managed to keep down three small snacks. I'm still a bit weak but I managed to get to the bush bathroom and not faint. I'll be able to ride the short distance to the town tomorrow I think.'

Her comment about the bush bathroom made me guffaw inside. She had staggered about twenty feet until she was behind the main bush, then made me turn my back. She did the business and managed to scrape dirt over it, and then called me for help to get back up again. I had to support her on the way back. But, no, she did not faint.

I could not fault her grit. Most people, male or female, would have wanted to be stretchered back. Most from our time would have pulled out after that first bite, to receive the best modern medical care. Not Mac, she didn't know the meaning of giving up.

'If you think you are up to it. Yes, we can ride there in a few hours tomorrow. But are you sure? I could go and get a wagon and be back here in less than a day.'

She shook her head. 'Tim, thank you for saving my life. From what you've said I could have died at least twice.'

'Equally I could have killed you with a misdiagnosis or too many jabs. No-one in their right mind puts their health in the care of an IT geek.' I carried on getting the fire together again and when I turned around it was to find that she was crying. If normal crying is a rain shower this was a thunderstorm. She didn't want me to see but it was unstoppable, a total release of feeling in the form of deep, constant sobbing. In typical male fashion I was useless. I went across and held one of her hands. 'It's just the relief, Mac. Understandable.' I fell back on my traditional facetiousness. 'I'm not at all surprised that you're relieved to be alive but it's possibly also shock. How would anyone with any sense expect to be alive after a few days of my care?' She sucked in some air and grinned at me. I went to do something unnecessary with the horses while she calmed down and wiped her face.

Next morning after I'd saddled the horses and packed up our few bits and pieces she let me help her onto her horse. We rode slowly back to the town with me riding close beside her just in case. This was why she'd been in the Special Boat Service – brave as a lion and stubborn as a mule.

As we rode gently to the lodging-house I had to stop myself grinning too much. Everyone was astounded to see us. Eyes were popping out of heads. And you should have seen the dismounting from our horses. I went manfully around to help Mac, she leaned down and began to topple, I grabbed whatever bits of her and her jacket I could grasp, and we both fell with a crash. She, of course, landed on top of me. When I'd managed to gasp down a couple of lungfuls of air she'd been picked up and carried into the lodging. I was abandoned, wheezing in the dust clutching my winded midriff. Someone gave me a hand up. The ostlers were already tending to the horses.

I limped tiredly onto the porch and into the gloom of the bar to find that the lady of the house had taken charge of Mac and was already getting her into bed. I nodded to her as a I passed Mac's bedroom and then threw myself onto my own bed, fully clothed. In the indescribable relief at having got back there, I then slept for twelve hours straight, and then dozed for the rest of the night until the sun had logged into work. I'd slept soundly in spite of the guns and knives in my pockets.

I took my time. Stripped off my clothes, washed myself thoroughly from the basin on the dresser, put most of the same clothes back on, combed my hair as best I could, and went downstairs. I was told breakfast was ready and was waved through to the back porch. I found Mac sitting with an empty breakfast plate beside her. She was staring out over the countryside with a very serious look on her face. I wondered whether she was considering how many Cape Cobras were out there. She was obviously not in a talking mood so I polished off a plate of cold meat and boiled eggs and dutifully drained a cup of mud-like coffee in total silence. Then Winston Churchill erupted onto the porch like a tornado. He made a bee-line for Mac.

'I was delighted to hear the news, Miss McKenzie. You have had a miraculous recovery. Never heard of anything like it. It's the subject of wonder and amazement among my men.'

Mac gave him the sort of smile I'd always wanted for myself. It rivalled the sun and clearly affected Churchill in the same way it did me. 'I am deeply beholden to my brother for his care and am infinitely grateful for everyone's help. We think the snake must have been a young one and that it did not give me a full dose of venom.' I snorted inside. On the ride yesterday we'd agreed that she must have been given a hefty serving of the venom and only modern antiserum in large quantities plus the two allergen pens had saved her life.

Churchill was bold enough to take her hand. 'It gives me immense pleasure to see you but even more when I can hope that you will someday soon visit me in England. Promise me you will do that.'

Mac was a superb actress. She looked him straight in the eyes and said, 'I cannot promise what might not prove to be possible but my brother and I will try our very best Lieutenant Churchill.'

He was to leave again the next morning and, over meals that day, we spoke at length about his recent expeditions and the final push towards Ladysmith. He seemed certain that, this time, the British would break the siege and, of course, we knew that they did. The following morning we accompanied him and several squadrons of cavalry on the first stage of the advance. Infantry were following but I have to say that the cavalry, alone, would have loosened my bowels if I'd been a Boer scout.

We parted from Churchill near the place of the snake-bite. He was extremely reluctant to leave us but I pleaded Mac's weakened condition. She needed frequent rests and we'd follow on at our own pace. We shook hands and wished him luck with the rest of the campaign. I told him that I had every confidence they'd relieve the siege of Ladysmith and thanked him for his devotion to the cause. I'm guessing but he might well have felt a little guilty at such praise. Churchill was certainly devoted to Britain but his ardour in those years was focused almost entirely on acquiring the fame that would gain him a seat in Parliament. Still, I suppose the two things were not incompatible.

In typical style he gave a confident snort. 'No question about it. We'll sweep them aside and, once that is achieved, we will break the Boer Army for good. We can all then look forward to a better future.'

If he only knew.

24

The Devil's Bargain

We returned to a very worried Reid. He'd sent a London team to try to find us but they'd arrived unprepared. One of them was wounded by a British sentry when they failed to shout the correct password for that night. They were forced to pull out. The fresh preparations for a better organised and informed team were almost complete. I found out afterwards that they'd have arrived after the snake-bite but before we'd returned to the town. All they would have found was that Mac was expected to die and I was alone in the bush. Their cover stories did not permit independent searches so they would have been stymied again..

So, it ended quite well. Reid was happy, Mac was taken into sickbay for observation and tests, and I was allowed to take refuge in my flat, where I showered several times and slept a great deal. The upshot of the medical conferences was that Mac was definitely on the mend and that 'rest is the best cure but keep an eye on her'. I submitted my report. Reid asked me to see him independently and seemed grateful that I had evidently saved his deputy security chief. For a moment it was quite a love fest and, if I had not been convinced that he desperately needed all the experienced psychics he could get, I'd have been quite touched.

That said, the gratitude was not effusive. This was John Reid after all, and he soon ground to a halt with nothing more to add. I tried to look pleased and complimented. From someone in a yellow jumpsuit that can be a very nauseating experience. Nevertheless, rather than avert his gaze, he was staring at me.

I became a little uncomfortable under that laser-like gaze. He never seemed to change. His hair seemed always to be immaculate. Who cut it I wondered? His shirt was crisp and his tie perfectly straight and even. His hands were neat, clean, and well-manicured. It crossed my mind, and I had to stop myself choking by pretending to get a tickly cough, that he could be a cyborg.

He examined my face for almost a minute without saying anything.

'Shall I go now?' I asked tentatively.

He straightened his shoulders by a millimetre or so. 'No, stay. You have completed four missions and you could now leave my employ.' My face must have given away my instant joy. He held up a finger. 'But I think you might want to consider a slightly different future.'

I'm sure my face again gave away the fact that such a turn of events would only occur over my dead body.

'I know how much money you have salted away.' He didn't. 'But please consider this. I can offer you infinitely more. I cannot tell you any more at this point but, if you were to decide to join Reid Research on a full-time basis, you would be exchanging your few millions in Sterling for billions of US dollars and more power than you have ever dreamed of.'

I decided to look interested. This might be an avenue to more information. 'Power?'

'Yes but that's all I can say at this moment. Give it some thought and let me know.'

'Is there a deadline?'

'Of course there is. I must get my final list of people together very quickly. Let's say the end of the week. Friday by six pm.'

As I left I was pondering his almost unprecedented slip of the tongue. Final list? If this was to be an ongoing business, why was there any need for a final list?

I went to check on Mac. She was sitting up in bed with a computer tablet in front of her. Typical that she should already be working. I was also back to being called Ward.

'Ah, Ward. The medics say I can leave, probably tomorrow. I've pencilled in a debrief with you the day after tomorrow at 1100 hours at the café.' As an answer, 'No' was clearly not an option. I asked her how she was feeling, agreed to the meeting, and scooted out of there before she could rope me into anything else.

I had a pot of tea and a small pastry by myself, a luxury I'd sorely missed, and then went to the base library on a whim. The Boer War had piqued my interest. I scanned a few relevant books. In Winston Churchill's memoires I found the following short passage indexed under 'Natal'.

'I learned a valuable lesson in Natal. We ran into an independent party; a man and a woman. Supposedly brother and sister, they travelled with my troop for many days. Their story was that they were headed for Ladysmith to rejoin their family but when we relieved the town we could find no-one who knew them by the surname they had given me. Neither did they reappear as they had promised. They were almost certainly Boer spies. I never again trusted new acquaintances as readily.'

I was a little disappointed to be branded a spy but that's history for you. After that I relaxed in the flat for an hour or so before going for a very stiff run to let off some steam. I had a gallon of adrenaline to wash away, so I ran myself to the limit at a very brisk pace for as long as I could manage. I saw everywhere on the base but at speed. I reached the west fence after running the perimeter twice and the whole array of roads in the main settlement and I was still not satisfied. I think I'd got rid of most of the adrenaline but a couple more miles of cross country followed by another perimeter should nail it. I headed into the woods.

It wasn't as easy as I hoped. Too much bracken and too many ankle-breaking traps hidden by broken branches. But it was hard work and that's what I wanted. I was slowed almost to a stop as I tried to evade a nasty patch of bramble when Henry appeared. I'd not seen him anywhere and his brown jumpsuit looked far too clean for him to have been stumbling around chasing after me. But there he was, quite a scary figure. Give him an assegai and a shield and I could readily understand why Lord Chelmsford had been defeated and forced to retreat at Isandlwana in 1879. Henry's sharp 'Come' brooked no argument. I followed him and we mounted the now familiar steps into the lodge.

He and Mrs Biddle pretended to ignore my sweat and mud.

'Where have you been?' asked Mrs B immediately grabbing a glass and moving towards the kitchen area. She handed me a brimming glass of cold water and retreated out of range of my smell. I told them the whole story of the final Churchill mission.

'Reid wants me to join the company,' was where I ended the monologue.

Henry made a rude sound and received a slap on the arm from Mrs B.

'You must think carefully about that Dr Ward,' was all she said.

'I intend to but I can't think how I could join such an outfit.'

Henry nodded. 'There's no way you should.'

'Yet I cannot see how he can refuse.' Mrs B was getting me another glass of water for which I was very grateful. 'The missions appear to be coming to an end and so is Dr Ward's usefulness.' She gave me a sad look. 'I cannot see how he could let you live to tell of his exploits if you chose to leave.'

I drank my water. 'My conclusion exactly. I must get back to my run or they will spot the additional time it has taken.' They agreed and walked me to the door. I remembered Reid's faux pas.

'He said that he was drawing up his final list of personnel.'

'Did he indeed,' Henry turned to Mrs B. 'He is closer than we thought.'

'Yes. It's the Devil's Bargain, Dr Ward, and you must make up your own mind. But you can be sure that we will be with you every step of the way from now on if you choose the right road.'

'And if I don't?'

She raised a pair of grey eyebrows that looked thick enough to hide a warren of rabbits. 'Then I believe we are finished – all of us.'

Friday dawned and I woke with the problem of how I would answer Reid at the forefront of my mind. The God of Indecisive Cyber-Geeks was on the job, though. I got called to Reid's office but it was not about joining the company. Mac was already there when I arrived. She looked a lot better - good enough to eat, in fact. I could say she was like her old self except that she actually gave me a tentative smile when I entered. It was moments like that which reminded my hormones how long it had been. Eventually I managed to calm them down and concentrated on what Reid was saying. He'd been speaking with Mac and wound up by saying that he would sort it out, whatever that was, with Mr Marshall.

Then he looked at me and the cyborg thing became a real possibility again. He had not forgotten what day it was.

'Your decision can be postponed if you wish, Dr Ward. We

have an urgent issue.' He waved us to the seats. 'One of the London teams has let me down badly. They will not get the chance again. I need you two, together with a specialist, to conduct what is now the final mission for this round of historical studies.' I was in awe of the man's ability to lie and dissemble. 'I need you to take on a difficult mission regarding the Earl of Marlborough.'

We remained silent even though I think we both took a mental step back in shock. This was further back than we'd gone so far and I had no idea how we would manage in the late seventeenth century. My schooldays provided a vague memory of Marlborough being famous for winning the Battle of Blenheim in 1704. A girlfriend had used the date as a password back in the innocent days before twenty-character passwords using everything on the keyboard. Marlborough won a couple of other ones that I couldn't remember, but, if this ran true to form, we'd be sent further back than that.

'He was a brilliant soldier, sir. I learned about his victories during my training at Sandhurst. One of Britain's finest generals.' Mac appeared to have donned her best brown-nosing hat.

I was not going to be outdone. 'Also, an accomplished statesman,' I added. 'He could keep a coalition together and,' I grinned directly at Reid, 'he knew when to change sides.'

Reid was on the same track. 'Yes, an important target for us. However, it's going to be historically and practically problematic because it is so long ago. However, our people have identified a three day period when he was in England and before he became a military and diplomatic colossus.'

'When was that, sir?' queried Mac in a quiet voice. I could almost feel her remembering what I'd suggested to her.

'The year 1693. He had been released from the Tower the previous summer and was awaiting the crown's pleasure as to his future employment.' Predictable, I thought. Get him while he is least protected and when his death would cause ripples to extend far into the future and negate a huge chunk of British and world history.

'You will not need historical costume. This is a covert operation which the Major here will be well used to. Surveillance and recording only, lots of film, accurate timings, all the detail. You both know the score.'

'What kit can we take?' He looked at me with a slightly puzzled frown.

'The usual stuff plus all the high tech equipment the Major decides upon.'

She coughed. 'And you mentioned a specialist, sir?'

He slid a file across the desk towards her. 'You can take this away, in confidence of course. The file is on Roger Hibbert. He specialises in audio work and this job will need long distance eavesdropping beyond the capability of the usual microphones. He's got the skills and the equipment and has been told he'll be going with you.'

'I see he has no time travel experience, sir. In fact he has never been on a jump.'

Reid gave an impatient grunt and waved his hands to dismiss such concerns. 'No, but you two are experienced enough to take care of him.' He gazed out of his vast window for a second. 'And anyway, this is extremely urgent and is a covert operation. He will not be communicating with any locals or wandering around much. Three days in the woods and you'll all be back without ever having so much as to bow or curtsey to an Earl or a Countess.' He loved his little joke did our Mr Reid.

Mac was not giving way though. She closed the file she'd been perusing. 'Sir, I must protest. It's against the protocols. Hibbert is just a boy. Our missions can get hairy at times and we need to rely on each other in tight spots. Is there no one else with experience but with the same skills?'

The response was cold. I'd never heard Reid speak to Mac in such a way.

'Major McKenzie, you are employed here as a deputy security chief and we all admire your knowledge and skill. I am the CEO of Reid Research and if I say that Hibbert goes on a mission, he goes. Is that clear, or should I find another team leader? I am sure Mr Marshall would jump at the chance.'

My blood ran cold for a few seconds, but Mac eventually complied.

'That's clear and understood, sir. With your permission we will start preparing.'

25

Not all missions are fun

If you are wondering what I was playing at going on another mission, I would remind you of the core aspects of my predicament. Vis: the certainty that I would be quietly disposed of if I decided against Reid, secondly, the risk I was taking with my money if I did join him, and thirdly the delay that this extra mission represented. And how did I know that he'd come through with his promise of billions and power beyond my wildest dreams, instead of millions and all the luxury I could handle?

The upside was that Mac was being much more friendly. She'd obviously thought about Reid offering me a permanent post. I suspected that she now saw me as a reasonable foot-soldier in the time business. I was not certain but I also suspected that Mac hadn't more than the vaguest inkling of what Reid was really planning.

Roger Hibbert turned out to be a boy, barely out of short trousers with the zits to prove it. He was short, untidy, bespec-tacled, and as timid as a mouse. Mac scared me, but she abso-lutely terrified young Roger. He seemed to regard her as being something between a souped-up Boadicea and the goddess Venus which, come to think of it, was close to my own appraisal. Except I thought Boadicea was probably much too gentle a simile. In our short private briefing, she laid down the law to him in no uncertain fashion. He was there to operate the high-tech listening gear, to eat his meals, and to do exactly what he was told. Roger said yes and no in the right places. His eyes followed Mac around the room as though she was likely to turn and rip him to shreds at any minute. I saw him glance at me more than once - presumably wondering how I'd survived so long.

The Black team then briefed us for 1693 and the mission as a whole. It was a year that seemed so barbaric to me that I was within an ace of refusing so that Reid would have me shot immediately. We were to take up a surveillance position as close as we could to Marlborough's mansion on his country estate. He was still the Earl of Marlborough in 1693 but even his recent incarceration in the Tower of London had not, apparently, dented his bank account by much. He had betrayed his sponsor James II, got himself under the ardent suspicion of King William's Queen – not to mention King William himself, narrowly escaped formal charges of treason, and was now presumably boot-licking himself back into favour. The times were those of dangerous intrigues, many changes of side by senior people, and the most barbaric punishments. Parliament was powerful but the monarchy still called most of the shots. William III had a love-hate relation-ship with the Earl. He needed Marlborough and eventually came to semi-trust him, but Queen Mary seems always to have believed that the Earl's loyalty was to the deposed James II, even though Marlborough had helped to depose him. Marlborough eventually got his fame and fortune but only after winning those world-famous battles … and from Queen Anne.

I mustn't forget that there was another small upside. I got to go on the mission dressed in smart green, brown, and black camouflage fatigues. I looked, if I say so myself, like a wicked special forces operative. A helmet and automatic rifle would have made me complete, and I told them so, but, for some reason, no-one was keen to press into my sweaty hands an advanced weapon like that. I could tell that Marshall was very put out by my outfit, a fact that pleased me no end. I didn't show it though.

We all donned the combat gear. Mac and I had a stun gun each. Mac decided we'd not need to take an automatic. Young Hibbert got a small stun gun locked to minimum power but he was told to use it only in the direst emergency. Mac had also specified IR/optical binoculars, long distance laser mics, food and med packs, the usual water purifiers (I remember that awful taste from somewhere) and nine bottles of beer. That was a real shock. Mac handed three each to me and Roger and took three herself. A beer each day each. Things really were looking up, but somehow I doubted this amount of alcohol would get her drunk and happy. If we'd had another ten missions, I was sure we'd be taking a case of beer and I might just get my evil way. But if you believe that, you'll believe anything.

Hibbert was bringing the advanced long distance listening gear. As far as I could see it consisted of a telescopic pole with a small parabolic dish that fixed to the end. The main secret he told me, with evident pride, was the software that he had written himself to collect the most indistinct sounds, separate them out into separate tracks, and then amplify them. For analysis one could combine the time-stamped tracks or keep them separate. As with our own recordings his were stored on solid-state hard drives but they were just ten times the size of ours.

'That's a big one,' I yelped, pointing down at where one of the drives was attached to the front of his pants. It went right over his head, while my own head got a slap across the back from Mac.

I waited for the signal to press the start button. Mac gave

me a despairing look and a slight shake of her head as she nodded to me to get things under way. She was not happy at being forced to take Roger and I felt exactly the same. It was even worse for Mac, though. Being saddled with me and Roger at the same time was a bit of a come-down from her SBS days when she led teams of highly trained professional soldiers.

I pressed the button and we arrived at the precise location set by the Black team. Seeing that it had been estimated using a seventeenth century map, painted over a twenty-first century Ordnance Survey grid using a set of not terribly accurate common landmarks and a mansion that had been consider-ably altered over the years, it was not a bad landing. I had got the impression from a series of briefings that the objective was always to land teams away from buildings, trees, and water, with just a hint that things might not have gone perfectly on some jumps. So, this time, the target was to land us in the fifty yard gap between the ornamental lake and a small stand of trees which lay closer to the main house and which would offer us good cover. The mansion's main rooms and bedrooms overlooked this vista - trees, grassland, and lake - an idyllic scene for any would be grandee.

So, at around 2 am on a dark and extremely blustery March morning, we three intrepid special forces soldiers found ourselves up to our middles in the shallows at the edge of the ornamental lake. Our sudden arrival disturbed the ducks from their well-earned slumber and the noise meant that Mac had us lying flat in the water for half an hour while our feathered neighbours got themselves calmed and ready for bed again. Luckily no-one came to check. Anyone who heard, probably thought a fox had spooked the ducks. Mac eventually gave an extremely cold me and Roger permission to slide slowly through the mud into shallower realms and from thence onto the grass at the side. We lay there for another fifteen minutes, allowing the water to drain from every orifice, while the boss worked out whether a night watchman might be coming to investigate. It was freezing, cold enough with the wind chill to freeze the whatsits off brass monkeys. Our gear was water-proof but the weedy liquid had filled my boots and soaked a long way up my arms and down my front. I noticed that Mac had carefully zipped her suit right up to the neck beforehand and had probably taken other precautions with the wrist and ankle bits. She'd be almost dry while Roger and I, casual and unzipped, had shipped enough cold, muddy water to fill two decent sized baths.

Following our intrepid leader, we crawled slowly to the copse of trees where Mac identified the best hiding places and made sure we had cover for our gear in the form of living grass and bracken. Mac did some careful exploring and found that the copse was more than a small stand of trees. More like a small wood which extended away from the house and even-tually curled around to join up with a veritable forest in the distance. Mac made us wait an hour before we could have a self-heating drink, eat a small pack of energy food, and get into our camouflaged sleeping bags. She placed Hibbert between herself and me and told him to stop whining about being wet.

'If you complain just once more about being cold or wet I will personally drag you back to the lake, drown you, and leave your body as food for the pike.'

It would all dry she promised. It did, but I was still a bit damp on day three. As soon as it got light we began the work. Mac and I took alternating shifts and our boy was allowed to be off-duty unless one of us called him to action having seen something that needed the top-level gear. He spent the time experimenting with the equipment and recording birds moving in trees about half a mile away. There were no real excitements. The Earl seemed to follow a set routine and, luckily, most of it was in rooms facing the view. He breakfasted alone and we got only brief snatches of conversation between him and his steward, the butler, and the housekeeper. Breakfast was obviously his time for making sure the estate was being run properly. I filmed him reading the newspaper and once had the exciting chance to observe him throwing it down in anger. But breakfasts turned out to be non-events.

The later parts of those days were much more rewarding. He had a meeting with two of the local gentry on day one. They mainly spoke of their retainers and how many could be mustered for warlike action at short notice. There were veiled references to the current King and Queen, the Dutchman, one of the gentry called him, and both expressed surprise at one point that they were not biting Marlborough's hand off to get him back into harness. Marlborough insisted on secrecy and he was assured that they would be ready to do their duty if needed. The three men had a fairly simple early dinner before the guests trundled off in somewhat decrepit carriages. The springing was almost non-existent so anything above a very short distance in them must have been torture. I'd rather have walked but that was not allowed for the gentry. Day two saw the arrival, at about 11 am, of a much more luxurious carriage. It was polished to within an inch of its life and the weak sun reflected from it into our cameras as two matched pairs of horses pulled it smoothly up to Marlborough's front entrance. It then rocked quietly to itself before Marlborough's butler opened the door, pulled down the step, and bowed obsequiously.

None of us could identify the coat of arms but it turned out to be the Duke of Shrewsbury, one of Marlborough's careful but determined supporters. We filmed the Earl bowing deeply to his guest before inviting him into the main front drawing room. From what we could see this was a large and very lavishly furnished place in which two people almost disappeared among the elaborate, carved furniture. We could not film their faces and the conversation proved impossible to record using our standard equipment. The speakers were too far away and yards behind thick masonry. Young Hibbert, however, had it cracked. His high tech mic with built-in, AI-assisted amps was more than up to the task. So, we listened, fascinated as two of England's most powerful men discussed how they could defeat intrigues and bring King William onto Marlborough's side. Roger surprised us both by telling us later that what they had said actually came to pass, but not for several years. He blushed as he told Mac that, when he'd been told he was going on this mission, he'd researched the period and the characters in some depth. Dinner for Shrewsbury was a much more luxurious affair than that of the previous evening. A grand table had been laid with the best silver and tableware. Marlborough offered his guest huge plates of appetisers, followed by trout, followed by roast pork, roast beef, and goose, all topped off by a selection of sweetmeats. The wines were so numerous and were poured so generously that I wondered whether humans in the past had far greater tolerance for alcohol. I'd have been under the table before the beef arrived.

There were no visitors on the third day but the Earl took to his horse with his steward after breakfast and we were forced to wait in the pouring rain for him to complete his estate duties. Miserable, but Mac's mood was far worse. She was irritated that we were not dressed to be able to follow him in some way. Our modern camo gear was a little inappropriate for the era. Both Roger and I were snapped at several times.

When the Earl returned at around 2 pm he took what we would call lunch with the Countess. The conversation was domestic, formal, and very boring. Not exactly a party-loving, amorous pair discussing their next vacation. Mac was never bored though. Her duty was to get intelligence and she was going to do that regardless of the tedium. When their snack was over, the Countess invited her husband to walk with her in the gardens. He didn't sound enthusiastic, but she said that she was very anxious to get his advice on the positioning of a new fountain. He sighed but agreed and they disappeared from the small drawing room.

It was the sort of situation we'd discussed but had never resolved. In any other mission we'd have been dressed for the era and would probably have been able to follow them around the gardens at the rear. But we were not garbed for the era. I looked at Mac, fearing the worst. It was an impossible situation which I, personally, would have ignored. Was a walk in the garden talking about fountains really so important?

26

A walk in the park?

You'll have guessed by now that Mac was beside herself.

'Ward. We have to get eyes and ears on them.'

I raised my eyebrows, which was as close as one could get to a mutiny with Mac. 'Is a fountain really that important?' I ventured. 'We'll be spotted. Even in this weather we'll stand out like sore thumbs. Wasn't the whole point to be covert and to stay in this hidden den of ours?' She narrowed her eyes at me. It was the final warning before shooting me in the kneecap.

'You two stay here. I'll do it myself.'

'No,' I objected. But I realised straight away that it was just an automatic reaction. I had not thought it through.

She shook her head. 'One of us could pull it off. Two of us ...'. She looked me in the eye. 'You know I'm the only one capable of doing this.'

I surrendered and, grabbing her gear, she was off. Roger and I watched her leave the copse and dash for a small stand of Alders down by the lake. The boy kept up a whispered running commentary. His admiration for her was all too clear. Until she came onto the comm channel.

'Shut up, Roger. I know what I'm doing. We don't need the soundtrack.' He shot me a wide-eyed glance and zipped his lips.

From the Alders Mac made a short run to a wall which overlooked the formal gardens at the rear of the house and at that point we lost sight of her. We didn't lose touch though. Through my earpiece I could hear her breathing steadily.

'They're in the middle of the garden ... I'll just get the recorders properly trained.' After some snaps and bangs we could now listen to the Earl and his wife discussing the earth-shatteringly important details of the new fountain.

A female voice. 'Perhaps where that small sapling is?'

The deep voice of the Earl. 'I think not, my dear. It must be sited a little lower. We must begin our consideration from the location from which the water pressure will come.' There was a pause as I imagined him pointing. 'There in the hillside. That is where the architect will want the water reservoir.'

'But why there?' She was clearly puzzled. The Earl put on his best patient voice.

'Because it has the two things he will require, my dear. Height and a constant supply of water from the brook.'

'But the brook does not run down to where we want the fountain.'

'That is true, my dearest, but on its way down to the far meadow it will fill the water header tank for the fountain.'

There was much more as the Earl tried to explain what a header tank did and why it was necessary. Then the two settled on a location for this fountain. It was all riveting stuff. Mac stayed hidden behind the wall until after dusk and then floated into our little den almost noiselessly. She was all sweet-ness and light now. She thanked Roger for his help as we packed our gear and even complimented me on another successful trip. We were almost finished. Hibbert was carefully stowing the last bits of his kit in preparation for going home, when a voice sounded behind us.

'Put yer 'ands in the air you three. See Dick, I told yer someone ran into these trees. Turn around slow and keep those hands high.'

We all obeyed but then, before either Mac or I could do anything about it, we heard a terrified whimper and Roger swivelled and ran. He was fast but he was silly. I watched him speed towards the lake. What he was thinking we'll never know. He ran in a straight line and when we heard the metallic thunk of the crossbow behind us we knew that it would not end well. In the faint moonlight I saw the brief flash of the bolt as it covered the distance in a second. The thud of its strike reached us even twenty or so yards away. Roger's puny body was flung forward, his arms and legs flailing randomly as he crashed to the ground. He twitched for a second or two and then lay very still.

'On the ground you two, hands out like youse on a cross. Don't move a muscle.' I could not reach my controller for the return switch. If I tried, I'd get a bolt between my ribs. I caught Mac's eye and did not like what I saw. I just hoped she would play this sensibly.

When the second gamekeeper returned, he shook his head. 'He's gone to his maker, God rest his soul. Let's get these two to the steward, Denny.' They stood back a bit and motioned for us to stand, which we did very slowly and carefully. Three dead suspected poachers would not faze these gamekeepers or the local Justice of the Peace, but it would put a crimp on my plans for the future. The taller of the two ordered the other to cover us while he searched our pockets. He found the stun guns but did not know what they were so put them back. Mac's knives, however, were instantly confiscated. Suddenly he stepped back in shock.

'One of 'em's a woman, by God.'

'They're wearing strange clothes, too. Best we get them to the Steward right quick. Up to him to decide what to do with 'em.'

'There's the Devil's business here, Dick. If 'twere me I'd string 'em up now and save our souls.'

The other was made of slightly sterner stuff. He waved us to get moving towards the east side of the house. 'Walk on you,' he pointed to me, 'and keep those hands in the air. The woman can walk in front of me.' Mac was almost half his size and weight so he felt very confident.

I allowed my shoulders to slump and turned for the house. They were making a mistake in treating me as the dangerous one and not Mac. I didn't see anything but I heard the blows. When I turned around, the two gamekeepers were spreadeagled on the ground and Mac was staring at them. She did not move so I bent to feel their neck pulses. Neither man had one. I gazed at Mac's expressionless face.

'I reacted as I have been trained. If a killer has a gun on you, you respond with lethal force.' This was not the time for rational discussion. I pointed back at the trees and we dragged the two bodies deep into the copse and hid them under a pile of brushwood and branches.

When Mac gave me the go ahead I pressed the return button and all three of us were instantly back at the base. Two of us alive and shocked, one of us very dead, with a crossbow bolt in his upper spine.

Reid took us immediately to his office and got us a stiff Scotch apiece. We told him what had happened and handed over the recordings, including Hibbert's high tech stuff. One look at Mac told me she was not yet totally composed, so I led the discussion.

'My biggest worry is that we'll have changed history in some way. Those gamekeepers lived their lives in the early eighteenth century and it would be highly unlikely and a huge coincidence if they'd both died childless.'

Reid seemed entirely laid back about the whole thing. 'We have the intelligence thanks again to you two. I have not noticed any changes in the world since you left.' I was astounded at his apparent naivety.

'Only McKenzie and I would notice any changes. If there were any, you'd be used to the world as it has changed. To you, nothing would appear to have changed but it still might have done in this new timeline.'

Marshall butted in. 'Can't follow that timeline mumbo-jumbo. Nothing's changed since you went and it's not likely anyway. We've had a couple of incidents with other teams without any apparent changes.'

'You mean other teams have killed people in the past?'

He scowled at me. 'O'course. Can't make an omelette, etc.'

Mac spoke up for the first time. 'But, sirs, we must be changing the world with every one of those deaths. They will have had consequences.'

'Right enough, McKenzie, but what about those Boers you killed in the fights in South Africa?'

I exhaled. 'We don't know that we killed any of them. I am a terrible shot and there were plenty of other British guns firing at the Boer fighters. I saw Churchill kill a Boer fighter but not Mac or I.'

Reid held up his hand. 'Enough. Let us put it this way. We haven't seen any changes that seem to affect our plans, so all's well that ends well.' I must have sighed because he turned on me. 'And you still have concerns Ward?'

'The current timeline will have been altered but those of us who have always been in this timeline will always have known the world the way it is. If Prime Minister Harold Wilson had never existed we would not know the difference, for example.'

Reid stared at me curiously. 'Prime Minister who?'

I laughed. 'You're joking.'

'Do I look like I am joking? Who is this Wilson character?'

My stomach lurched. 'I learned about him in school. Labour Prime Minister in the 1960s and 1970s.' Another thought knifed into my mind. 'Did we join the EU in 1970?'

Reid looked at Marshall and frowned. 'No, that was 2002. We joined with the Czech Republic and Slovakia.'

'So, who was PM during the Labour Governments of the sixties and seventies?

'Reid thought for a moment. 'There was only a short-lived 1964 Labour government under James Callaghan. And that appalling disaster of a government was the cause of the military coup that led to the period of the Junta between 1966 and 1976. They handed over to the Tories under US pressure and they have governed almost unbroken since then.'

I gazed at both men. 'Case proven then. Messing with people in the past can cause important changes in the present. You are lucky neither of those gamekeepers was one of your own ancestors.'

Mac had been listening quietly to all this but now stirred in her chair. She addressed Reid. 'Sir, regardless of the changes to the timeline, What we did was a terrible waste of a young life,'

He looked at her with cold eyes. 'Hibbert was told what he was getting into and he accepted the risks. Sounds like he brought about his own demise through stupidity. Anyway, there are always casualties in any risky venture.'

'This should not be risky at all. We are after all, just acquiring academic information. Lives should never be put at risk. It was a total waste of a young and promising youngster.'

Against the wall in his usual confident position Marshall pointed at her. 'It sounds to me, McKenzie, like it was you who caused his death by getting yourself spotted. If you'd stayed put and not gone on that silly goose chase, Hibbert would still be alive.'

Mac blanched. She was furious. Her hands clenched and unclenched several times. She was very close to a killing fury but her self-control was magnificent. 'Mr Marshall.' She exhaled through gritted teeth, 'as far as I know, you spent your years in the forces in a training capacity. You have no idea what a real-life combat situation can do to a person, especially one who is inexperienced and untrained.' I was in awe of this Amazon. She was more than magnificent as she stood and glared at the two men. 'As I said before we left, the boy should not have been sent on a jump.'

She stormed out, giving Marshall no chance to respond.

For my own part, I was physically sickened by his callous attitude. Yet it was simply a mirror of Reid's own cold-blooded approach. I ignored Marshall and gave Reid a disgusted look. 'If that's the way you regard your employees, if that is the way you treat them, why should I sign up with you?'

He was staring at the door through which Mac had just left. When it came, his voice was like a cold-shower. 'We take care of our own, Ward ... as far as we can. Of course, that does not mean that we can predict the decisions of field commanders.'

'McKenzie makes good calls in almost every situation and she made the right one for Hibbert as well.' I got up and moved towards the door. 'Her view was that the poor boy should never have been sent on that stupid mission. And she was right.' I slammed the heavy door behind me and headed out to find Mac.

It took almost an hour and I began to think she'd retreated to her flat but I eventually tracked her down in the bar of the Admin building. That bar tended not to be frequented by those in black or blue, so was a relatively safe place to brood in uninterrupted peace. The lights were low, so I had to scan the place carefully, but there she was, sitting alone at an isolated table at the rear of the bar.

'Do you come here often?' I asked quietly. She glanced up and pushed a seat out with her foot. I sat down, miming to the bar staff for a beer and another for Mac.

'They were right, Tim. It was my fault and now a poor boy with his whole life ahead of him lies dead in our morgue. He was so young, and it was all for nothing. Just my stupid pride. I was determined not to return without every scrap of intelligence no matter how small or inconsequential and look at the cost of my ego trip.' She didn't look at me during this speech and I stayed silent. I did not know how to help her.

I continued to refrain from speaking while the waiter brought our beers and spilled the obligatory cupful on the table. Mac was correct, of course. It was her fault. 'You of all people, Mac, should know that shit happens. We take decisions and we have to live by them. Some are good and we can regale our grandchildren with them, but some are bad. We are none of us perfect. All we can do is learn from our mistakes and try not to commit them again.' I noted she'd been shedding a few tears. 'Roger was a nice lad, but you hit the nail of the head when you told Reid that he should never have sent such an untrained, unblooded novice on a mission. Reid was so desperate to get this mission finished and the worst thing is that he doesn't care a hoot now that we've got the data. The vast majority of the blame is his but he and Marshall just don't care.'

'I noticed.' She took a huge gulp of the beer. It looked to be at least her third glass. 'Damn Reid. I thought he was a better man but you may be right about both of them. They're just heartless, arrogant, avaricious shits.'

I raised my glass. 'Hear, hear.'

There followed a few minutes of silence while we both concentrated on the serious business of getting legless. After a while, I changed the subject to her plans now that the 'first set' of missions was complete. I wanted to get her mind focused on practical problems and we talked about her options, and mine, for another hour or so. In my gut I knew the conversation was a waste of time. There was unlikely to be a normal period of time ahead of us once Reid pressed the start-button on his plot. But it was a harmless way of grounding Mac again for at least a short while. We left the bar together and I said goodnight to what seemed to be an amazingly sober Mac at the door of her residential block. I could not help reflecting on my way back to my own apartment that young Hibbert would have loved Mac's performance in Reid's office.

27

Who's a silly wizard, then?

It took a few days for me to get the worst of the bad taste out of my mouth. Mac blamed herself but, when push came to shove, this was all Reid's fault. It was his company, his plan, his impatience, and his decision to throw a boy into a time mission without proper preparation and totally without experience. Mac had to take some responsibility. She made the wrong decision about the garden surveillance. And I am sure I could have been more determined to stop her doing it. But it was with Reid that the vast majority of blame lay. On second thoughts it was also Reid's fault that I had been dragooned into it all in the first place.

The amazing thing, though, was that my biggest beef with him was for his callous disregard for how the event had affected Mac. I was furious that he and the despicable Marshall had just stood aside and let her take all the guilt on herself. I kept out of Marshall's way most of the time but his face when I did see him around the base was every bit as cocksure and complacent as it had always been. The pair of them had thrown Mac to the wolves for no other reason than they simply did not care. They didn't even know what they'd done.

Meanwhile she wandered the base like a zombie, her face

set, her focus only on the task of the moment. I tried to speak to her, but she would only pass a few words my way and then speed off to some other 'important job'. McKenzie was arguably the most difficult person I'd ever met. She was pig-headed, stubborn, single minded, inflexible, and almost always distant. Yet I'd come to see her as fundamentally decent. I even admitted to myself that it would be good if we became friends. I was sure she felt the opposite and that was a conundrum that puzzled me to heck. I thought about it regularly but I could not get a handle of any sort on what was behind her intense dislike for me. She'd come round from total frigidity, almost hatred, to being reasonably warm, but that was it.

I wanted to avoid Reid altogether but he eventually called me in. He was happy that all the missions were complete and made his feelings very clear as I sat across the familiar desk from him.

'I will repeat what I said the other day. I am marginally satisfied with the way you have adjusted to the life here … after some deviations from acceptable parameters. The offer of a permanent post is still open. How do you feel about that?'

'The recent Marlborough mission is still uppermost in my mind, I'm afraid. It's difficult to forget what happened and to ignore what it might mean for the future – my future.'

He sighed quietly. 'I can see what you mean.' He was silent for a while. 'You must understand Ward, that neither myself nor Mr Marshall wanted that unfortunate event to occur. If we sound callous it is only because we have great responsibilities and we cannot allow ourselves to get too involved or too emotional about anything.'

'I understand that, but what about Major McKenzie. She's taking this very hard.'

He looked genuinely surprised. 'Is she?'

So much for caring leadership, I thought. 'She is. She feels responsible and even though, technically, it wasn't her fault, her current mental state might impair her operational efficiency.' I can be a devious bastard at times, can't I!

Reid nodded and told me that he would ask the psych staff to arrange counselling and some help for the Major. It was probably all I could hope for.

'Under the circumstances I can give you a little more time but I stress that I need a decision from you soon.'

'Can I ask why?'

'Why I need the decision?'

'No, why me? Why do you think I'd be a good employee for Reid Research to have? I'm certainly not in line for employee of the year.'

'There are several reasons. You are intelligent and resourceful. We've had ample proof of that. You have shown that you can be brave and determined in action. And … you have a character which does not flinch at illegal or even immoral activity.' He was spot on. 'I will give you a few more days but then I will have to insist on a final decision.'

'And if I don't want to join you, I can leave?' He held his arms wide, palms uppermost. Butter wouldn't melt in his mouth.

'As I said before, you can leave tomorrow if you want and get your money and the life you planned. We will not stand in your way and there will be no hard feelings.' He stopped there and I suspect it was purely for effect. 'However, you would be standing aside from a chance to acquire wealth beyond your imaginings as well as gaining a position of power that, also, you would not dare to imagine in your wildest dreams.'

'You keep mentioning power. Where would that come from? Would I be in line to be made a department head of some sort?'

He actually laughed. Well, I think it was a laugh. He made a choking sound and coughed into his hand. 'Far, far more power than that, Ward. I need good men to run … to run larger organisations. But if you would still prefer to think small and go back to your little stashes of money, that is fine.'

In my heart I knew I was being fed a large pile of BS but even the slim prospect of being able to return to my original plan was like him opening a door to paradise.

I lay in bed that night pondering things. Realistically, there was only one thing I could do and that was to accept Reid's offer. Otherwise, he'd either have me killed, probably in a car 'accident' once I was twenty miles away, or he would arrange something more exotic but equally satisfying. Perhaps I'd be thrown into a secure mental hospital? The well documented background from the base would be that I thought I was a time traveller and that people were changing history. To add a bit of danger he would make up a story of how I used weapons against his people in the company. Neither of those possibilities were futures I would look forward to. If I accepted the offer, however, I would stand to be included in his new order - whatever that was. He mentioned billions and power. While the latter had never been my priority, the former sounded just a little enticing.

I'd tried to talk to Mac about it but she stonewalled the subject. Whenever I mentioned it she would adopt a formal voice and tell me that it was a marvellous opportunity, great conditions of service, interesting work, what more could I ask? She also pointed out that the pay would be at least treble what I would get outside the company. And, she added, if Reid was also offering to forget my indiscretions and keep me out of a military prison she could not see why I was hesitating. All true, but the whole fragile story, everything about Reid's offer, was about the company she *thought* she knew. It was not about the one I was fast becoming convinced was about to explode onto the world.

At that moment, however, my deepest concern was about Mac herself. She was half the girl she'd once been. Remembering Reid's promise, I asked her if she'd seen a counsellor. She'd shaken her head. 'Told him I was not interested.'

So, if I could not talk to Mac I had only one alternative. I had not seen Mrs Biddle and Henry around the place for days, so I looked for them on my runs. They were nowhere to be found and I began to think they might have gone away. That evening, though, they stepped out of the bushes as I was returning from the west fence. I jumped a mile as Henry stepped out in front of me and ushered me into the undergrowth. The pleasantries were quickly disposed of - well, I only had to be pleasant to Mrs B. Henry glowered and I tried to annoy him by nodding a casual greeting. Bringing them up to date was a lengthier affair. When I stopped, Henry grunted dismissively and Mrs Biddle sighed.

'Mr Reid is being economical with his facts, I believe, Dr Ward. If his scheme works and you opt not to join him, the consequences will be extremely serious.'

'I know,' I agreed. 'He'll have me put somewhere I cannot do him or his company any harm … ever.' I got a sharp punch on the shoulder from Henry. 'Ouch, what was that for?'

'Mrs B is referring to far more serious consequences than merely your own demise.'

I smiled at them. 'Far as I have been led to understand, there simply is nothing worse than not being alive.'

Not for the first time, the tiny cleaner placed a restraining hand on her giant colleague's arm. 'Dr Ward please sit on that dead branch.' It was not a request. They sat themselves down on a stump opposite. As a group we were well hidden. 'Mr Reid's plot is not about making huge amounts of money from time travel, Dr Ward. His objective is to change history in his favour and dominate the world.' I must have been staring at them vacantly because Henry leaned across and tapped my forearm.

'Pay attention Dr Ward, this is important.' I shook myself

and tried to look as if I was believing what I was being told. But Mrs B was speaking again.

'Can you imagine a world in which 95% of it has been thrown back to an early industrial phase, when all high technology is reserved for one relatively small country, where most humans are little more than slaves providing raw materials, food and basic metals for the fantastically rich 5%?' I shook my head. It was quite literally unbelievable, but I did my best to look as if I was swallowing it all. 'If Mr Reid manages to assassinate world leaders in several centuries, he will be able to mould the world to his own design. Empires will not exist, whole modern nations will remain divided into tiny principalities or feuding statelets, scientific advances will not be made except in his own artificial nation, he will be able to steer technology into only one area of the world - which he will control.'

'But that's impossible, it's unthinkable. How could a single organisation like Reid Research rewrite history so completely?'

Henry entered the fray. 'By assassinating the most influential leaders, by using his knowledge of their movements to remove them from the world stage and change history, by literally moulding history to produce the world he wants. It will mean millions of deaths and billions of people consigned to short, poverty-stricken lives so that he and his chosen people can live in luxury. He'll keep the rest of the world divided and underdeveloped - supplying raw materials, human labour, and basic foodstuffs for his Orwellian state.' This was just too much. It was not even believable in a science-fiction way. I grasped at the only solid thing in my life at that moment.

'Even if what you say is true, and I suspected something similar, I will have to join him. You know that.' Henry was the most obstreperous person I knew but even he saw the sense in this.

'That's as may be, join him, but do not turn gamekeeper.

What Reid is planning is beyond horrific. The whole world will become a slave camp supporting one advanced nation.'

'But, surely the rest of the world will gradually develop better weapons and will eventually rise up and defeat Reid's brave new order? You said yourself they will only be about 5% of the population.'

He shook his head sadly. 'How did the British conquer India, Australasia, most of Africa, and all of North America? They kept the advanced weapons to themselves and established garrisons to keep the natives under strict supervision and control. After independence, how did the Americans conquer North America? They had an almost monopoly of advanced weapons and, when they took land, they kept it by setting up forts and using troops of soldiers to keep the natives quiet and underdeveloped. That is what Reid wants to do with the whole world. Every country will have its own Reid-appointed Governor supported by garrisons of well-armed troops with modern weaponry and sophisticated aircraft. They will ensure that no-one ever develops anything to threaten the new order. If they do, they will be thoroughly crushed.'

'Reid's people will be in the minority though.'

'So were the British. So was the US Cavalry.'

'But you must see. I can't do anything about it, I'm just one man.'

Mrs B had been playing with a dead twig. Now, she pointed it at me. 'We can't say any more, but you are not an ordinary man, Dr Ward. You have an incredible natural ability to set your mind free and accomplish almost anything you set your mind to. Just think for a minute. Where have all your 'dreams' come from? How did you manage to steal all that money without being caught? Why does Reid want you so badly in the time-travel business?'

Those were easy questions. 'The dreams were probably the result of stress. It's not been easy being locked up here, you know. And I managed the crimes because I have a certain natural talent plus some very good cyber-skills. The whip-backs prove that I am not terribly good at time travel.'

Henry stood up and dragged Mrs B with him. 'You are a stubborn man, Dr Ward, you are refusing to see the truth. Could it not be that, far from being a phenomenon that you cannot control, the whip-backs were actually engineered by your own mind? My God man, wake up and extract your head from your nether regions.'

When they had gone, I resumed my run down the now very familiar hill. When I reached the main gates I turned and kept running around the perimeter. I needed time for my mind to digest what I had been told. If I stopped running I knew that I would probably scream. The story was impossible. It was preposterous and insane. I would be a fool to accept what two cleaners told me. And yet, they were far more than cleaners. I had definitely had some very strange dreams, I had dreamt of the assassination of a President, and I had seen the inside of the Blue Building without being there. On top of all that the list of time travel targets contained all the most crucial leaders in the history of the world. Would the USA continue as a single nation if Reid assassinated Lincoln and Grant? Would China be a united nation if they killed some of the Emperors at strategic times? What if Mao was killed at the early stages of the Long March? Could a united Germany form without Bismark? Without characters like Marlborough, the two Pitts, and Churchill it is highly unlikely the British Empire would have been created or maintained.

Careful selection of targets and a short campaign of killings could be used to create whatever world Reid wanted. We'd already acquired the detailed intelligence he needed to direct his killers when the time came. How many targets were there in all? In view of the number of teams, I would think a hundred at the least and possibly as many as two hundred.

Once he had his Orwellian State, the future would be

bleak for the vast majority of the human race. He'd have all the technology, all the science, all the modern weapons, the aircraft, the bombs to keep the rest of the world in a state of primitive industrialisation for many centuries to come. And only Reid's new state, wherever that was, would be wealthy and advanced. Only in that tiny part of the world would people have the best food, gadgets, entertainment, travel, and medical care. Each nation would need a Governor who would live in well-protected luxury. Is that what Reid meant by money and power?

The more I thought about it the more my breath was taken away by the audacity and ambition of the plot and the horror and suffering it represented for billions. There was no doubt about it. Reid must be stopped. I very much doubted I was the special hero painted by Mrs Biddle and Henry but I could use a gun and I could wait for an opportunity.

28

The game's afoot

The very next day I was in Reid's office at ten am. I was told this was his earliest appointment and that I was very fortunate to get the slot. The meeting was short. He asked me if I had now made up my mind. I said yes, thank you for the opportunity, I accept. He said that he was pleased and that, within a week or two he would arrange for me to become part of the Black team and, miracle of miracles, I would be paid a substantial salary from now on.

'Not the blue team?' I asked innocently. He pierced me yet again with those keen eyes. He had a habit of dropping his head slightly when looking at you that way. Intimidation personified.

'Not yet, Mr Ward. You have many more brownie points to accumulate before I consider that particular promotion.'

I thanked him again and left quickly. There was much to do.

Henry and Mrs B were where they said they'd be. In a small alley behind one of the admin buildings. I gave them the news that I was now a full-time employee of the Reid Research Corporation and, while they expressed a little disappointment, they understood. I used the occasion of them being slightly on the back foot to ask them for a couple of weapons.

Mrs B almost dropped through the floor and Henry responded with his favourite word. But I was determined.

'I need something if I am to stop this character,' I pleaded. 'You may have all sorts of theories about how good I am, but I, personally, do not know what exactly I am supposed to be good at. So, I will need to have weapons and ammunition. You got me the laptop. Can you not acquire some decent hardware?'

There followed a muted but heated conversation between the two cleaners. I caught words like 'stupid', 'useless', 'dangerous', and 'pathetic' and I took a wild guess that all of them related to me. I was adamant though. This situation was likely to get very bloody and all the blood would be mine if I did not have something to fight with. In the end the discussion died down and Mrs B passed on the Board's decision. They did not believe them to be necessary, but they would acquire two automatic pistols and a couple of bags of magazines and ammunition. I thanked them and made to go. Mrs B coughed and I halted in mid stride.

'Did you know about the moves, Dr Ward?' She was gazing at me curiously and I asked her what she meant. 'Henry was eavesdropping around the Black Building yesterday. It seems that half of the London staff are already on their way and we've noticed a drift of staff out of this base too.'

'Where are they going?'

'New York, I think,' said Henry. 'The discussion was mainly about arrangements for two dignitaries who would be arriving here in a few days. Possibly Reid's partners or his financial backers.'

'We believe that Mr Reid is almost ready to leave this base. Once he and his backers are in New York the historical killings will begin and the world will begin to change.' I had never seen Mrs B so serious. 'We will be ready when you are Dr Ward.'

It sounded like the two of them would be taking up a couple of AK-47s and getting stuck in alongside me. That would certainly end in tears, but they seemed set on trying to stop Reid at any cost and, although she looked far from the type, I could easily picture Mrs B doing a 'do-or-die' final charge at the massed security men.

I tried to find Mac to have a chat and tell her at least part of what was going on. The Rottweilers in the guard house sneered at my yellow jumpsuit but eventually informed me she was in a planning meeting with the senior staff and was not expected back before her shift ended. I did, however, pass the great man himself as he walked briskly towards the Black Building. He shouted to me and I strolled across. Casualness irritated him beyond measure. It was one of my few high-points that day.

'I forgot to tell you to start getting your stuff together, Ward. I have not yet agreed the exact schedule but you will be leaving with the final group - with myself and the other senior staff.'

'Keeping me close, Mr Reid? Where are we going?'

'The precise location is confidential but our chartered aircraft will be taking us from Newcastle to the United States.' He looked to be on the top of his game; positively bouncing with eager anticipation. I was all toadying eagerness. I would be ready, I told him. 'Good. Expect the code 'Orwell' in a few days' time. That will be the only signal to finish packing every-thing. Be prepared to leave at a moment's notice.'

'Can I ask what my role will be in the organisation?'

He seemed to ponder this. It was an eminently reasonable request. 'Everything will all be explained once the action is initiated. Your role will not be time travel, at least not in the early stages, it will be coordinating the action teams.'

'Sounds exciting. What are these action teams going to be doing?'

'It is more than exciting. You'll be fully briefed when we get to our final base in the USA.' With that he strode off, turning only to inform me that I would be helping to create a new world.

I was surprised to find the two cleaners in the yard behind my residential block. They were not working, merely waiting by the bins.

'Are you waiting for me?' I asked jokingly. Mrs B's response was a shock.

'Yes. We thought you might seek us out after that chat with Mr Reid. We have fixed the two cameras that could see us here. They are showing an empty area.' I was taken aback again.

'You knew I'd met Reid?' They nodded. It was best not to ask. Instead, I told them what Reid had said. It would be easy to panic, I thought. I had wanted to leave the base for months but now that it was about to happen I could feel the fear soaking into my bones. I had no plan and as yet no guns. When the proverbial brown stuff hit the fan I would also be short of the fifty armed men I'd prefer by my side for any sort of final showdown. When I told them this, Henry laughed. As you will know by now this was not a common phenomenon and three crows that had been pecking at a dead rat behind the bins took noisy flight. Henry had to duck as one of them tried to get back at him for disturbing a delicious snack.

When he had recovered his dignity he looked at his colleague. 'It is as we suspected.'

Mrs B agreed. 'We knew the time was near. Dr Ward you must prepare yourself.'

'That's why I need the guns. Is there any sign of them?' Henry's sigh could have blown the heavy bin down the hill, but he informed me stiffly that they would be hidden in my wardrobe before lunch tomorrow.'

'What will you do, Dr Ward?' Mrs B looked worried.

I gazed into that creased and pleasant face. 'I don't know, Mrs B. I have only the vaguest of ideas at present but I will be thinking hard, believe me.'

'You'll know when the time comes.'

'But where will you and Henry be? I would not want you to be hurt.'

'We will be close at hand.'

'You don't need to risk yourselves. Both of you should get out of here while you can. Use the tunnel to the lodge.'

'This is too important for cowardice to rule our actions,' announced Henry. 'We will be here and ready to help you.'

'The code-phrase is 'Orwell', that's the signal that Reid and the last staff will be leaving. It will also be my chance to stop him because the number of remaining staff will have been pared down to the minimum.'

'How many people on the final day do you think?' There was a calculating gleam in the Zulu's eyes. I could not help thanking my lucky stars he was on my side - well, partly on my side.

I raised an eyebrow. 'Can't say but knowing Reid he'll want to get almost everyone away before he himself departs. There were around a hundred and fifty people on the base a week ago. The population is already a third down, I would guess, so about a hundred left as we speak. He could clear most of those in the next two days. So, not sure. Probably between fifteen and twenty in the final group?'

Henry nodded. 'That's what I would say, too. Reid is a very cautious and very organised man. His character is secretive and almost cabalistic.'

'What?'

'He revels in the idea that he is at the centre of a secret plot. He does not believe that he is an evil genius, but he embodies the worst characteristics of that type. He is the archetypal sociopath. His weakness for showmanship will win out for the leaving party - it will be very senior, very devoted to him, and quite small. Reid will pare down the people to the bare minimum, to a top-level gang of which he is the undisputed boss. He'll not be able to resist the massive thrill of being the very last to get into a car from his English base.' The tall black man squared his shoulders and his face glared hatred at the bits of the base he could see. 'Reid will see himself as a successful Hitler - the man who did what that monster could not achieve. When he leaves, he will want to imagine the bands playing martial music and the flags waving as he watches his generals mount their armoured SUVs.'

Mrs B and I were stunned to silence for a few seconds by this unaccustomed eloquence. 'I think Henry has missed his vocation as an orator,' she murmured. 'We agree with your figures Dr Ward and we will try to be nearby on the day.'

29

Better late than never

I'm a genuine hypocrite, but then you'd probably already guessed that. In spite of my intense dislike of Reid and my hatred of what he seemed to be planning, I still revelled in a minor triumph. My black jumpsuit arrived the next morning and I immediately put it on. Better late than never. It was a good fit and I was even grateful to Reid for not forgetting, until I realised that it was not due to his generous nature. He would not want the embarrassment of a tame banana getting on his plane with all the other sinister-looking staff. I threw the hated yellows under the bed.

Mac was busy that day. I tried my best but she dashed about furiously and waved me aside as I attempted, half-heartedly I will admit, to get in her way. There was no point in getting myself injured at this stage. The base was a hive of activity. Vans were loading from almost every building before heading, presumably, for the airport. The cafés were handing out lavish packed lunches. Security guards were everywhere. Some were carrying their kit bags and were clearly leaving with different vans while others were obviously staying for the time being. They were carrying their weapons almost casually now. No-one was expecting trouble.

I sat in the main café watching a large luxury coach and a smaller equivalent loading staff and luggage. I estimated about seventy or eighty people in all. So Henry and I had been roughly correct. The café was adorned with notices advising customers to serve themselves and to take what they wanted from the counter-fridges and the small freezer at the rear. There were no waiting staff visible. All either laid off to the local community or already on a coach or plane.

By two o'clock I was almost alone. The vans had loaded and departed in clouds of diesel fumes, the coaches had glided away with a discreet swish of air brakes. Only a few security guards remained on the gates. They wandered into the café occasionally and grabbed a drink or a pastry but none spoke to me. I sighed to myself. It would not matter. Within a few days everything would be decided … one way or the other.

It took precisely twelve minutes to pack the last of my stuff. So, I decided to take a walk around the nearly deserted base. I had spent a few months here desperately wanting to get out. Now that my exit was imminent I was a little nostalgic. I'd been beaten up in that gate house, I'd had numerous briefings in the Black Building, I'd had that unique evening with Mac in the Admin Bar, and almost everywhere reminded me of clandestine meetings with the two cleaners. The memories were stark and very recent. I knew virtually every crack in the concrete of the base's roadways and I certainly knew every camera and security sensor on the perimeter. But this was senseless. I had to plan. I walked quickly back to the café just in time to witness the arrival of a single black SUV which disgorged two black-suited security people from the front seats. The guards opened the rear doors and a passenger descended from each. One was male, short and very expensively dressed. Probably in his late forties he had a crew cut in the latest fashion. He wore fawn sneakers rather than shoes and was dressed to be seen as unconventional, a rebel, a bit of a lad.

He stared around at the base, his gaze proprietorial. I

quickly had him marked as an entrepreneurial type, perhaps a self-made man who had made his money by hard decisions and back-stabbing. Watching him examining the buildings it became all-too-clear that most, if not all, the bricks belonged to him and he would want an explanation why the fiftieth one down on the left was chipped.

The woman was very different. She was older, probably in her late fifties, and conventionally dressed in a navy blue skirt-suit. Her hair was almost certainly dyed which made her look younger. But her neck gave her age away. Like many older women she made the mistake of trying to wear lower neck-lines in order to look younger. As always, it had not worked. She was a sun-worshipper who had spent many hours getting her skin seared to a deep red-brown. Consequently her neck was a mass of wrinkles and sunburn scars. She glanced at the base but gave it scant attention and, unlike her male colleague, was more interested in watching the approaching John Reid. She was dressed like a civil servant and I was certain that that was what she had been for a great many years. Even the way she moved was careful and considered. Small steps and little body movement. Her head moved like a small bird's – with quick pecking motions and rapid scanning of the surround-ings. I'd guess her subordinates had been terrified of this crea-ture. Jurassic Park came vividly to mind as I watched her eyes assessing Reid like a top-predator. Kill him now or keep him for later?

How had Reid met this fearsome creature? Had they been civil servants together at one point? When he shook her hand she did not smile. But then neither did he. They did not speak much and the way they turned to get on with the day said that they were old acquaintances. When Reid shook the hand of Mr Wide-Boy, on the other hand, there were false smiles all around and a few small jokes which everyone pretended were funny. That they were Reid's equals was obvious. This was definitely the group that had set up the Reid Research Corporation.

While they chatted their way back to Reid's office, their SUV was turned around and parked a little down from the café. I was left alone again with my thoughts. Their body language spoke of them being business acquaintances rather than friends. They may have known each other a while but there was a wariness between them, almost as though they were still sparring for position as top dog. If the woman was an ex-senior civil servant and the man was the source of the money I could well imagine how each of them would imagine themselves the most valuable … and, therefore, the most senior.

I went back to my own planning while drinking myself steadily through some of the remaining stores: tea, coffee, and soft drinks only, of course. I've already said that I have an aversion to writing notes about personal or secret matters. This topic was one of those and I memorised the main elements. I'd closed my eyes for a second to memorise a particular point and, when I opened them again, Mac was standing silently opposite me.

'Hi. Sit down and I'll get you a drink.' She just wanted water, which was easy enough. 'What have you been up to? When I saw you earlier you looked run off your feet.' I tried not to show it but I was worried. Mac's usually precise appearance had become frayed at the edges. To be frank, she looked haggard. Her eyelids drooped, her complexion was a little sallow, and those beautiful eyes had dark lines beneath them. Her shoulders, usually held back and up, were down. She had had only once before looked so tired and washed out and that was when she was recovering from an almost fatal snake bite.

When she spoke, her voice was soft. I had to concentrate to hear her properly. 'Marshall wanted me to supervise the staff who were leaving. That's why I was so frantic.' I passed her a Danish pastry but she waved it away. 'What are your own plans?'

'I accepted Reid's offer so in theory I'll be leaving with the last group.'

Her nod was a satisfied one. 'Good. It's the right decision.'

I told her I was still not sure of that, and hinted at the fact that I did not understand what Reid had planned once we all got to the States. She fired back the authorised responses but I could tell her heart was not in the same place. Her eyes never held mine for long, her mouth was tense. I could see her breathing deeply to calm whatever tension was eating her up.

'You *are* coming with us aren't you?' I blurted out. It had never crossed my mind before, but the current Mac was not the same person who had been so enthusiastic a few weeks ago. It shocked me how much I did not want the answer to be negative. But she nodded.

'Thanks for the water Tim. I'll see you around before we go, I expect.' I watched her walk out. It was a weary walk. A month ago, no matter how tired she'd been, she would have considered it a matter of pride to march briskly. I was really worried about that girl.

Everything was very unsettling now. The base was eerily deserted. Dinner at the restaurant was a self-service affair with a tiny number of people scattered around the place. Reid had contracted a local company to provide food and service for the last few nights but they were nowhere near as good as Reid's own staff. I ate quickly and left, passing Mac on the way out. On a whim – and because I was pretty lost myself – I asked her if she wanted a drink in the bar. No. Packing was her excuse.

My residential building was empty except for myself and two security people who had flats on the floor below. The corridor leading to my front door was quite dark, so I did not see Henry until it was almost too late.

'You'll be the death of me one day if you keep surprising me like that.'

'Just take these.' He handed over three smallish but heavy hessian bags and moved closer. 'I did some listening this afternoon. Reid's friends will be travelling with him. The woman is an ex-Principal Secretary at the Ministry of Defence named Celia Wilcox. The chap is Denny Carruthers, CEO of WuT.'

'The wifi company?'

He nodded in the dim light from the reduced number of ceiling lamps. He laughed mirthlessly. 'Carruthers told Reid that he'd bought him.'

I smiled. 'Did he indeed? Is it Reid and the woman against the wifi guy?'

'I don't think so. She and Reid worked at the Ministry at roughly the same time. I got the impression she'd been his boss. It was she who recommended Carruthers as the financer. The whole meeting seemed tense. Mainly centred on who did what and who had what position once the plan moved to what they called the next phase. She and Reid had a bit of a spat about roles in the USA. She suggested herself as CEO with Reid as Chairman and the other chap as Chief Operating Officer. The WuT chap thought he'd paid enough to be Chair and CEO with the other two in subordinate roles. Reid had other ideas entirely and, after a very fraught few minutes, they left it undecided.'

'Did it get feisty?'

Henry shook his head reluctantly. 'I'd have loved them to have shot each other but Reid did a good job of diplomacy. He is quite good at that. He delayed a showdown until they are all settled in the States.'

'What are the other two like as people? She looks ferocious.'

'She is. In different ways they make Reid seem a bit of a pussy-cat. At one point Ms Wilcox asked Reid whether he had terminated the 'offending parties' – whoever they were. He said not yet and she was quite animated about him getting it sorted very soon. She said they could not afford loose ends. Reid told her that no matter what loose ends they left, the action teams and the forthcoming changes would eradicate them.'

'And Mr WuT?'

'Carruthers is just your standard, super-rich, amoral, gangster-businessman. Perhaps not as bloodthirsty as Wilcox but ruthless. I would not like the pair of them as my co-conspirators. There is no doubt that, of the triumvirate, two will wake up one day with their throats cut. Just a matter of time.'

'Thanks Henry and thanks for the equipment.' He was turning to go.

'The new place is in upstate New York near the Canadian border.'

I took the guns and ammo straight into the bathroom. I sincerely doubted that there would be more than one security guard on duty watching monitors tonight but best to take no chances. The most important cameras were those watching the gates and perimeters. Reid would not want anything to go wrong at the last minute. Watching what was going on in the residences was almost certainly the lowest priority, especially now he thought I was hooked on the promise of billions of dollars.

Henry had somehow purloined two of the latest Glock 17s – the Gen 5 model. They were standard NATO issue but with the full nineteen round magazine. I'd used an earlier model when training. The RAF Regiment used them as well. In the third bag were enough magazines and cartridges to start a medium-sized war. I checked them all carefully, loaded each gun and then put three spare magazines for each weapon into each of two bags. The remaining magazines and shells went into the third bag. I'd be dead long before I ran out of magazines and needed a complete reload.

30

Well, you wanted action!

It was happening faster than I had thought. The next morning I went to the restaurant for breakfast and passed a small people-carrier which appeared to be taking more staff, looked like eight or ten, to the airport. That would leave only a few for the last group, which was better than I had hoped. The fewer in the final group the more chance I had of putting a spoke in Reid's wheel.

I was walking up the steps into the front door of my building when another black SUV whooshed down the hill and came to a halt below the one that had been parked yesterday. My stomach began to churn as I went into the bathroom and retrieved the guns from behind a panel in the under-sink cupboard. I checked again that they were fully loaded with safeties on, and then stashed them in a small briefcase where they were easy to reach but could not be seen on the surveillance system.

I kept watch by standing back from the window which overlooked the café. From there I could see one of the SUVs but not the other. They were seven-seater brutes so that made a total of possibly fourteen people in the two cars for the final trip to the airport. I counted by placing teabags on the kitchen table so that I would not make a mistake. There was Reid and his two conspirators, Marshall and McKenzie and me, the two security people who'd arrived with Reid's partners, and probably another six of Reid's own guards. Fourteen in all. That figure included no less than ten armed and well trained security people. The total included Mac but I could only work on the principle that she would side with her boss. She'd shown little sign of antipathy towards her employer. I had no idea at all what she'd do. More to the point, what would I, myself, do if she and I came face to face with guns pointed at each other? I knew me. I'd hesitate and not want to shoot her. Mac on the other hand would go with her training and instincts. So, I'd be dead.

There was a knock on my door and a shout of 'Orwell'. This was it. I would dearly like to say that I grabbed my guns and ran furiously into battle without a care for my own safety. That didn't happen. First, I was shaking so much I could barely hold the gun never mind aim and fire it. Secondly, I wasted valuable seconds, hesitating while trying to decide whether to take my bags downstairs ready for the drivers to collect them. WHAT? There followed a lot of mental face slapping and telling myself to pull myself together. At least I'd prepared a little. I'd kept a bottle of brandy in the kitchen for the past couple of weeks. It was now almost half empty. When I left the room that morning it was less than a quarter full but I felt a whole lot better. I grasped the bags with the guns and took the bottle to the window where I stayed back out of sight, sipping steadily with what I hoped was a determined expression on my face.

Make your own mind up. The brandy was having an effect, though. My hands had stopped shaking and I could feel the fire coursing through my body. Whoever denigrated Dutch courage has never been alone and about to take on ten armed killers.

Near the café I could see two security guards loading the

SUV belonging to Wilcox and Carruthers. Mr Wifi and Mrs Starched-Shirt were strolling down the hill with John Reid. They were accompanied by two security men including the one I'd nicknamed Mr Goon. We'd known each other a long time. The group acted like tourists, looking around and pointing things out, chatting away merrily. When they were outside the café, Reid said something to his guards and they loped off. I saw them pass the new SUV and assumed they'd be helping to load Reid's own wagon. The three conspirators stopped and Wilcox and Carruthers nodded to Reid before heading for their car. My plan had been to wait until this moment and then open fire from the cover of a wall at the end of my building. From there I would have a complete field of fire from the gates to the Blue Building. But I was truly, knee-wobblingly terrified. Why on earth was I doing this? Was I really sure that killing people was a good idea when no-one had stirred a finger against me? Perhaps I could just shoot out the tyres and make them miss their flight? I was being a total coward. As I turned to go downstairs my attention was drawn by a flash in my peripheral vision. Another figure had come into my field of view, walking quickly down the hill towards Reid. It was Mac.

I groaned inwardly. Would she be there when I opened fire? I desperately hoped not. I couldn't see Marshall but I guessed that he and the other guards would be in the gate-houses. I hesitated again. There would be no one behind me now and I should get moving. But I was glued to my view of the interchange between Reid and Mac. There was no sound of course but he looked agitated and she was waving a hand around uncharacteristically. Perhaps more seriously she had put her face well within his personal space. The two guests had got into the back of their SUV. The guards, one of whom was driving, also got in. I guessed they would drive down to the gate and pick up another three of Marshall's men and then head for the airport.

Suddenly Mac pushed Reid violently. He staggered and fell to the ground using an arm to save himself. Mac swivelled in a single smooth motion and stepped quickly down to the SUV where she said something to the occupants and threw two small black objects. One went through the front and one into the rear window. She began to run back up the hill as she threw another object towards Reid's own SUV. I heard the explosions of the grenades as I ran down the stairs, conscious that I'd left the flat door open. It's incredible what you think of in such situations.

As I got outside, I saw Mac running towards me, jinking all the way. Reid was not armed. He was shouting to his guards and Marshall to 'get McKenzie'. They were not focusing on me so I had time to run the few steps down the outside of my building and throw myself behind the wall. Now that the action had started I was easy in my mind about getting into the fight. I took out one of the guns, flipped off the safety and began to fire, one carefully aimed shot at a time. Mac landed in a breathless lump beside me.

'Trouble with these armoured SUVs is they are armoured in different ways. The idiots were relaxed and had their windows down.' She took out her own pistol and began a steady fire towards Marshall and the gates. 'I didn't get Reid's car though. But, one of his men took some shrapnel I think.'

I gave her the bag with the spare ammo. 'You can use this better than me.' I took another couple of shots.

The once pristine black wagon belonging to Carruthers and Wilcox was a flaming mess. The doors had been blown out and the interior was a furnace. No-one survived. Mac was hopeful about the fuel. It had caught fire and was running in a flaming rivulet towards the Reid's SUV. Marshall was frantically trying to move the relatively undamaged SUV. He got it rolling away from the flaming petrol and, leaning out of the window, he beckoned to Reid, dusty and bedraggled after Mac's push, to get in.

At the same time he was shouting confusing instructions. He evidently wanted all four remaining guards to attack us, but he did not give them clear directions. Mac was peeking out of the side of the wall.

'Tim, I'm going to get around them. You keep them busy from here. If they get too close get back to the residence and try to get to the second floor. I'll join you there from the fire-escape at the back.' I did not have time to acknowledge. She was gone and I was trying to deter the four gate guards who had now joined up with Reid's own guards. The one who had taken some shrapnel appeared to be fine. His left arm was bloody but his gun arm was unscathed. I was up against six of them, seven if you included Marshall. I changed magazines as quickly as I could and risked a look over the wall. Two of them had worked around to the café. They were now diagonally across from me, forming a second front to my left. Another two had moved further to my right, presumably to split my attention, while Reid's two continued to fire at me from the cover of his SUV. Always keep changing your position was what I'd been taught. I shifted closer to the wall of the building, aimed carefully and fired. There was a yelp of pain. Maybe I'd winged one.

Bullets were pinging off the top of the wall, thudding into the building behind me. I changed position again and lay on the floor looking out of the side of the wall. A guard was running up the hill towards me while the other fired at where he thought I was - near the building itself. I rested the pistol on the floor and breathed out as I had been taught. I gave the man a slight lead and fired. The shot caught him in the lower leg. I'd aimed too low. He fell over, yelling in pain. He'd dropped his gun and was holding his leg as he rolled around.

A quick check of the café showed one man limping back towards Marshall and another lying still on his face. Mac was sprinting towards me.

'Into the building … now!' she shouted.

31

Here comes the reaper

I needed no more encouragement. Discounting the one Mac hac killed at the café and the one writhing in agony from a leg wound, there were at least four guards plus Marshall closing in on us. We raced for the familiar front door and skidded into the hallway and up the stairs as bullets thudded into the exterior walls behind us. As we went, I heard Marshall shouting for men to follow us.

Mac entered and immediately crouched by the door. 'The odds are with us now. Five against two. We'll destroy them!' She grinned at me. 'Get upstairs and into your doorway. Cover the stairs. I'll keep them honest for a while. Eventually they'll think about the back entrance and I'll move there, so watch the stairs.'

I did as I was told and heard Mac yell that she'd got another one as she dashed for the back. The guards who rushed the front door used a spray of automatic fire to kill anyone who was still stupid enough to be in the entrance hallway. When that ended I knew two or three were in the building. I waited until the first man up the stairs was in full view, allowed him to take two steps up the corridor and then shot him squarely in the chest. He fell backwards against the wall and lay there. I could hear shots from the rear. That would be another of the guards trying to outflank us.

A rapid succession of shots struck the door and wall above where I was lying. I stuck the gun out without aiming and fired two shots. I was pinned down. When I needed to change magazines they'd be on me instantly. I took the decision to retreat further into the flat and hid behind the kitchen island. There were two sets of cupboards back-to-back, so they might stop a few shots. I heard two more shots in the building. Had Mac got another … or had they got her?

No sooner had I lain behind the island than a black suited guard stepped in. It was the one I'd shot in the chest. Would I never learn? His bullet proof vest had stopped my shot and, now that he had regained his breath, he was quite understandably out for vengeance. I vowed not to make that mistake again. It would probably never happen again in a thousand years but I rolled smoothly into view, aimed the pistol before he could react, and shot him in the head. Very, very messy. His body crashed to the floor in a shower of blood and … other stuff … just as yet another guard stumbled through the door and fired some shots at random. I aimed again and fired. There was a dull click.

I fumbled for my bag, clicked the old mag out and began sliding the new magazine in. It took about three seconds but he was already standing over me gloating. 'Got you, you bastard, It was you what winged me.' he snarled. I watched his automatic come up and then watched it fall to the floor. His boot bashed my head as he staggered under the headshot. He hit the small coffee table on the way down and would have cracked his skull if he had not already been dead. Another mess of blood and brains. The cleaners were going to have a job on their hands.

I tried to still my heart by taking deep breaths. I peeked out towards the door. Mac was standing inside the room with a huge smile on her face as she looked around.

'Not bad for an IT geek. I got two at the back.'

I grinned back but then another shot exploded in the small space. Mac almost flew towards me, falling to the floor just in front of me. And there, behind her, was the creep Marshall, smiling that smug, bastard's smile. He was watching Mac fall to the floor and it took him couple of seconds to identify my location. That was enough even for an amateur like me. My gun was loaded and already raised in my attempted defence against the last guy. I just had to adjust aim slightly. At that range my grandmother could have hit him. I was incandescent with fury and I emptied half a magazine at him – eight shots one after the frigging other with my hatred and fury travelling with every single one. Four of the bullets hit his vest, two went wide, and two smashed his right arm. They impacted in the same place just above the elbow almost severing his arm. The shots blasted him backwards and took the wind out of him as well as giving him a satisfying amount of pain. Even as he was settling into a semi-conscious heap by the bathroom door, I scrambled to my feet. I was not going to make the same mistake twice with bullet-proof vests. I picked my way carefully across the slippery floor, grinned at his confused face, and shot him twice in the head. It did not give me any pleasure. In fact I felt completely drained of emotion but I was getting used to the idea of finishing a job properly.

I checked that the corridor was empty of threats. I'd lost count but there had to be one or two guards and Reid to worry about. He'd not leave himself unguarded. I dashed back to where Mac was lying. She was struggling to turn herself over. The wound was high in the back and very central – it looked as if it had broken her spine. I reached up to grab the kitchen towels and used them to pad the wound. If she lay on her back that would apply pressure and slow the bleeding. My old running fleece was on one of the kitchen chairs. It was worn and old and I had decided to leave it. It now became a cushion for Mac's head.

When I had finished, she grasped my arm weakly.

'Tim. Reid. Get him quickly. I can wait.'

I was torn. Should I stay and try to save her - but how? The medics had all left and the nearest doctor was in a town about ten miles away. I'd need to get Reid first and then phone the ambulance. But she was right, Reid was the priority. If we failed to get him, it had all been for nothing.

So, I squeezed her hand, stroked her cheek, promised to be back soon, and ran.

Three dead bodies on the way down the stairs. I grabbed an automatic rifle from one of them. As I went, I ran through the numbers again. At the beginning of the day there were twelve people left on the base excluding Mac and myself. Four had been killed by Mac in that grenade explosion, she'd got another at the café and probably another two at the back stairs. There were three bodies on the stairs and in the flat including Marshall. Which, excluding Mac and myself, left two. Reid was one of them. I took the chance that they would be more interested in getting away than dealing with me. Considering there had been just me and Mac as the opposition we'd done exceedingly well. And Reid would know that, if he died here, the whole scheme would fail. His partners had been incinerated over a warm fuel tank in the back of that SUV and the whole Orwell plot now depended on him catching that aircraft in Newcastle this afternoon. So, I ran out of the door and down the hill towards the gate.

I had passed the café before I got sight of Reid. The car was standing in the gap between the first and second gates. He was shouting something to someone inside the gatehouse. Probably the guard I'd shot in the shoulder. I took a knee and let go a couple of shots with the rifle. I saw one ping off the roof of the SUV but both missed Reid. He was screaming at his man to hurry up and get the last gate open. The security had been very well designed. The gates were not just a couple of bars to be raised and lowered, they were full height, steel jobs. Two of them opened inwards and, from what Mac had told me when trying to scare me off trying to escape, their operation was quite a business. They were rigged to open and close at high speed if necessary but the operator had to insert a passcode which was changed twice daily. The question was whether this guard knew it or whether Marshall had taken that little secret on his journey to hell.

I kept running. By now Reid had taken cover inside the SUV so it was not worth the effort to shoot at it. When the guard emerged from the gatehouse I could see he was not the one I'd wounded in the shoulder. That sparked the memory that he had been one of the bodies on the stairs. This was the chap who'd taken a shot in the leg and he was in a bad way. The gates were opening but on the usual slow setting. He was trying to limp towards the SUV using a rifle as a crutch. I tried a shot but it must have been very high and wide. The SUV was moving slowly. It could not go any faster until the gates opened properly. The guard was almost at the front passenger door. He seemed to grasp it and then fling himself back. The sound of the shot came next. Reid had killed his own injured guard.

As the gates opened further, the car began to pick up speed. I flung myself against the stanchion for the first gates and let the SUV have every bullet in a copious magazine. I could see sparks fly as my shots hit home but they had no effect. The wagon sped up, made a skidding right turn onto the main road, and disappeared from sight.

Reid had escaped.

I almost cried with rage. We had got so far only for him to get away. I knelt beside the gate stanchion, my head lowered in defeat. A cold hand began to crush my heart. After everything I'd been through, after all the sacrifice and deaths, after all that I'd been told by Mrs Biddle and Henry, I had failed and failed in the most important way possible. Reid was on his way, free and clear, to the airport. By this evening he would be well on his way across the Atlantic and, as soon as he arrived in upstate New York the plan would be launched in all its horrific detail. He would be without his partners but that was probably something he'd celebrate. He had enough people to act as time controllers and masses of killers. The world would be changed forever and all I could do was to wait and see what happened if, indeed, I existed that long.

Mrs B had said that, if this came to pass, we would notice nothing. One moment we'd be in the early twenty-first century with all our luxuries and technology, the next our lives would be very different. We'd be living in a world that had only managed to reach basic industrialisation and steam power. Our working lives would be brutal and short. Lung disease, industrial accidents, heart problems, cancers, viral diseases, all would cut lifespans by decades. Every so often we would see a jet aircraft cross the sky and more frequently the Orwell police stationed to control the rest of the world would show their power. The slightest resistance to Orwell would be punished by instant death. Their modern weapons and high-tech equipment would make any resistance totally futile. It would be like putting a First World War regiment up again a modern company-sized unit with their advanced weapons, missiles, drones, artillery, and air support. The despair was so deep that I was frozen in place at the gate. Nothing now mattered. I flung the rifle to one side and put my head in my hands.

We'd lost.

'Do not be so gloomy, Dr Ward,' said a familiar voice, which angered me beyond bear.

'Don't be so stupid,' I shouted. Mrs B was standing only about four feet from me and Henry was just behind her. 'He's escaped. We've failed. Which bit of this do you not understand?'

'Dr Ward …Tim …' she murmured. 'It is not over. You have tried it your way and it did not work. You got close but …'

'I can't stay to listen to this drivel again. I have a friend who is dying. Can you do surgery?' I was in the advanced stages of meltdown and I didn't care who I hurt. 'I thought not. If you want to be useful, phone an ambulance at once from the gatehouse phone.'

With that I ran back up the hill and up the stairs. On the way into the flat I took my fury out on Marshall's dead body by giving his torso a solid boot.

32

Okay, they were right all along

She was still with us but her eyes were clearly not focusing very easily and she could not raise her hands. I knelt down and gripped one hand. It was ice cold.

'Mac, hold on, the ambulance will be here shortly.' Her eyes flickered. 'Why didn't you wear a vest?' I wasn't wearing one myself but that was not the point.

'Tim. Is that you? No time for vest. I want to say sorry before I go.'

'What do you mean? It's me who should be apologising for getting you into this.'

'No … Reid had to be stopped. I meant something else.' There was the slightest pause. 'I took this job so that I could kill you.'

'What?' There had been some shocks and surprises recently but this was something else. It crossed my mind that she was delusional. 'Why would you want to do that?'

'Because of Betty.' Now I was sure she was losing her mind. Did she think she was talking to someone else?

'I'm sorry. Who is Betty?'

'My sister. You went out with her for quite a while back in

the day and then you broke her heart by breaking it off. She took her own life shortly afterwards.'

I froze as a dark shadow crept up my spine. Yes, there had been a Betty. Years ago when I was still at the RAF College. Lovely girl and we had lots of fun. But she had been a bit clingy for me, her hints about settling down, and having lots of children came much too early in my life. I just wasn't ready. One day I decided to cut the strings and I told her one evening over a drink. She'd cried a little but got up and left. I never saw her again.

I squeezed Mac's shoulder, looking into her beautiful face. I had always known, somehow, that it was familiar to me. 'Bloody hell, Mac, I am so, so … desperately … sorry. I had no idea she'd done that …' I broke off because I had deliberately not contacted Betty. I was afraid she'd think I wanted to start it up again and I did not.

'I could have spoken to her. I could have helped her. I can't tell you how sorry I am.'

Mac gave a croak that I interpreted as a scoff or a laugh. 'I know, Tim. I hated you with a vengeance and was determined to make you pay with your life. I almost did it on a couple of occasions on our time trips.'

'How did you track me down?'

'Didn't. Was going to look for you and settle your hash when I got some leave from this new job. Never happened. Then you showed up here and when Richie was killed I took my chance to get you on my team. Seemed like … gift from heaven.'

I was quiet for a while. 'Why didn't you do it?'

'Would have done earlier, but you were infuriatingly nice. And then you saved my life. And then you stuck up for me on the Hibbert thing. And then this Reid thing. You were right all along. Nasty bastard. Did you get him?'

I crossed my fingers. 'Yes, Mac. He'll not trouble anyone again.'

'You're more than half a good man, Tim Ward. I was wrong about you. We can all be too self-centred at times. Do what is right … for me … and for Betty.'

Her eyes closed and I watched helplessly, the tears flowing down my face, as her breathing slowed. When it stopped I cried for many minutes. And all the time I was kicking myself for being so selfish for so many years and for hurting so many people. But the worm does not turn with a single traumatic event. Tim Ward was going to have to work very hard to justify Mac's judgement. But I would try and, more importantly, I would kill Reid if I had to walk to the USA and if it was the last thing I ever did in this world.

And again, the timid cough of a small female cleaner. My fury had not abated.

'For the love of God - get out of here. I do not want to see or hear from you or your friend ever again.' For a split second I even thought of picking up my pistol and killing both of them where they stood.

'We will go if you really want us to, but first we must deal with Reid. He is still our main concern.'

My mouth opened but no words would emerge. I stared at them without seeing them. My brain was floundering with all the stupidities surrounding those words. In the end I merely said.

'He's gone. I will have to get a car and follow him.'

She shook her head. 'No. We will deal with this from here. Please come into the sitting room where we can be comfortable.' Comfortable? Had she not seen the blood and devastation around her - the dead bodies, the body bits, the bullet holes, the smashed furniture? 'Please,' she said again. Henry pulled her back and they went into the sitting room as though they had just come around for a cup of tea and some cakes. I looked down at Mac and the tears returned. She was with her sister now but that thought did not assuage my grief and guilt. It was my fault that both of them had died young and with most of their lives ahead of them. The pain coursed through me again, together with the anger. It was so intense that I couldn't think properly. I was pure automaton as I stood and walked into the sitting room to confront the two cleaners. I didn't notice but I was still carrying my gun. My feet left bloody footmarks on the carpet. The two of them were sitting on the sofa, faces composed and serious.

I sat in an easy chair opposite them and put the pistol on the arm.

'I'm going to leave in a moment to try to find a car or something that will get me to the airport. If I am too late, I know where I can get money and passports and I will be on one of the next flights following Reid's. I will kill him, come what may and whatever the consequences for me.'

Henry leaned forward and, for the first time that I could remember, spoke softly. 'Please listen to us, Tim. We cannot make things happen, we cannot lead you into this. It must all happen because you, yourself want it, because you create it. But if you do, we need not leave this room to handle Mr Reid.'

I gazed at them both blankly. 'Are you still trying to sell this crap?'

'Yes, Tim. But it's not … it will work if you want it to.' I can only think that I was so tired, so emotional, so drained. My shoulders slumped and I found myself saying, 'What do I have to do? But be warned, if it doesn't work, I'll be out of here like a flash and you will never see me again. You have three minutes.'

'It will take a little longer than that,' said Mrs B. 'Please come and sit between us … right, lean back, relax, and close your eyes. We will be doing the same.'

I did as I was asked. Henry's voice was soft and compelling - so much so that I feared I was being hypnotised. I recalled, however, that a person cannot be hypnotised without permitting it so I relaxed and listened to his voice giving me instructions.

'You have travelled a long, hard road, Tim, and it has become even harder in recent weeks and days. Normally you would want to forget the pain, the anger, the frustration, the grief ... but now you must look deep into yourself and gather it all together. Remember all the bad the times, recall every incident where you have been frustrated by your apparent impotence, remember your beating, bring out the anger and hatred, gather all the pain from the death of your friend. Gather it all before you in your mind.'

I was breathing hard. The images and thoughts crowded into my mind and pushed each other aside as they clamoured for my attention. Reid, Marshall, prison vans, razor wire fences, being savagely beaten, seeing Richie die, my constant humiliation in my yellow jumpsuit, knowing what Reid planned, reliving the moment a crossbow bolt took the life of an innocent young man, and most of all watching Mac's young and beautiful life ebb away because of that bastard Marshall. I saw Reid kill his wounded guard in cold blood, I watched again the assassination of Roosevelt, I felt my searing anger about the way they'd treated Mac after Hibbert had been killed. I swallowed and gripped my legs as the feelings mounted to a crescendo. I could not contain them. In my mind there was a white-hot fury building into something I somehow knew would be an H-bomb of emotional energy. I saw Marshall's sneers and Reid's disdain, I saw the pity and scorn of people around the base, I saw my own impotence in the failed escape attempt, I saw Mac's face telling me to get Reid.

And I heard Mrs B and Henry saying to me over and over ... 'See Reid's face, bring it up from all that pain and anger ... send it all at that face ... we will help.'

The words somehow got through everything. I saw Reid

sitting in that all-too familiar pose behind his desk. His bald head, his self-satisfaction, his arrogance. Then, a split second before I thought that I would explode, I threw the whole white-hot ball of resentment, frustration, hatred, and fury at Reid's face.

As the ball of energy sped to Reid, it turned into a spear of light which penetrated his face just above his nose causing the whole face to contort in agony. I did not have time to feel any satisfaction although I was briefly aware of a black SUV hurtling through a dry-stone wall and down a steep drop towards a river. Mrs B and Henry were shouting at me to keep going. I didn't know what they meant, but I kept pushing that spear of light down through Reid's face, deeper and deeper. I half recognised a younger Reid and even a much younger one before they were replaced by faces I did not know at all. Face after face came briefing into view and the rainbow-coloured spear pierced all of them. It seemed to go on forever as scores of people's faces were obliterated by the fury I was directing at them. Men and women screamed briefly and disappeared, to be replaced by others, and yet others. I did not know how long I could maintain this even with the support I could now feel coming from my companions. Mrs B and Henry were adding their strength to my fury.

Suddenly there was a single face in my mind. It was of a man with long dark hair and a white collar. His mouth was set in a sneer. I had never seen him before in my life but I instinctively hated him. I heard Mrs B shout 'Finish him' and I thrust the spear deep into his face. It grimaced in agony and swept from side to side as though to evade the thrust. I kept pushing even though my strength was failing fast. The man's eyes flashed once with shock as he recognised his own death.

After that I recall only an explosion of darkness interspersed with flashes of what had just happened. Time and space seemed to collapse into a tiny ball and I had a profound impression of being sucked into the ball myself. It was the end, I thought, but I could die with the immense satisfaction that I had ended Reid before I myself faced eternity.

33

Decisions, decisions

I came to my senses in bed, in a strange bedroom. I gazed around sleepily. It was neither Reid's base, nor my RAF quarters. It was larger than the bedroom at Barrow Briggs, but less modern and certainly not as smart. I was in a king-sized bed wrapped in soft, warm sheets and duvets.

I could think of more appealing sights to greet me as I woke up after … after whatever had just happened, but, no … Mrs B and Henry were standing by the side of the bed watching me while I got my eyes to work properly.

'Welcome back Dr Ward,' she said, with a broad smile on her face. She looked younger in ways I could not fully describe. Her face was much less lined, her mouth firmer, her eyes even brighter. But there was something else, an indefinable beauty. Panic must have registered on my face for she went on quickly. 'Don't worry. Henry has placed us in a time bubble. No one can see us - any more than they could see us at the base. It may not last long but Henry's spells are usually robust.'

I was feeling rested and relatively alert. The memories of what had happened were still terrifyingly fresh, but somehow this place felt safe. 'Okay. I'll ask the question. Where am I? Oh, and when am I?'

Henry grinned. It was terrifying. 'You're at RAF Deepwood, in Gloucestershire. You are in your own bed and your wife is currently getting you both a cup of tea to prepare yourselves for the day.'

Come on now. Tell me honestly. Had I not suffered enough recently? Had there not been enough twists and turns in my life. Why did I deserve another huge load of change being dropped on me? I needed time to come to terms with what had happened – especially the death of Mac.

My mind simply refused to process the data. 'What? Never mind. How did you get me here?'

Mrs Biddle chuckled. 'It was not us but you who chose this new reality. We had nothing to do with it.'

I looked around frantically and she laughed. 'Don't panic. It is not necessarily fixed yet. You have a decision to make.'

'What sort of decision?'

'You were exhausted by the attack on Reid and it appears your mind took control and brought you to a different reality. The only thing certain is that it must have been one that your mind genuinely liked and wanted above all else. And before you ask … you succeeded.'

'*We* succeeded,' corrected Henry.

'Yes of course. Together we were able to resolve matters.'

'Reid's dead?' More in hope than belief.

'Reid is not dead. Reid never existed. You have eradicated his line back to the nexus at which this all began. But to put your immediate fears to rest, if you wish you can close your eyes and wake up on the train to London the day you left RAF Sneddon Downs. Everything will be as it was but Reid will not have existed and your little peccadillos will not have been discovered. You left the base a well-liked and respected officer and have all that money and a life of sublime luxury to look forward to.'

My heart took a little skip. But then it tripped over a nasty thought. 'Won't I just be arrested again?'

Henry reverted to type. 'No. Reid never existed. You made certain of that. In this reality the time experiments ceased when the government of the day lost the will to continue. We must hope that no-one discovers the dusty files buried in the cellars of Whitehall. So, no-one knows of your crimes and you can get on with your decadent life the way you originally planned. You could be in Brazil tomorrow and there is not a soul in the world who would want to stop you.'

'There's an 'or' in there somewhere by the sound of it.' I braced myself.

'Yes. Alternatively, you could choose a life in this new timeline. Your mind created it so we guess that it is close to your real desires.'

'But what happened? Tell me what's going on. Surely you can do that now?'

'Put simply Tim,' smiled Mrs B, 'you are a channeler - a person who has the power to channel inner emotions, feelings, and desires and use them to see things, to change things, and where necessary to eliminate things.' I knew better than to call it nonsense.

'I've never heard of such a thing.'

'Think of it as being a sort of wizard. The two are not totally comparable because you do not, as we do, need to cast spells. But it is close enough. Perhaps more to the point you are a powerful channeler. We saw this as soon as Reid selected you to be 'arrested'. He had been told that you had minor psi-powers. He had no idea just how powerful you are.'

'Me, powerful? How did that happen?'

'Do you remember that final face that you eliminated in the old reality? I don't think Henry and I will ever be able to forget it.'

'The glaring, wide eyed fanatic of a chap with the long greasy hair and the white collar?'

She nodded. 'That was a man of the cloth who never deserved the status. He was an evil man. He preyed on others and was particularly fond of preying on women, especially young and pretty ones, whether they were married or not. He was the Reverend Reede. He lived in the early eighteenth century and, through vile, twisted revenge, was responsible for the execution of your most important ancestor - a lovely lady by the name of Lucy Brimham. She was a witch who refused the Reverend's advances and, to her credit, hurt and embarrassed him. She also passed down powers to her children and they down, eventually, to you. By taking Reid and his forebears – right back to the evil Reverend – out of reality you have restored Lucy to her life.'

'Sorry, Mrs B, but how do you know all this. It's like you've been time travelling too.'

She laughed. 'Not at all. Henry and I cannot do that over long spans of time. You are underestimating the close and faithful community that we witches exist in. We have an enduring loyalty to the community past, present, and future and that means that every generation leaves detailed accounts of their lives and activities. Lucy's daughter left us a comprehensive account of her mother's life – and her own – and the generations since then have naturally followed suit.'

I was quiet for a bit, while I tried to absorb all this.

'If you like we can show you her grave. She lived to a ripe old age and helped hundreds and hundreds of people. Her daughter was a famous witch and we think her son was a very capable channeler. As far as Henry can tell, you inherited your own channeling abilities through Lucy's son and one of her great-great grandsons.'

The information was piling up on me like an avalanche. My mind switched to more recent events and particularly to Mac. 'If I am so powerful it's a pity I couldn't save some of the others who died due to that bastard Reid. Sorry Mrs B.'

She smiled at my crudity and inclined her head to accept

my apology. There was surprise in her eyes . 'Oh, but you did … save them I mean.' I sat up straighter. 'Your … sorry Henry … our … eradication of Reid's whole family line means that he never existed. No-one bought the rights to the time-travel experiments and the plot never came to anyone's mind. The base at Barrow Briggs is still there but it is just an old government site consisting of crumbling buildings, surrounded by rusting barbed wire, full of bats and birds' nests. The people who died are still alive.'

I shook my head in amazement. 'Even Marshall?'

'Yes, even him. He is a security chief at a big London bank, as arrogant a pompous arse as he ever was.'

And then it hit me. 'And Mac?'

'Yes, she also is alive and thriving. She is happily married to an ex-SAS Colonel. They have a child with another on the way we think.'

'But not her sister?'

Her mouth turned down. 'No. It seems that incident occurred in what we are calling both realities.' My mouth dropping open was the sign for Henry to take over.

'Think about it, Tim. The reality that Reid was in and in which we defeated the plot is reality number one. By getting rid of Reid you have cleaned that reality up a lot and all the deaths except Reid's never happened. It is also the reality in which you stole a lot of money and plan to live out your life in cossetted luxury. Reality 2 is this one.'

'But Betty killed herself in both?'

Mrs B sighed. 'Tragically, yes. I can understand that you could not have known what she'd do, but your lack of interest did not help. You may want to do some explaining and apolo-gising there.'

I sighed even more deeply. 'So, not everything is sweetness and light.' Henry had gone quiet and seemed drawn into himself. When he looked at me he gave a small smile.

'No. But Mac seems very happy in her new life. She is content. I'm sure she will understand and forgive you.'

'So, what's next?'

He shook himself and was every inch the disgruntled Zulu again. 'The decision. It has to be quick because we cannot hold this time bubble open for too much longer. You can choose to resume the life you left, go and collect your ill-gotten gains, and live a life of pampered wealth. Or you can choose this reality.'

'I know about my old reality, what about this one - what is it? All I can see is a slightly tatty bedroom.'

Henry looked to Mrs B but she motioned for him to continue.

'You might want to brace yourself, and … ' he narrowed his eyes meaningfully, 'remember it was you who selected Reality 2, not us. We are blameless.' I rolled my eyes and motioned for him to get on with it. 'Alright. In this reality you signed a new contract with the RAF. You married Emma …' Mrs B interrupted.

'It was a lovely day, Tim, at a beautiful local hotel. I think it used to be a stately home. It had the most wonderful …'

'Tim doesn't need all the flowery, fashiony, foody details, Mrs Biddle.' When Henry was irritated he never hid it. She subsided with an apologetic smile. 'You did another four months at Sneddon Downs. Why they promoted you I will never understand, but they did. You got posted to take charge of the cyber-warfare centre at this base.' I remembered Deep-wood; one of the central hubs. A good posting. 'Your life is not a wealthy one. It will not be like your other life would be, but there are benefits.' He waved around him. 'This house is the married quarters assigned to a certain Squadron Leader Tim Ward.'

I gazed around the room, frowning. 'Back in the RAF again. Really?'

My hand received a playful slap from Mrs B. 'Don't be awkward. You'll find that Squadron Leader Ward is going places in the forces ...'

'Sorry to interrupt but how long have I been married?'

'Three months.'

'She's a lovely girl,' interrupted Mrs B. It was not exactly a surprise but I was stunned that I'd taken the plunge. I'd be lying to say that I'd never thought of asking Emma to marry me. But it had always seemed the closest thing to a life sentence with hard labour, so I had always pushed those insidious thoughts to the back of my mind. Even now I felt a little pang of angst at the thought of being with one girl for the rest of my life.

But, always looking for the upside, I had another thought.

'Is my money still here?'

Henry grunted dismissively. 'Ever the greedy bugger. I'm pleased to say, no, that never happened in this timeline. You never committed the crimes and therefore there's no mountain of bank accounts containing millions of pounds. Equally there is no gaggle of law-enforcement agencies after you.'

I took a deep breath. 'So, if I did not commit the crimes, I must be a different person in this reality?'

'Well done. That's an unusually incisive thought for you. You are definitely different. Something happened in the old reality that changed your character a little ... or perhaps a lot.' I nodded and thought of Mac, and of what Henry and Mrs B had said to me over the past few months. Yet there was still a lot of the old Tim lurking in the background.

'What do I have in this timeline, then? As far as I can see, I've just been thrown back into the RAF, consigned to a life-time of drudgery, and had all my hard-won cash disappeared.'

Mrs B slapped my hand again, harder this time. 'Don't be so naughty. You have a beautiful and talented wife, a valuable and satisfying career that will help keep millions of people safe, and a group of friends who, for some unknown reason, respect and admire you.' There was a long pause. 'You can be an ungrateful man at times, Tim Ward.'

I stared into the distance for a long time and they were good enough to turn away and study the view outside. After a minute Henry's nerve broke.

'Have you made up your mind yet,' he demanded impatiently. Mrs B shot him one of her looks.

'He has to make up his own mind, Henry, this is a very important choice.'

I nodded my thanks. Out of the bedroom window I could see a building which was very obviously of World War Two RAF design. It was just across the road. The windows were dirty, the frames needed painting, the brickwork needed a good pressure wash, and there were a few weeds growing out of the gutters. I closed my eyes and turned inward. This time there was no anger and frustration, just peace and quiet, a sense of everything being right. I remembered what Mrs B had said. I had chosen this new reality. No-one had forced it upon me.

As I was staring out of the window, a face formed in my mind. I closed my eyes to see it more clearly. It was Mac and she was repeating her final words to me. I looked past her and there stood Betty, her sister. She was also smiling at me, but she said nothing. Mac's voice echoed in my head. 'You are a good man at heart, Tim. Silly at times and prone to running off the rails without some wiser spirits around you.' She exhaled in that typical tetchy Mac way. 'But essentially you're good.' The face scowled. 'Don't take the wrong decision or I'll come there and break both your legs.'

Then the vision was gone and Mrs B was gently shaking me, asking if I was alright. I braced myself.

'Okay I'll take the right path.'

'Does that mean what I hope it means?' asked Henry, suspiciously.

I smiled at him. 'Yes, you miserable old bugger, it means I'll stay with Emma and make a go of this poverty-stricken life that I appear to have chosen for myself.' Then I had a terrible feeling. 'Will I stop being what you called me, a Channeler?'

They shook their heads in almost perfect synchrony. 'Not at all.' Mrs B was smiling at Henry. 'You cannot stop, ever. In fact all you will do is keep getting better and stronger and helping people in more and more ways.'

'Will you two still be around?' I was shocked at the pleading in my voice.

Henry gave an immense grin. 'You'll not get rid of us that easily, and anyway, you will need us.'

'What for? Not that I don't want you to be here.'

His voice dropped. 'The world is not a stable place, Tim. We are but two - sorry three - and we cannot be everywhere and everywhen. There is always work to be done.'

'We will be in touch, Squadron Leader. You will need to practise, so we will not be away long. A matter of a week at the most.' Mrs B waved and, with that promise, one that could also have been a threat, they turned and walked through the wall. As they went I swear I could hear them arguing again.

Their disappearing through the wall acted like a switch. Noise returned to the world. The first things I was aware of were voices on the street outside, the sound of a truck going past, and footsteps on the stairs. The bedroom door burst open and there was Emma beaming as she carried in a tray with two mugs. Her hair was unkempt and her dressing gown untidily fastened by an uneven belt but that was the moment I knew that I'd taken the right decision. She was so incredibly beautiful, she radiated such warmth and love, my heart felt like it was going to burst.

'Come on sleepy-head. Your secretary has already been on the phone to ask when you'll be showing up. It seems there's a bit of a stir down at HQ; new attempt to hack somewhere important was all she would say.' She placed the mug on the bedside table and gave me the nicest kiss I could remember from any reality. It was, I knew, the still centre of what might be a very trying day, but I cradled her face in my hands and told her that she filled my heart with joy. She flicked my nose.

'Don't be silly. Drink your tea and get yourself out of that pit. It's time to be up and at 'em.'

Notes

I tried for historical accuracy where the period characters are concerned but I have taken liberties with dates and places. I have no idea whether JFK was in Atlanta on the dates in the story and he certainly would not have made untoward advances to a young lady. Where the Elder Pitt is concerned the dates and the location in London are both of my own invention. His importance to British history, however, is unquestionable. The country estate of the then Earl of Marlborough is not intended to be any existing property. He too – flawed as he was – was incredibly important to the way Britain and Europe developed in the eighteenth century and beyond. We know that Winston Churchill dashed off to South Africa as soon as the second Boer War began, that he was captured and escaped and fought in several battles, but his adventures in this book are, of course, totally fictitious.

Nevertheless, Churchill is arguably in the top five most colourful and fascinating characters of the twentieth century. He was brave – sometimes extremely foolhardy. He was intelligent, resourceful, and extremely driven. His target was to get into Parliament and make a career of it and he moved heaven and earth to make it happen. Few people plan their careers as meticulously as Winston Churchill. His exploits during the war in South Africa are legendary and he went on to add to them with a political life which saw him shape the Royal Navy – alongside Admiral Jackie Fisher – during World War One – and make an everlasting name for himself as Prime Minister in the Second World War.

David Lloyd George's name is not one that comes easily to modern lips but he played a pivotal role in shaping modern Britain particularly in social reform.

FDR was another clever and brave leader during World War Two. In spite of his own deepest convictions and the opposition of members of both parties he helped Britain even before the Japanese bombed Pearl Harbour.

The view from the present for most of us is extremely limited. There are evil people who see farther and try to manipulate our world to their ends. Thank goodness there are also good people with equivalent vision who fight for the right.

About the Author

James T Abbott worked in academia for many years and led a well-known research company for over thirty years. Alongside his career he has authored and contributed to many non-fiction and fiction books. Among the earliest were very successful textbooks on applied economics, business, and politics. More recently he spent ten years researching and writing two very successful books on the background and reality behind the UFO phenomenon. The two current volumes in The Outsider's Guide to UFOs series, (2017-2022), have attracted such descriptions as 'one of the best', 'refreshingly balanced', and 'devoid of conspiracy nonsense'. Volume 1 of the series has recently been revised, expanded, and updated. In 2023 he published the result of further in-depth research in the form of his well-received 'Paranorm 2.0' investigation and assessment of the paranormal. Paranorm 2.0 reviews most aspects of the paranormal – from ghosts to reincarnation – and discusses the vital importance of consciousness in the way we view all paranormal phenomena. James has written several novel but 'Osiris' is the first of the Tim Ward Tales - a series of lighter, time-travel and paranormal novels. Since 2017, James has been a guest on dozens of podcasts and radio shows and has been the subject of news and magazine articles on both sides of the Atlantic- including interviews with Politico and CBC of Canada, and appearances on Coast to Coast and TalkRadio UK. He was also the subject of an article in Mechanics Illustrated! James' new book – 'Osiris' – continues the paranormal theme but, this time, with a lighter look at how such matters could affect the lives of ordinary people … and witches. He and his wife live in the depths of sheep country, in Yorkshire, UK, where paranormal events are frequent but usually turn out to be the grandchildren.

Also by James T Abbott

The Outsider's Guide to UFOs Volume 1: Mystery and Science

The Outsider's Guide to UFOs Volume 2: What are they?

Paranorm 2.0: The New Reality